GIOVANNI VERGA

W9-ADA-505

THE

SHE-WOLF

and Other Stories

Second edition, revised and enlarged

Translated with an Introduction by
Giovanni Cecchetti

University of California Press
Berkeley   Los Angeles   London

University of California Press
Berkeley and Los Angeles, California
University of California Press, Ltd.
London, England

Second edition, revised and enlarged, 1973
Copyrights © 1958 and 1973 by The Regents of the
University of California

ISBN: 0-520-02153-3
Library of Congress Catalog Card Number: 79-181437

Printed in the United States of America

INTRODUCTION

In 1880, when Giovanni Verga published "The She-Wolf," "Cavalleria Rusticana," and the other stories in Part One of this volume, he was forty years old and had achieved a measure of popularity as a writer of sentimental novels of passion. His aristocratic and upper-bourgeois heroines had exotic names and were driven by a devouring sensuality. One of them died in a cloister with passion frustrated; another killed herself in the arms of her lover as a supreme act of devotion. His southern Italian heroes, living in Florence, were preoccupied with conquering beautiful women. Some felt disillusioned after attaining the objects of their quests, and some died of consumption.

The titles of those first novels are indicative: *A Sinner, Story of a Blackcap, Eva, Royal Tigress, Eros*. Their plots are standard; their themes and style reflect the influence of second-rate contemporary French writers such as Alexandre Dumas *fils* and Octave Feuillet. Now and then the prose sparkles, but those artificial novels lack depth and breadth, and are of interest mainly because they helped the author to purge himself of autobiographical dross.

Verga left his native Catania, Sicily, at the age of twenty-five, after publishing a long historical novel, and went to Florence, then the cultural center of Italy, the capital of the newly established kingdom. There he mingled in the upper strata of society and had some love affairs, but no more than normal for a brilliant young man of his age. In 1869, however, he met a Florentine girl with whom he was to fall deeply in love. In 1872 she became the wife of one of his friends, the Sicilian poet Mario Rapisardi. Some years later, when Verga went back to Catania after writing *I Malavoglia,* he saw her again and the two had an affair which resulted in scandal. This was the only extraordinary event in the otherwise uneventful life of Giovanni Verga.

In 1873 he moved to Milan, where he enjoyed other love relations, but we know very little about them. He was restrained and distant when it came to personal matters. With his friends he usually discussed literary art, to which he was truly dedicated. During his first years in Milan he wrote *Royal Tigress* and *Eros. Eros* is the last and possibly the most interesting of his sentimental novels. Although weak in many ways, it occasionally affords us a glimpse into some of the features of the author's future great works.

In 1874, one year before publishing *Eros,* Verga discovered a new and more genuinely human source of art. For the first time he focused his attention on the poor Sicilian people among whom he had spent his adolescence, although not as one of them but as the son of a landowner. He wrote *Nedda,* the story of a Sicilian peasant girl who loses her mother, her fiancé, and the child born of her love. She accepts her destiny in stony resignation and, pressing her dead child to her breast, exclaims: "Blessed you who are dead! Blessed you, Virgin Mary, who took my little girl so that she wouldn't suffer what I had to suffer!" The story is marred by obvious flaws, but it marked a turning point in Verga's career. He was conscious of having discovered a new world, and in 1875 he announced a similar short work, dealing with the lives of poor fishermen in a Sicilian village, to be entitled "Padron 'Ntoni." This story was never published as such, but toward the end of 1880 it achieved its final form as *I Malavoglia* ("The House by the Medlar Tree"), one of the most compact and original novels of the last century, unanimously acclaimed by critics as Verga's masterpiece.

During the 'seventies, Verga was working toward two goals which were actually one: a fresh human content and a style to render it in the best possible way. Milan was then full of ferment: new theories of art were passionately debated by young writers and composers seeking new forms of expression. In literature the trend most closely watched was French naturalism. Under its influence, Giovanni Verga and his friend Luigi Capuana, also a Sicilian, developed Italian realism, a school known under the name of *verismo*. But while French naturalists tried to explain the behavior of the corrupt and the degenerate in pseudoscientific terms, Verga and his fellow realists brought to light the unrefined, somewhat primitive, but intensely human drives and impulses of the poor and the humble.

Although Verga was considered the leading figure of

verismo, he cannot be identified with any school. His masterpieces, as well as those of all great writers, transcend the narrow boundaries of a school and defy classification. He was undoubtedly influenced by contemporary trends, but he assimilated those influences and transformed them into something definitely his own. The only element which was not assimilated and therefore remained external, was the conception of a cycle of five novels to be entitled "I Vinti" ("The Vanquished"), a conception that he borrowed from the general framework of Zola's *Les Rougon-Macquart.* This plan proved an artificial superimposition. He wrote only two of the five novels—*I Malavoglia* and *Mastro Don Gesualdo*—and they are not part of a composite picture but independent masterpieces.

For Verga, realism was a discovery of himself, or, as Croce puts it, *una spinta liberatrice,* "a liberating impulse" that led him to abandon a sophisticated world for a more genuine one to which he felt instinctively attracted. It helped him to acquire a more direct vision of life and to understand the joys and sorrows of common men and women.

Verga published all his mature works in a period of approximately ten years, starting in 1880. His two great novels and all his finest short stories appeared then. The development of his maturity is reflected by his short stories even more than by his novels. Unquestionably the best collections are *Vita dei Campi* ("Life in the Fields") and *Novelle Rusticane* ("Rustic Stories"). They represent two separate stages in the author's conception of life. In *Vita dei Campi,* which includes such stories as "The She-Wolf," "Cavalleria Rusticana," and "Ieli," his vision of life is heroic in a sense: tragedy seems to be the cathartic element which is necessary whenever human values must be saved. In *Novelle Rusticane,* as in *Mastro Don Gesualdo,* Verga is more pessimistic: human values cannot be saved any longer, and men and women are the helpless victims of uncontrollable forces and have no choice but to accept their fate. In the subsequent collections, from which Part Three of the present volume is derived, this helplessness is colored with bitter humor; then the author's attitude toward life becomes still more pessimistic, and even cynical at times.

His native Sicily provided the setting for nearly all Verga's best work. The poor people of the ancient island enabled him to observe and recreate humanity at its simplest, free from all the complications of city life. During the 'eighties, however, after writing *Vita dei Campi, I Malavoglia,* and some *Novelle Rusticane,* he occasionally returned to his early non-Sicilian world, as he did in *Il Marito di Elena* ("Helen's Husband") and in many short stories. Although his style had become more personal and direct than in his sentimental novels, the products of this return are lacking in real significance. Only when he portrayed the poor, common people, even if they were not Sicilians, did he attain greatness, as in "Buddies" and "The Last Day."

In 1893 Verga left Milan permanently and moved back

to Catania. His work was done. The last decades of his life were spent in a long and dignified silence. He died January 26, 1922.

II

One of the recurrent themes in the writings of Verga's second period is economic. His people are constantly engaged in a struggle for the most elementary means of survival. Their incessant need for material security often determines their actions and leads them to tragedy and ruin.

The novel *I Malavoglia* tells of a family of Sicilian fishermen prompted to speculate on a cargo of lupins to better their lot. But unfortunate circumstances bring about the loss of the cargo, the death of the oldest son, the eventual loss of the family house, and the disintegration of the family itself. The theme of poverty is equally evident in the short stories. In "Cavalleria Rusticana," Lola jilts Turiddu because Alfio is better off; in "Malaria," the disease seems to prostrate only the poor because they cannot afford to move away from the infested region; in the "Story of the Saint Joseph Donkey," the animal is of some use as long as it produces financial benefits for its owners, but its misery becomes identified with the misery of the people who are trying to make a living with its help; in "The Orphans," Meno cries over his wife's death because with her he has lost her dowry, and can finally find some comfort in the possibility of marrying Alfia, who owns property; in "Black Bread," Santo and the Redhead fight constantly because they are poor ("The trouble is we aren't rich enough to love each other all the time. When chickens don't have anything to peck at in the coop, they peck at each other"), Pino the Tome marries the crippled widow and abandons the beautiful Lucia only because the widow is well off ("It was for love of bread," he says), Lucia gives in to Don Venerando because he gives her money for her dowry, her fiancé pushes her into the affair because he wants the dowry, and her brother and sister-in-law forget all moral considerations as soon as they realize that she has earned it; in "Consolation," poverty drives Arlia from one delusion to another until she sinks into stupefied resignation; in "The Last Day," the protagonist resorts to suicide because he cannot support himself; and in "Nanni Volpe," Raffaela marries the old man only because he has property.

But even when Verga's characters have accumulated considerable wealth, they retain the psychology of the poor with its feeling of insecurity: they are driven by a compulsive desire for more wealth and thus unconsciously nourish the drama of their emptiness. Such a person is Mastro Don Gesualdo. By laboring day and night he acquires a large fortune. Then, to improve his social status, he marries a penniless aristocratic girl, but is disliked by his wife's relatives as well as by the people of his former class. Finally he dies alone, in the palace of his son-in-law, neglected by his daughter and laughed at by the servants. Similar is the story of Nanni Volpe. He spends the best years of his life making money and buying property; when he feels that he has enough to start a family, he gets married, but it is too late, and his marriage is a total failure. All he is able to do is to try to get out of his money whatever personal advantage he can, by playing wife and nephew against each other. Still more tragic is the story of Mazzarò in "Property": all his life he has done nothing but amass money and buy land, until everything in sight belongs to him; he has no children, no grandchildren, no relatives of any kind, he has only property. But as he realizes that death is near and sees the inadequacy of his riches, he goes mad with despair. Verga's rich are in truth poorer than the poor.

But for Verga poverty is also a deterministic factor in an environment where passions may explode with unexpected violence. Love and jealousy, the two main passions of his characters, are as prominent in his world as the struggle for survival and the desire for wealth.

Love enables him to portray the fundamental gentleness inherent in humble people, as in the section of "Ieli," where he beautifully recreates the childhood idyll of the two protagonists. Sometimes, however, he sees love as a dark passion ruling human lives inexorably. In "The She-Wolf," Nanni falls under the spell of his mother-in-law and has no way of freeing himself except by killing her. Pina is depicted as invincible, as the symbol of the inescapability of the flesh, in whose presence even religion loses its effectiveness. "The She-Wolf," which Verga called "the most accentuated" of the stories of *Vita dei Campi,* is a drama of unusual power. It has been compared to the tragedies of incest found in

Greek literature. The closing paragraph is certainly one of the most impressive passages in all of Verga's stories.

A different treatment appears in "Gramigna's Mistress." Peppa falls in love with a bandit because he is her ideal of strength and manhood; she ignores all conventional rules of respectability and follows him. When Gramigna is captured, she lives by her memories of him, working near the jail and doing little jobs for the policemen. She moves within a dream of love which has become the only reality of her life.

Although love may have its tender, poetic moments, jealousy either generates tragedy or tortures a man with unreasonable suspicions. In "Cavalleria Rusticana," Turiddu feels betrayed by Lola and wants to make her jealous in order to win her back; by so doing he makes Santa jealous, and tragedy ensues. Ieli, in the story that bears his name, cannot believe that his old friend has taken Mara away from him; after a long period of revery, during which he refuses to accept the facts, he suddenly sees the truth and kills Don Alfonso without a moment of hesitation. What happens to "Stinkpot" is not very different. Jealousy seems to spring up as an integral part of the psyche of these characters.

"Cavalleria Rusticana" and "Ieli" also reveal a primitive moral code by which Verga's people live. If they offend, they know that they must pay; if they are offended, they know that they are entitled to justice, and are ready to take the law into their hands in order to get it. Turiddu is conscious that he has offended Alfio ("I know I've done wrong") and that he deserves to be killed. Ieli instinctively feels that he must kill the man who has defiled his home. And after the crime, he is sure that it was the least he could do; when they arrest him, he exclaims candidly: "What! I shouldn't even have killed him? . . . But he'd taken Mara! . . ."

Jealousy is a basic passion that prompts these men to protect their families and their honor, and therefore their own lives. But of course there are times when it may be only the product of unfounded suspicions and may consequently cause unnecessary mental suffering. This is the theme of "Donna Santa's Sin," in which Doctor Brocca becomes the humorous and yet pathetic victim of his own apprehensions—fostered as they are by the delirious utterances of his wife and the unscrupulous insinuations of his friends.

Like all human beings, Verga's people are simple and complex at the same time. We can single out some major traits, some stronger impulses, but these are merely elements in a total picture. The only way to perceive the full humanity of these characters—as of the characters in any work of art—is to follow the continuous interplay of their actions and aspirations, their drives and passions, their sorrows and joys.

III

With *Vita dei Campi* (1880), not only did Verga discover and recreate a world which was in sharp contrast with the one of his early work, but he also forged a style by which that world could be brought to life in the most direct and unmistakable way. Before publishing that book, he had spent many years in search of a "form," as he called it, which was to be "one and the same with the subject matter." And by form he meant language, images, structure, and everything these terms imply. His objective was to attain that ideal of impersonality, set forth in the preface to "Gramigna's Mistress," whose main tenet was that the work of art should appear to have "matured and come into being spontaneously, like a fact of nature." Obviously Verga's impersonality, like Flaubert's *impassibilité,* does not exist. The author can never efface himself: the very choice of a subject matter, the particular manner of approaching the characters, and the preference for certain means of expression unavoidably bear the imprint of his personality. But the pursuit of such an impossible and nonexistent goal helped him to reject worn-out expressive patterns, approach reality more directly, and achieve an often naked but always lyrical prose.

What Verga actually wanted to do was to interpret his Sicilian world not in literary terms but in the terms that were ideally those of that world itself. For this purpose he adopted a very limited vocabulary, which consisted of words that were popular in quality, or would sound so in a given context. He condensed the narration as much as possible, eliminating everything except what seemed absolutely indispensable and could not be suggested between the lines. His syntax became linear, and kept some traces of the syntax of Sicilian dialect—the language most of his characters would have spoken in real life. His sentences acquired certain peculiarities of everyday speech. The conjunction "e" ("and") was employed repeatedly to connect coördinate clauses and sentences, as is common in popular narration.

Most of all—and this may be the primary source of all the characteristics of Verga's style—he had his people "narrate themselves," without apparent intrusions on his part; that is to say, he told the story with the words of his characters, or of a chorus of villagers who witnessed, or participated in, the action. The stories and novels of his second period, in fact, seem to be told by the very people the author writes about; they are all written in *style indirect libre,* or "free indirect style." In the first page of "Cavalleria Rusticana," for instance, we find this sentence: "As soon as Turiddu found out, damn it! he was going to tear that Licodian's guts from his belly, he was!" Here Verga relates the words of Turiddu, without omitting either his curse or his habitual repetition, and inserts them into the narrative stream, merely changing the personal pronouns and placing the verbs in the past tense, giving no indication that Turiddu might be speaking. Generally, in Verga's stories, when a character is mentioned, his speech follows. This technique was remarkably original for the time and contributed greatly to the power and freshness of Verga's prose. In our century it has been adopted by most major writers.

The speech of the chorus can be heard almost everywhere. In some cases Verga makes it evident by introducing such popular phrases as "God save us!" "God forbid!" and similar utterances. But it is usually discoverable through the language, the syntax, and the references to local customs and beliefs. Nearly all of "Stinkpot," for example, is related in the words of the villagers or the spectators.

This strict adherence to the world of his characters leads Verga to eliminate conventional description. He treats nature and all external elements as integral parts of his people. The grueling Sicilian sun that scorches the countryside, and the fogs and rains that destroy the crops, are never considered for their own sake, but are felt as components of the toil and struggle of his men and women. One of the best examples of this approach to nature can be found toward the end of "Ieli." Ieli asks Mara to go with him to Salonia, where he works as a shepherd, but Mara answers "that she wasn't born to be a shepherdess." Her words immediately suggest to Ieli how hard the life of a shepherd is, and convince him that it is better for Mara to stay home:

In fact, Mara wasn't born to be a shepherdess, and she wasn't used to the north wind of January when your hands stiffen on the staff and your fingernails seem to be falling out, and to the furious rainstorms when the water goes through to your bones, and to the suffocating dust of the roads when the sheep move along under the burning sun, and to the hard bed on the ground and to the moldy bread, and to the long silent and solitary days when in the scorched countryside you can see nothing but a rare sun-blackened peasant driving his little donkey silently ahead of him on the white, endless road.

Introduction

These are Ieli's thoughts; they spring from his everyday life and from his feelings for Mara. Through them we become aware of what the deserted countryside at Salonia looks like, and of the changing of the seasons, but we see these facts as part of the life of the protagonist.

In the "Story of the Saint Joseph Donkey," the writer goes even so far as to look at the surrounding fields through the very eyes of the poor animal:

> His eyes [were] lifeless, as if he were tired of looking at that vast white countryside which was clouded here and there with dust from the threshing floors and seemed made only to let you die of thirst and to make you trot around on the sheaves.

In the opening pages of "Malaria," the apparent description of the Plain of Catania is in reality the picture of the disease itself, of the desolation it causes, and of the people who cannot escape it:

> In vain Lentini, and Francofonte, and Paternò try to climb like stray sheep up the first hills that break loose from the plain . . . malaria snatches up the villagers in the deserted streets and nails them in front of the doors of their houses . . .

At the beginning of "Property," our eyes do not rest on the orange orchards, the huge storehouses, the immense vineyards and olive groves, the endless lines of oxen, and the herds filling the pastures of Canziria, but on Mazzarò, who becomes instantly identified with all of them. From the very first lines of that truly "symphonic" beginning, we know that all that property *is* Mazzarò, and that Mazzarò is nothing but his property.

Thus in Verga external factors are interiorized and charged with the inner life of his characters; they are, in other words, transformed into images and symbols. This is the essence of his lyricism.

Only a few words are sufficient for Verga to present a psychological situation in all its richness and suggestiveness. Who can forget the two sentences that introduce the She-Wolf? Her figure, her eyes, her red, devouring lips give us her picture and suggest the symbol she embodies. How delicately, on the contrary, the writer says that Santa had fallen in love with Turiddu: "The tassel of the *bersagliere*'s cap had tickled her heart and was always dancing before her eyes"—which is, among other things, an admirable way of expressing the most common of human events. And of Peppa, when asked by Gramigna if she wants to stay with him, Verga writes only that she nodded "avidly"; and of the dejected protagonist of "The Last Day" he mentions a pair of shoes that are falling apart. In "War Between Saints," the misery of the whole town is evoked in a sentence depicting the women, immobile in their despair: "It was one of those long years when the famine begins in June, and the women, with stunned eyes, stand idle and disheveled at the doorways."

The beginning of "Rosso Malpelo" is especially vivid from this point of view: "He was called Malpelo because he had red hair; and he had red hair because he was a mean and bad boy, who promised to turn into a first-rate scoundrel." Here Verga uses a touch of popular psychology: the traditional prejudices of the people join to introduce the unfortunate victim, who will be forced to become an outcast, if he wants to be an individual in a hostile environment. A beginning like this would be considered striking even today.

With his tightly knit prose, his immediacy and directness, his powerful conciseness, and his lyricism, Verga was ahead of his time. This might be the reason why his major works did not enjoy much popularity during an era when the general public was used to fiction of a Victorian type. The only work of his that became widely known was "Cavalleria Rusticana," thanks to the theater version and to Mascagni's opera.[1] Fame was to come to Verga after World War I, when readers and critics finally realized his greatness. Since then he has been a profound influence on contemporary Italian literature. This should not be surprising, for most of the narrative devices of twentieth-century fiction were already his.

Giovanni Cecchetti

---

1. "Cavalleria Rusticana" was originally an episode of the first drafts of *I Malavoglia*. Verga expunged it from the final version of the novel and published it as a short story in 1880. In 1884 he rewrote it as a one-act tragedy, which was immediately successful and became a cornerstone in the history of Italian realistic theater. In 1890 Targioni-Tozzetti and Menasci turned the tragedy into a libretto which was set to music by Mascagni and is the universally known version of the story. The original piece is artistically superior to both the one-act tragedy and the libretto. "The She-Wolf" was also rewritten by Verga as a tragedy (this time in two acts), but again the story remains the superior piece.

A NOTE

ON THE TRANSLATION

The short stories collected in this volume are, in my opinion, Verga's best and most representative. In Part One, the reader will find the famous collection *Vita dei Campi* almost complete; in Part Two, a rather large selection from the equally famous *Novelle rusticane;* in Part Three, the most significant stories subsequently written by Verga ("Donna Santa's Sin" is among the very last ones); and in "The Mark X," an example of the author's early writings. Part Three and "The Mark X" appear in English for the first time.

The selections in Part One have been translated previously. Toward the end of the last century most of them were done by Alma Strettel (*Cavalleria Rusticana and Other Tales of Sicilian Peasant Life,* London, 1893) and by Nathan Dole (*Under the Shadow of Etna,* Boston, 1896). Miss Strettel's book includes "Cavalleria Rusticana," "Rosso Malpelo," "Gramigna's Mistress," and "War Between Saints"; and Dole's "Cavalleria Rusticana," "The She-Wolf," "Jeli, the Shepherd," and "Gramigna's Mistress." These versions can be considered commendable attempts to render Verga into English, but they contain errors and, above all, they are outdated and consequently their English does not come alive to us.

In the twenties D. H. Lawrence translated *Vita dei Campi* (*Cavalleria Rusticana and Other Stories,* New York, 1928) and *Novelle rusticane* (*Little Novels of Sicily,* Boston, T. Seltzer, 1925, reissued by the Grove Press, New York, 1953). Lawrence's translations are by far the best known. Although they have some good passages, on the whole they are rather unsatisfactory. Lawrence did not know Italian sufficiently well, nor did he have enough time to do justice to the original. As a result, his Verga is full of oddities. He misunderstood or misread many Italian words, so that "a picnic in the country" became "the ringing of the bells," a "fiancée" became a "wife," a "mother" a "midwife," a "hard bed on the ground" a "hard biscuit," a "storeroom" a "millstone," a "rump" a "group"; the olive trees instead of "fading gradually in the twilight," "fumed upon the twilight," etc. He translated southern Italian idioms literally, and thus the common expressions meaning "they had spent a fortune" and "as happy as a king" became "they had spent the very eyes out of their head" and "as happy as an Easter Day." He even altered some stories by making additions that clashed with the immediate context; for example, he had Nanni stretch out his arms in order "to keep off" the She-wolf, on that memorable afternoon. —All these factors point to the need for a new translation.

The present translation is as literal as possible, and

attempts to render the spirit as well as the letter of the original. A constant effort has been made to convey Verga's style and the rhythm of his sentences, to preserve his mixture of popular and semilearned language, and to keep the economy of words of the Italian text. Very few liberties have been taken: the prefixes *compare,* *comare,* and *gnà,* which in the speech of southern Italians carry only a musical significance, have been left out. *Compare* was kept when it was not a prefix. The other prefixes, which indicate a difference in social status, are given in Italian: *massaro* is a man who owns or rents the land he farms; *curatolo,* one who cares for a farm and is usually in charge of the sheep; *mastro,* a skilled laborer or an artisan; *Don,* a professional man or a landowner; and *Donna,* the wife of a *Don.* Names of old currencies are also given in Italian: an *onza* was a Sicilian gold coin worth about thirteen *lire,* a *tarì* a silver coin worth about forty-two-hundredths of a *lira,* and a *grano* a very small copper coin worth about one-twentieth of a *tarì.* A few footnotes have been added where necessary, to explain untranslatable words occurring only once or twice, to clarify local customs and beliefs, and to indicate the location of the most important places mentioned.

The text translated is the "critical" text currently in print, which, at least for *Vita dei Campi,* I have helped to establish. For most of the stories included in Part One, this text differs markedly from the one commonly known before, and therefore from the one used by Strettel, Dole, and Lawrence.

Note

The date at the end of each story is the date of its first publication.

The first edition of this book appeared in 1958 and was reprinted in 1962. For the second edition all the stories in Part Two were added, and the introduction was expanded to include references to the new material.

G. C.

Los Angeles, July 1971

CONTENTS

PART ONE

THE SHE-WOLF

She was tall, thin; she had the firm and vigorous breasts of the olive-skinned—and yet she was no longer young; she was pale, as if always plagued by malaria, and in that pallor, two enormous eyes, and fresh red lips which devoured you.

In the village they called her the She-wolf, because she never had enough—of anything. The women made the sign of the cross when they saw her pass, alone as a wild bitch, prowling about suspiciously like a famished wolf; with her red lips she sucked the blood of their sons and husbands in a flash, and pulled them behind her skirt with a single glance of those devilish eyes, even if they were before the altar of Saint Agrippina. Fortunately, the She-wolf never went to church, not at Easter, not at Christmas, not to hear Mass, not for confession. —Father Angiolino of Saint Mary of Jesus, a true servant of God, had lost his soul on account of her.

Maricchia, a good girl, poor thing, cried in secret because she was the She-wolf's daughter, and no one would marry her, though, like every other girl in the village, she had her fine linen in a chest and her good land under the sun.

One day the She-wolf fell in love with a handsome

young man who had just returned from the service and was mowing hay with her in the fields of the notary; and she fell in love in the strongest sense of the word, feeling the flesh afire beneath her clothes; and staring him in the eyes, she suffered the thirst one has in the hot hours of June, deep in the plain. But he went on mowing undisturbed, his nose bent over the swaths.

"What's wrong, Pina?" he would ask.

In the immense fields, where you heard only the crackling flight of the grasshoppers, as the sun hammered down overhead, the She-wolf gathered bundle after bundle, and sheaf after sheaf, never tiring, never straightening up for an instant, never raising the flask to her lips, just to remain at the heels of Nanni, who mowed and mowed and asked from time to time:

"What is it you want, Pina?"

One evening she told him, while the men were dozing on the threshing floor, tired after the long day, and the dogs were howling in the vast, dark countryside.

"It's you I want. You who're beautiful as the sun and sweet as honey. I want you!"

"And I want your daughter, instead, who's a maid," answered Nanni laughing.

The She-wolf thrust her hands into her hair, scratching her temples, without saying a word, and walked away. And she did not appear at the threshing floor any more. But she saw Nanni again in October, when they were making olive oil, for he was working near her house, and the creaking of the press kept her awake all night.

4

"Get the sack of olives," she said to her daughter, "and come with me."

Nanni was pushing olives under the millstone with a shovel, shouting "Ohee" to the mule, to keep it from stopping.

"You want my daughter Maricchia?" Pina asked him.

"What'll you give your daughter Maricchia?" answered Nanni.

"She has all her father's things, and I'll give her my house too; as for me, all I need is a little corner in the kitchen, enough for a straw mattress."

"If that's the way it is, we can talk about it at Christmas," said Nanni.

Nanni was all greasy and filthy, spattered with oil and fermented olives, and Maricchia didn't want him at any price. But her mother grabbed her by the hair before the fireplace, muttering between her teeth:

"If you don't take him, I'll kill you!"

The She-wolf was almost sick, and the people were saying that when the devil gets old he becomes a hermit. She no longer roamed here and there, no longer lingered at the doorway, with those bewitched eyes. Whenever she fixed them on his face, those eyes of hers, her son-in-law began to laugh and pulled out the scapular of the Virgin to cross himself. Maricchia stayed at home nursing the babies, and her mother went into the fields to work with the men, and just like a man too, weeding, hoeing, feeding the animals, pruning the vines, despite the northeast and levantine winds of January or the

The She-Wolf

August sirocco, when the mules' heads drooped and the men slept face down along the wall, on the north side. "In those hours between nones and vespers when no good woman goes roving around," [1] Pina was the only living soul to be seen wandering in the countryside, over the burning stones of the paths, through the scorched stubble of the immense fields that became lost in the suffocating heat, far, far away toward the foggy Etna, where the sky was heavy on the horizon.

"Wake up!" said the She-wolf to Nanni, who was sleeping in the ditch, along the dusty hedge, his head on his arms. "Wake up. I've brought you some wine to cool your throat."

Nanni opened his drowsy eyes wide, still half asleep, and finding her standing before him, pale, with her arrogant breasts and her coal-black eyes, he stretched out his hands gropingly.

"No! no good woman goes roving around in the hours between nones and vespers!" sobbed Nanni, throwing his face back into the dry grass of the ditch, deep, deep, his nails in his scalp. "Go away! go away! don't come to the threshing floor again!"

The She-wolf was going away, in fact, retying her superb tresses, her gaze bent fixedly before her as she moved through the hot stubble, her eyes as black as coal.

---

[1] An old Sicilian proverb, which refers to the hours of the early afternoon, when the Sicilian countryside lies motionless under a scorching sun and no person would dare walk on the roads. Those hours are traditionally believed to be under the spell of malignant spirits.

But she came to the threshing floor again, and more than once, and Nanni did not complain. On the contrary, when she was late, in the hours between nones and vespers, he would go and wait for her at the top of the white, deserted path, with his forehead bathed in sweat; and he would thrust his hands into his hair, and repeat every time:

"Go away! go away! don't come to the threshing floor again!"

Maricchia cried night and day, and glared at her mother, her eyes burning with tears and jealousy, like a young she-wolf herself, every time she saw her come, mute and pale, from the fields.

"Vile, vile mother!" she said to her. "Vile mother!"

"Shut up!"

"Thief! Thief!"

"Shut up!"

"I'll go to the Sergeant, I will!"

"Go ahead!"

And she really did go, with her babies in her arms, fearing nothing, and without shedding a tear, like a madwoman, because now she too loved that husband who had been forced on her, greasy and filthy, spattered with oil and fermented olives.

The Sergeant sent for Nanni; he threatened him even with jail and the gallows. Nanni began to sob and tear his hair; he didn't deny anything, he didn't try to clear himself.

"It's the temptation!" he said. "It's the temptation of hell!"

The She-Wolf

He threw himself at the Sergeant's feet begging to be sent to jail.

"For God's sake, Sergeant, take me out of this hell! Have me killed, put me in jail; don't let me see her again, never! never!"

"No!" answered the She-wolf instead, to the Sergeant. "I kept a little corner in the kitchen to sleep in, when I gave him my house as dowry. It's my house. I don't intend to leave it."

Shortly afterward, Nanni was kicked in the chest by a mule and was at the point of death, but the priest refused to bring him the Sacrament if the She-wolf did not go out of the house. The She-wolf left, and then her son-in-law could also prepare to leave like a good Christian; he confessed and received communion with such signs of repentance and contrition that all the neighbors and the curious wept before the dying man's bed. —And it would have been better for him to die that day, before the devil came back to tempt him again and creep into his body and soul, when he got well.

"Leave me alone!" he told the She-wolf. "For God's sake, leave me in peace! I've seen death with my own eyes! Poor Maricchia is desperate. Now the whole town knows about it! If I don't see you it's better for both of us . . ."

And he would have liked to gouge his eyes out not to see those of the She-wolf, for whenever they peered into his, they made him lose his body and soul. He did not know what to do to free himself from the spell. He paid for Masses for the souls in purgatory and asked the priest and the Sergeant for help. At Easter he went to confession, and in penance he publicly licked more than four feet of pavement, crawling on the pebbles in front of the church—and then, as the She-wolf came to tempt him again:

"Listen!" he said to her. "Don't come to the threshing floor again; if you do, I swear to God, I'll kill you!"

"Kill me," answered the She-wolf, "I don't care; I can't stand it without you."

As he saw her from the distance, in the green wheat fields, Nanni stopped hoeing the vineyard, and went to pull the ax from the elm. The She-wolf saw him come, pale and wild-eyed, with the ax glistening in the sun, but she did not fall back a single step, did not lower her eyes; she continued toward him, her hands laden with red poppies, her black eyes devouring him.

"Ah! damn your soul!" stammered Nanni.

1880

CAVALLERIA RUSTICANA

When Turiddu Macca, Nunzia's son, came back from the service, he used to strut in the square on Sundays in his *bersagliere*[1] uniform with the red cap that looked like the one worn by the fortuneteller who sets up a bench with a cage of canaries. The girls, on the way to Mass, their noses in their mantillas, eyed him longingly, and the urchins buzzed around him like flies. He had also brought a pipe with a carving of the king on horseback that seemed alive, and he lit matches on the rear of his pants, lifting his leg as if giving a kick.

But in spite of all this, *massaro* Angelo's daughter, Lola, had not shown herself at Mass or on her balcony, because she had become engaged to a certain man from Licodia,[2] a cart driver who had four Sortino[3] mules in his stable. As soon as Turiddu found out, damn it! he was going to tear that Licodian's guts from his belly, he

[1] The *Bersaglieri* are a famous Italian army corps, especially trained for quick movement and swift action against an enemy. For full dress they used to wear beautiful hats with plumes and for informal dress a red cap with hanging tassel.

[2] A large village near Vizzini, on the western slopes of the Iblei Mountains, about thirty miles inland from Syracuse.

[3] Another large village, about halfway between Syracuse and Licodia.

10

indirect discourse

was!—but he did nothing of the kind, and vented his rage by singing all the scornful songs he knew under the girl's window.

"Doesn't Nunzia's Turiddu have anything to do," the neighbors were saying, "that he spends his nights singing like a lonely sparrow?"

He finally ran into Lola, who was returning from a pilgrimage to Our Lady of Peril; and seeing him, she turned neither white nor red, as if it were none of her business.

"It's a lucky person who sees you!" he said.

"Oh, Turiddu, they'd told me you came back the first of the month."

"They've told me things too!" he answered. "Is it true you're going to marry Alfio, the cart driver?"

"If that's the will of God!" answered Lola, pulling the two corners of her kerchief over her chin.

"You make the will of God yourself, just as it happens to suit you! And the will of God was that I should come home from so far away to hear this fine piece of news, Lola!"

The poor devil was still trying to act brave, but his voice had grown hoarse; he walked behind the girl, swaying while the tassel of his cap danced here and there on his shoulders. She, in all honesty, was sorry to see him with such a long face, but hadn't the heart to encourage him with nice words.

"Listen, Turiddu," she told him at last, "let me catch up with my friends. What would they say in town if they saw me with you?"

Cavalleria Rusticana

"That's right," answered Turiddu, "now that you're going to marry Alfio who has four mules in his stable, you mustn't make people talk. Instead my mother, poor woman, had to sell our bay mule and that little vineyard on the highroad while I was in the service. The good old days are gone, and you don't think any more of the time when we talked together at the courtyard window; and before I went away, you gave me that handkerchief— and God knows how many tears I've wept in it, going away so far that even the name of our town was lost. But now, good-by, Lola—'Let's pretend it's rained, then cleared up, and our friendship is over.'" [4]

Lola married the cart driver; and every Sunday she sat on the balcony with her hands on her stomach, displaying the huge gold rings her husband had given her. Turiddu kept going up and down the little street with an air of indifference, his pipe in his mouth and his hands in his pockets, eyeing the girls; but gnawing away inside him was the fact that Lola's husband had all that gold and that she herself pretended not to notice him when he went by.

"I'll get even with her right under her eyes, the dirty bitch!" he muttered.

Across the street from Alfio lived *massaro* Cola, the winegrower, who was rich as a pig, people said, and had a daughter on his hands. Turiddu managed to get a job as field watchman at *massaro* Cola's and began to

---

[4] A Sicilian saying that means "Let's forget completely about everything connected with the past."

hang around the house, saying sweet words to the girl.

"Why don't you go and say these nice things to Lola?" answered Santa.

"Lola's a big Lady! Lola's married to a crowned king now!"

"I don't deserve crowned kings."

"You're worth a hundred Lolas, and I know someone who wouldn't look at Lola or her patron saint when you're around; Lola doesn't deserve to carry your shoes, she doesn't!"

"When the fox couldn't reach the grapes . . ."

"He said: how beautiful you are, my sweet little grapes!"

"Hey! watch those hands, Turiddu."

"Are you afraid I'll eat you?"

"I'm not afraid of you or your God."

"Eh! your mother was from Licodia, we know that! You've got fighting blood! Uh! I'd eat you with my eyes."

"Go ahead and eat me with your eyes, and we won't leave any crumbs; but now help me lift that bundle."

"For you I'd lift the whole house, I would!"

To avoid blushing, she threw a wooden block that she happened to have within reach, and that she missed him was a miracle.

"Let's hurry up, talk won't get us anywhere."

"If I were rich I'd try to get a wife like you, Santa."

"I won't marry a crowned king like Lola did, but I'll have my dowry too, when the Lord sends me someone."

"We know you're rich, we know it!"

"If you know it, hurry up; my father may come any minute, and I wouldn't want him to find me in the courtyard."

Her father began scowling, but the girl pretended not to notice it, because the tassel of the *bersagliere*'s cap had tickled her heart and was always dancing before her eyes. When the father threw Turiddu out the door, the daughter opened the window and stood there chattering with him every evening, so that the entire neighborhood spoke of nothing else.

"I'm going crazy because of you," said Turiddu, "I'm losing my sleep and my appetite."

"Nonsense!"

"I wish I were Victor Emmanuel's son, so I could marry you!"

"Nonsense!"

"By the Holy Virgin, I could eat you like bread!"

"Nonsense!"

"On my honor!"

"Ah! For heaven's sake!"

Lola, who listened every evening, hidden behind a pot of sweet basil, and turned pale and red, one day called Turiddu:

"And so, Turiddu, old friends don't greet each other any more?"

"Well . . . ," sighed the young man, "it's a lucky person who can greet you!"

"If you want to greet me, you know where I live!" answered Lola. Turiddu went back to greet her so often that Santa noticed it and slammed the window in his face. The neighbors pointed out the *bersagliere* with a smile or a nod, when he passed. Lola's husband was making his round of the fairs with his mules.

"Sunday I want to go to confession, because I dreamed of black grapes[5] last night!" said Lola.

"Forget it! Forget it!" begged Turiddu.

"No, now that Easter's coming, my husband would want to know why I didn't go to confession."

"Ah!" muttered *massaro* Cola's daughter Santa, while on her knees awaiting her turn at the confession box where Lola was washing her sins away. "On my soul, it's not to Rome I'll send you for penance!"

Alfio came back with his mules and loaded with money, and brought a beautiful new holiday dress as a gift for his wife.

"You're right to bring her presents," his neighbor Santa told him, "because when you're away your wife makes a cuckold of you in your own house!"

Alfio was one of those cart drivers who carry a chip on their shoulders, and hearing his wife spoken of that way, he changed color as if he had been knifed.

"Damn it!" he exclaimed. "If you haven't seen right, I won't leave you eyes to cry with, you and your whole family!"

"I'm not used to crying!" answered Santa. "I didn't even cry when with these eyes I saw Nunzia's Turiddu enter your wife's house at night."

"Fine," answered Alfio, "many thanks."

[5] In Sicily, an ominous dream.

Now that the cat had come back, Turiddu didn't hang around the little street any more during the day, and drowned his ill-humor at the tavern with his friends. On Easter Eve they had a plate of sausages on the table. As Alfio came in, Turiddu understood, just from the way he fixed his eyes on him, that he had come about that business, and laid his fork on the plate.

"What can I do for you, Alfio?" he asked.

"No favors, Turiddu; I hadn't seen you for some time and wanted to talk to you—you know what about."

At first Turiddu had offered him a glass of wine, but Alfio brushed it aside with his hand. Then Turiddu stood up and said:

"Here I am, Alfio."

The cart driver threw his arms around Turiddu's neck:

"If you want to come to the cactuses of Canziria[6] tomorrow morning, we can talk about that business."

"Wait for me on the highroad at sunrise and we'll go together."

With these words they exchanged the kiss of challenge. Turiddu bit the cart driver's ear, thus making a solemn promise to be there.

His friends had abandoned the sausages in cold silence, and accompanied Turiddu home. Nunzia, poor woman, waited up for him until late every evening.

"Mother," Turiddu said to her, "remember when I went into the service, and you thought I'd never come

---

[6] A hilly farm area near Vizzini.

home again? Give me a nice kiss as you did then; tomorrow morning I'm going far away."

Before daybreak he got his clasp knife, which he had hidden under the hay when he had been taken into the army, and started out for the cactuses of Canziria.

"Oh! for Christ's sake! where are you going in such a rush?" whined Lola in dismay, when her husband was about to leave.

"I'm not going far," answered Alfio, "but it'd be better for you if I would never come back."

Lola, in her nightgown, prayed at the foot of the bed, pressing to her lips the rosary Father Bernardino had brought her from the Holy Land, and recited all the Ave Marias it had beads for.

"Alfio," began Turiddu, after having gone a certain distance with his companion, who remained silent, his cap over his eyes, "I swear to God, I know I've done wrong and I'd let you kill me. But before I came here I saw my old mother who got up to see me leave, pretending she had to feed the chickens, almost as if she knew; and I swear to God I'll kill you like a dog not to make the poor old woman cry."

"That's fine," answered Alfio, taking off his jacket, "so we can really fight it out."

They were both good fighters. Turiddu was hit first, and was quick enough to take the stab in his arm; as he struck back, he struck hard and fast, and aimed at the groin.

"Ah, Turiddu, you really intend to kill me!"

"Yes, I told you; now that I've seen my old mother in the chicken coop, she seems to be always before my eyes."

"Open 'em well, those eyes!" shouted Alfio. "I'm going to give you a good one!"

While he was on guard, all doubled up to keep his left hand on his wound, which hurt him, and almost trailing his elbow on the ground, he quickly grabbed a handful of dust and threw it into his opponent's eyes.

"Ah!" howled Turiddu. "I'm dead."

He tried to save himself, jumping desperately backward; but Alfio caught him with another stab in the stomach and a third in the throat.

"And that's three! That's for making a cuckold of me in my own house. Now your mother will let the chickens alone."

For a while Turiddu staggered here and there among the cactuses and then fell like a log. Blood gurgled up and foamed in his throat, and he couldn't even gasp: *Ah, mamma mia!*

1880

IELI

Ieli, the horsekeeper, was thirteen when he met Don
Alfonso, the rich boy, but was so small that he didn't
come up to the belly of Bianca, the old mare who carried
the herd's bell. You could always see him straight and
still on the edge of a cliff or squatting on a big rock, here
and there, on the hills or on the plain, wherever his
animals were grazing.

His friend, Don Alfonso, while in the country on his
summer vacation, went to see him every day that God
sent to Tebidi,[1] and the two shared the good things of
the little baron and the barley bread of the herd boy,
or the fruit stolen from the neighbor. At first Ieli called
the rich boy "Your Excellency," as people do in Sicily,
but after they had a good fight, they became very close
friends. Ieli taught his friend how to climb up to the
magpies' nests, at the top of the walnut trees higher
than the bell tower of Licodia, how to hit a sparrow in
flight with a stone, or how to mount with a running
jump on the bare backs of the yet-untamed mares, grab-

---

[1] The name of a group of houses and of the farm land
surrounding them, in the region that lies west of Vizzini,
where most of the present story is set. Tebidi was owned
by Verga's family.

bing by the mane the first that passed within reach, without being scared by the unbroken colts' angry neighing and desperate leaping.

Ah, the wonderful chases over the mown fields, manes in the wind! the beautiful days of April, when the wind piled up the green grass into waves and the mares neighed in the pastures! the beautiful summer afternoons, when the whitish countryside lay silent under the hazy sky, and the grasshoppers crackled among the clods, as if the stubble were catching fire! the beautiful winter sky through the naked branches of the almond tree that shivered in the north wind, and the path that sounded frozen under the horses' hoofs, and the skylarks that sang high up in the warmth, in the blue! the beautiful summer evenings that came up very slowly, like fog, the good smell of the hay in which you sank your elbows, and the melancholy humming of the evening insects, and those two notes of Ieli's pipe, always the same—ee-oo! ee-oo! ee-oo!—that made you think of faraway things: of the fiesta of Saint John, of Christmas Eve, of the dawn of a picnic day, of all those big events gone by, which seemed sad so far away, making you look up, your eyes wet, as if all the stars that were lighting themselves in the sky rained into your heart and flooded it!

But Ieli didn't suffer from that melancholy; he squatted on the ridge, his cheeks puffed out, all intent on his playing—ee-oo! ee-oo! ee-oo!— Then he rounded up the herd by yelling and throwing stones and drove it into the stable, beyond Poggio Alla Croce.

Panting, he went up the slope on the far side of the valley, at times shouting to his friend Alfonso:

"Call the dog; hey, call the dog!"—or: "Throw a stone at Zaino,[2] who's acting up and playing around with the bushes in the valley and is coming along much too slowly"—or: "Tomorrow morning bring me a needle, one of Lia's."

He knew how to do all kinds of things with a needle; and he had a little bundle of rags in his canvas sack to patch his pants or the sleeves of his jacket when necessary; he also knew how to weave braids of horse hair, and he washed with the clay of the valley the kerchief he wore around his neck when it was cold. In short, as long as he had his sack on his shoulder he needed nobody in the world, whether he was in the woods of Resecone or lost deep in the plain of Caltagirone. Lia used to say:

"See Ieli? He's always been alone in the fields, as if one of his mares had brought him into the world, and that's why he knows how to do everything with his own hands."

As a matter of fact, it was true that Ieli needed no one, but all the people at the farm would have been glad to do things for him, since he was a helpful boy and there was always a chance of getting something from him. Lia baked him bread, out of Christian charity, and

---

[2] The name of a chestnut colt. Words that are used as names of animals in the original have generally been left in Italian, but when they refer only to the animal's coat, they have been translated.

he repaid her with well-made little wicker baskets to carry eggs in, cane winders, and other trifles.

"We act like his animals," said Lia, "that scratch each other's necks."

At Tebidi they all knew him since he was a baby, when you couldn't see him among the tails of the horses that were grazing on the Piano Del Lettighiere; and he had grown up under their eyes, you might say, though nobody ever saw him, and he was always wandering here and there with his herd. "He rained down from the sky, and the earth picked him up," as the saying goes; really one of those who have neither home nor family.

His mother was working at Vizzini and saw him only once a year, when he went to Saint John's fair with the colts; and the day she died they came to call him—one Saturday night—and on Monday Ieli went back to the herd, so that he didn't even lose the day's pay; but the poor boy had come back so upset that at times he let the colts break into the wheat fields.

"Hey, Ieli!" *massaro* Agrippino shouted at him from the threshing floor. "You want an extra good taste of my whip, you son-of-a-bitch?"

Ieli started running after the scattered colts and drove them dejectedly toward the hill. But his mother was always before his eyes, her head wrapped in a white kerchief, and not able to speak any more.

His father herded cows at Ragoleti, beyond Licodia, "where you could mow malaria," said the peasants of the neighborhood; but in malaria country the pastures are rich, and cows don't catch the fever. So Ieli stayed in the fields all year long, either at Donferrante, or at the Commenda, or in the Valle Del Iacitano, and the hunters or the travelers who took the short cuts would always see him here and there, like a dog without a master.

He didn't suffer from all of this, because he was used to staying with the horses that walked along step by step in front of him nibbling the clover, and with the birds that swirled around him in flocks, for the whole time the sun was making its slow, slow journey, till the shadows grew long and then vanished; he had the time to watch the clouds pile up little by little and picture mountains and valleys; he knew how the wind blows when it brings a storm and what the color of the clouds is when it's about to snow. Everything had its look and its meaning, and there were always things to see and things to listen to, every hour of the day. So toward sunset, when Ieli started playing on his pipe of elder-wood, the black mare would draw near, listlessly chewing clover, and would stand looking at him with her big, pensive eyes.

The one place where he suffered a little melancholy was on the desert lands of Passanitello, where neither a bush nor a shrub grows and in the hot months not a bird flies overhead. The horses gathered together in a circle to make shade for one another, with their heads drooping, and on the long days of the threshing, that great silent light rained down always the same and suffocatingly hot for sixteen hours.

But where feed was abundant and the horses liked to

linger, the boy would busy himself in some other way. He made reed cages for crickets, pipes with carvings on them, and little rush baskets, using a few twigs; he could set up a little hut, when the north wind drove the long files of crows through the valley, or when the cicadas beat their wings in the sun that scorched the stubble; he roasted acorns from the oak grove in the embers of sumac branches, as if they were chestnuts, or toasted his big slices of bread when they began to get hairy with mold—for when he was at Passanitello in the winter, the roads were so bad that fifteen days would pass without a living soul going by.

Don Alfonso, who was kept in cotton by his parents, envied his friend Ieli the canvas sack where he kept all his things: his bread, his onions, his little flask of wine, his kerchief for the cold, his little bundle of rags with his thread and needles, his tin box with flint and tinder; he envied him also the haughty speckled mare, that animal with the tuft of hair sticking out on her forehead, who had mean eyes and swelled her nostrils like a surly mastiff when anybody wanted to mount her. Instead she let Ieli mount her and scratch her ears, which were especially sensitive, and she kept sniffing him to listen to what he had to tell her.

"Leave that mare alone," Ieli advised, "she's not bad, but she doesn't know you."

After Scordu, the man from Buccheri,[3] led away the Calabrian mare that he had bought at Saint John's fair

---

[3] A large village about twenty-five miles west of Syracuse.

with the agreement that they would keep her in the herd until vintage time, the chestnut colt, left an orphan, didn't want to quiet down, and ran around on the cliffs of the mountain, with long lamenting neighs and his nostrils in the wind. Ieli ran after him, calling him with loud shouts, and the colt stopped to listen, his neck stretched tight and his ears restless, lashing his flanks with his tail.

"It's because they took his mother away from him, and he doesn't know what he's doing any more," observed Ieli. "Now he'll have to be watched, because he's liable to let himself fall over the cliff. It's like me, when my mother died I couldn't see straight any more."

Then, after the colt began to sniff the clover and take a couple of bites halfheartedly:

"See? Little by little he's beginning to forget all about her. —But he'll be sold too. Horses are made to be sold, like lambs are born to be butchered, and clouds bring the rain. Only the birds have nothing to do but sing and fly all day."

Ideas didn't come to him clear and straight one after the other, for there had rarely been anybody for him to talk to, and so he was never in a hurry to dig them out and disentangle them from the back of his mind, where he was used to letting them sprout and grow until they came forward little by little, like the buds on the branches under the sun.

"The birds, too," he added, "have to hunt up food, and when snow covers the ground they die."

Then he thought it over awhile:

Ieli

"You're like the birds; but when winter comes you can sit by the fire without doing anything."

Don Alfonso, however, answered that he went to school, to learn. Then Ieli opened his eyes wide and was all ears when the rich boy started reading, and he looked at the book and at him suspiciously, listening with that slight winking of the eyelids that shows intensity of attention in those animals that come nearest to man. He liked poetry, which caressed his ears with the harmony of an incomprehensible song, and sometimes he knitted his brow and pointed his chin, and a lot of work seemed to be going on inside him; then he would nod yes, yes, with a cunning smile, and he would scratch his head. When the rich boy started writing to show how many things he knew how to do, Ieli would have stayed there for whole days to watch him, and suddenly a look of suspicion would escape him. He couldn't understand how one could repeat on paper those very words he had said, or that Don Alfonso had said, and even those things that had never come out of his mouth at all, so that he ended by drawing back incredulously with his cunning smile.

Any new idea that knocked on his head to get in made him suspicious, and he seemed to sniff at it with the savage mistrust of his speckled mare. But he showed no surprise at anything in the world: if somebody had told him that in town horses rode in carriages, he would have remained impassive, with that mask of oriental indifference which is the dignity of the Sicilian peasant. He seemed to entrench himself instinctively in his ignorance, as if it were the strength of poverty. Every time he found himself short of answers, he repeated, with that obstinate smile that was intended to be sly:

"I don't know anything about it. I'm poor."

He had asked his friend Alfonso to write Mara's name for him on a piece of paper he had found, God knows where, for he picked up everything he saw on the ground, and he had put it in his little bundle of rags. One day, after having been silent for a while looking here and there deep in thought, he said very seriously:

"I've got a girl friend."

Alfonso, even though he knew how to read, opened his eyes wide.

"Yes," repeated Ieli. "Mara, the daughter of *massaro* Agrippino, who used to live here and who lives at Marineo now, in that big house on the plain, that you can see from the Piano Del Lettighiere, up there."

"Then you're going to get married?"

"Yes, when I'm grown up and make four *onze* a year. Mara doesn't know anything about it yet."

"Why haven't you told her?"

Ieli shook his head and became lost in thought. Then he unwrapped his little bundle of rags and spread out the paper he had had Alfonso write for him.

"It really does say 'Mara'; Don Gesualdo the field watchman read it, and Brother Cola too, when he came down to collect broad beans for the monastery.

"Anybody who knows how to write," he observed then, "is like one who keeps words in his tinder box, and can carry them in his pocket, and even send them here and there."

Ieli

"What are you going to do with that piece of paper now, when you don't know how to read?" Alfonso asked him.

Ieli shrugged his shoulders, but continued to wrap up carefully in his little bundle of rags the piece of paper with the writing on it.

He had known Mara since she was small, and they had begun by beating each other up, when they had met in the valley while picking blackberries in the wedges of bramble. The little girl, knowing she was "on her own ground," had grabbed Ieli by the collar as if he were a thief. For a while they pounded each other on the back, one blow for you and one for me, as the cooper does on the hoops of the barrels, but when they grew tired they began to calm down little by little, still clutching each other by the hair.

"Who are you?" Mara asked him.

And since Ieli, who was the wilder of the two, didn't say who he was—

"I'm Mara, the daughter of *massaro* Agrippino, who's the watchman of all these fields here."

Then Ieli let go his hold without saying anything, and the little girl started picking up the blackberries that she had dropped on the ground, peeking now and then at her opponent with curiosity.

"On the other side of the bridge, in the hedge of the vegetable field," added the little girl, "there are lots of big blackberries and the chickens eat them."

Meanwhile, Ieli was slinking away very softly, and Mara, after she had followed him with her eyes as far as she could see him in the oak grove, also turned and ran home as fast as her legs could carry her.

But from that day on they started to become tame and get used to each other. Mara would go to spin hemp on the parapet of the little bridge, and Ieli would slowly drive the herd toward the foot of Poggio Del Bandito. At first he kept his distance, circling around her, looking at her suspiciously from afar, and little by little he kept going closer with the cautious movements of a dog used to stones. When at last they happened to be side by side, they remained silent for hours, Ieli attentively watching the intricate work of the knitting Mara's mother had assigned to her, or she looking at him while he carved fine zigzags on sticks of almond wood. Then they went off, one in this direction, the other in that, without saying a word, and as soon as she was in sight of her home, the little girl began to run, making her skirt go high up on her little red legs.

Then when the prickly pears were ripe, they spent their time in the thick of the cactus bushes, peeling prickly pears all day long. They wandered together under the century-old walnut trees, and Ieli knocked down so many walnuts that they fell as thick as hail; the little girl worked hard picking up as many as she could, shouting with pleasure, and then she fled away swiftly, holding out the two corners of her apron and wobbling like a little old woman.

During the winter Mara didn't dare stick her nose out, the weather was so cold. At times, toward evening, you could see the smoke of the little fires of sumac wood that

Ieli

Ieli was making in the Piano Del Lettighiere, or on Poggio Di Macca, in order not to freeze to death like those titmice he found in the morning behind a stone or a clod of earth. Even the horses enjoyed swinging their tails a little around the fire, and they huddled together to keep warmer.

With March, skylarks came back to the plain, sparrows to the roofs, leaves and nests to the hedges; Mara began to go for walks with Ieli again, in the soft grass, among the flowering bushes, under the trees that were still bare but were starting to show dots of green. Ieli plunged into the thorny scrub like a bloodhound, to root out the nests of the blackbirds who looked at him in bewilderment with their little eyes of peppercorn. Inside their shirts the two children often carried almost naked baby rabbits, freshly taken from their holes, but with their long ears already uneasy; they ran around the fields following the horses, going into the stubble behind the reapers, step for step with the herd, stopping every time a mare stopped to crop a mouthful of grass. In the evening, when they came to the little bridge, they left each other, one in this direction, the other in that, without saying good-by.

So they spent the whole summer. Meanwhile, the sun was beginning to set behind Poggio Alla Croce, and the robins went after it toward the mountain, following it through the cactus bushes, as darkness was coming. The grasshoppers and the cicadas were not heard any more, and in that hour something like a great melancholy spread through the air.

At that time to Ieli's hut came his father, the cowherd, who had caught malaria at Ragoleti, and could hardly hold himself up on the donkey that was carrying him. Ieli lit a fire immediately and ran to "The Houses" to get him some eggs.

"You'd better put some straw by the fire," his father said, "I feel the fever coming back."

The chills of the fever were so strong that Menu, buried under his big cloak, the donkey's saddlebag, and Ieli's sack, shook like the leaves in November, in front of that huge blaze of branches which made his face look as white as a dead man's. The peasants from the farm came to ask him:

"How do you feel, Menu?"

The poor man answered only with a whine, like that of a suckling pup.

"It's the kind of malaria that kills you better than a gunshot," said his friends, warming their hands at the fire.

They sent for the doctor too, but it was all a waste of money, for the disease was one of those simple and familiar ones that even a boy would know how to cure, and if the fever hadn't been one of those that kill you anyhow, quinine would have cured it right away. Menu had spent a fortune buying quinine, but it was like throwing it down a well.

"Take some good strong eucalyptus tea, which doesn't cost anything," suggested *massaro* Agrippino, "and if it doesn't help any more than the quinine, at least you won't ruin yourself by spending money."

Ieli

He took the eucalyptus tea also, but the fever kept coming back, and it was even more violent. Ieli helped his father as well as he could. Every morning before going away with the colts, he left him the tea ready in a bowl, a bundle of branches within reach, eggs in the hot ashes, and he came back early in the evening with more firewood for the night, and a small flask of wine and some mutton that he had run as far as Licodia to buy. The poor boy did everything carefully and well, like a good housewife, and his father, following him with tired eyes as Ieli did the little chores here and there in the hut, smiled now and then, thinking that the boy would be able to take care of himself when left alone.

On the days the fever stopped for a few hours, Menu got up, his features all distorted and his head wrapped up tight in a kerchief, and he waited for Ieli at the doorway, while the sun was still warm. As Ieli dropped the bundle of firewood at the doorway and put the flask and the eggs on the table, his father said to him:

"Put the eucalyptus on to boil for tonight"—or: "When I'm gone remember that Aunt Agatha's keeping your mother's gold for you."

And Ieli nodded yes.

"It's no use," repeated *massaro* Agrippino each time he came back to see Menu. "By now your blood is all infected."

Menu listened without batting an eye, his face whiter than his cap.

He didn't get out of bed any more. Ieli began to cry

when he wasn't strong enough to help him turn from one side to the other; little by little Menu couldn't even speak any more. The last words he said to his boy were:

"When I'm dead go to the owner of the cows at Ragoleti and have him give you the three *onze* and the twelve *tumoli* [4] of wheat that he owes me for my work from May until now."

"No," answered Ieli, "it's only two and a half *onze,* because you left the cows more than a month ago, and we have to be fair with the master in figuring out the salary."

"That's right!" said Menu, half closing his eyes.

"Now I'm really alone in the world like a lost colt that the wolves can eat!" thought Ieli when they had taken his father to the cemetery of Licodia.

Mara also had come to see the house of the dead man, with that morbid curiosity that frightening things arouse.

"See how I'm left?" Ieli said to her. The little girl stepped back startled, fearing that he would make her go into the house where the dead man had been.

Ieli went to get his father's money, and then he left with his herd for Passanitello, where the grass was already tall on the fallow land, and the feed was abundant; so the colts stayed there to graze for a long time.

Meanwhile, Ieli had grown up—and Mara must have grown too, he often thought to himself as he played his pipe; and when he returned to Tebidi, after a long time,

---

[4] The *tumolo* was a Sicilian measure of grain equivalent to about forty pounds.

driving the mares very slowly in front of him on the slippery paths of the Fontana Dello Zio Cosimo, he kept searching with his eyes for the little bridge in the valley and the hut in the Valle Del Iacitano, and the roofs of "The Big Houses" where the pigeons were always flapping their wings.

But at that time the master had fired *massaro* Agrippino, and Mara's whole family was moving away. Ieli found the girl, big now and rather pretty, at the door of the courtyard, keeping an eye on her things while they were being loaded on the cart. Now the empty room seemed darker and smokier than usual. The table, the bed, the chest of drawers, and the images of the Virgin and of Saint John, and even the nails to hang the gourds with the seeds, had left marks on the walls where they had been for so many years.

"We're moving away," Mara said as she saw him looking around. "We're moving down to Marineo where that big house is, on the plain."

Ieli began to help *massaro* Agrippino and Lia load the cart, and when there was nothing left to carry out of the room, he went to sit with Mara on the edge of the watering trough.

"Even houses," he said to her when he had seen the last hamper piled on the cart, "even houses, when you take their things away from them, don't seem the same any more."

"At Marineo," answered Mara, "my mother said we'll have a room that's nicer and as big as the cheese house."

"Now that you'll be away I don't ever want to come

here again, because it'll seem like winter's back, seeing the door closed."

"At Marineo, though, we'll find other people, Pudda the Redhead and the field watchman's daughter; we'll have fun; at harvest time more than eighty reapers will come with bagpipes and there'll be dancing on the threshing floor."

Massaro Agrippino and his wife had started out with the cart, and Mara ran gaily behind, carrying the basket with the pigeons. Ieli followed her as far as the little bridge, and when Mara was about to disappear in the valley, he called after her:

"Mara! Oh! Mara!"

"What do you want?" she said.

He no longer knew what he wanted.

"What're you going to do here all alone?" the girl asked then.

"I'll stay with the colts."

Mara went skipping away, and he remained there motionless as long as he could hear the noise of the cart that bounced on the stones. The sun was touching the high rocks of Poggio Alla Croce, the gray foliage of the olive trees faded gradually in the twilight, and in the vast countryside, far, far away, you could hear nothing but the bell of Bianca in the widening silence.

After going to Marineo, where there were new people and so much to do at vintage time, Mara forgot all about him; but Ieli was always thinking of her, because he didn't have anything else to do in the long days he spent watching the tails of his animals. Now he no longer had any reason to go down into the valley, beyond the little bridge, and he was not seen at the farm again. So for a long time he didn't know that Mara had gotten engaged—so much water had passed and passed meanwhile under the little bridge. He only saw the girl again the day of the fiesta of Saint John, when he went to the fair to sell the colts: a fiesta that turned completely to poison for him and made him lose his bread, because of an accident that happened to one of his master's colts, God save us!

The day of the fair,[5] the factor had been waiting for the colts since dawn, walking up and down in his shiny boots behind the rumps of the horses and the mules which were arranged in rows on both sides of the highroad. The fair was already almost over and still there was no sign of Ieli and his animals around the curve of the highroad.

On the scorched slopes of Calvario and Mulino A Vento there still remained a few small flocks of sheep, huddled together in circles with their muzzles to the ground and their eyes lifeless, and a few yoke of oxen with long hair, the kind that you sell to pay the rent of the farms; they were waiting motionless under the broiling sun. There below, toward the valley, the bell of Saint John's sounded High Mass, accompanied by the

---

[5] This fair takes place on the 24th of June, St. John's Day, at Vizzini, which is a small town on the Iblei Mountains, about thirty miles west of Syracuse. The names of places occurring in this section of the story are either points near Vizzini or streets in the town.

long crackling of firecrackers. Then the fairground seemed to quiver, and a loud cry ran through the town, lingering among the peddlers' awnings that were spread along the Salita Dei Galli, going down the streets and then seeming to return from the valley where the church was. *Viva San Giovanni!*[6]

"Damn it!" screamed the factor. "That bastard of an Ieli will make me miss the fair!"

The sheep lifted their muzzles in wonder and began bleating all together, and the oxen took a few steps slowly, looking around with big, intent eyes.

The factor was furious because the rent for the "big fields" was due that day, "as Saint John arrives under the elm"[7] the contract said, and the money from the sale of the colts had been counted on to complete the sum. Meanwhile, there were as many colts, horses, and mules as God had made, all groomed and shiny, and decorated with tufts and tassels and little bells, swishing their tails to while away the time and turning their heads toward everyone who passed, as if waiting for some kind soul willing to buy them.

"He must have gone to sleep somewhere, that bastard!" the factor kept shouting. "And he leaves me stuck with the colts!"

Instead, Ieli had walked all night so that the colts would arrive at the fairground fresh, and would be able to get a good place when they arrived, and he had

---

[6] "Long live Saint John!"

[7] The procession of Saint John. The elm refers to a specific location of the kind used in old rural contracts.

reached the Piano Del Corvo when the *Three Kings*[8] had not yet gone down and were shining on Monte Arturo with their arms crossed. Along the road, carts and people on horseback going to the fiesta passed continuously; so Ieli kept his eyes wide open to make sure that the colts, scared by the unusual traffic, didn't scatter, but went together along the edge of the road behind Bianca, who walked calmly straight ahead, the bell on her neck. From time to time, when the road ran over the crest of the hills, even way up there you could hear the bell of Saint John's, so that also in the darkness and silence of the countryside the fiesta was in the air; and all along the highroad, far, far off, as far as there were people on foot or on horseback going to Vizzini, you could hear the cry: *Viva San Giovanni!* And rockets rose straight and shining behind the mountains of Canziria and they were like the stars that rain down in August.

"It's like Christmas Eve," Ieli was saying to the boy who helped him drive the herd, "when all the farmhouses are lit up and the people are celebrating, and here and there you can see bonfires all over the countryside."

The boy was half asleep, slowly pushing ahead one leg after the other, and didn't answer; but Ieli, who felt all his blood stirred by that bell, couldn't stay quiet, as if each one of those rockets sliding silent and shining on the darkness behind the mountain burst from his soul.

"Mara must have gone to Saint John's fiesta too," he said, "because she goes every year."

[8] Three stars of the constellation of Orion.

And not caring that Alfio, the boy, didn't answer—

"You don't know? Mara's so tall now that she's even bigger than her mother who brought her into the world, and when I saw her again I couldn't believe she was the same girl I used to go with to pick prickly pears and knock down walnuts."

And he began to sing out loud all the songs he knew.

"Hey, Alfio, are you asleep?" he shouted when he had finished. "Watch out that Bianca keeps following you, watch out!"

"No, I'm not asleep," answered Alfio with a hoarse voice.

"See the Puddara[9] winking at us up there above Granvilla, as if rockets were being shot off at Santa Domenica too? It can't be long before daybreak, but we'll get to the fair in time to find a good place. Hey, my good Morellino! You'll have a new halter, with red tassels, for the fair! and you too, Stellato!"

And he went on talking to each of the colts, so that they would take heart hearing his voice in the dark. But he felt sad that Stellato and Morellino were going to the fair to be sold.

"When they're sold they'll go away with their new master, and we won't see them in the herd any more, just as it's been with Mara after she went away to Marineo. —Her father's doing very well down there at Marineo; when I went to see them they put in front of me bread, wine, cheese, and any other food you could think of, because he's almost the factor, and he's got the

[9] The Sicilian name of the Pleiades.

keys to everything, and I could have eaten the whole
farm if I'd wanted to. Mara almost didn't know me
any more, it'd been so long since she'd seen me, and
she began to shout: —'Oh look, it's Ieli, the horsekeeper,
the one from Tebidi!' —It's like when you come back
from far away; and if you only see the tip of a mountain
you recognize right away the place where you grew up.
Lia didn't want me to use *tu* with Mara any more, now
that she's big, because people who don't know talk
easily.[10] But Mara laughed, and she was all red in the
face as if she'd been putting bread in the oven that very
minute; she spread out the tablecloth and set the table
and she didn't seem the same any more. —'Do you still
remember Tebidi?'—I asked her as soon as Lia had gone
to draw some fresh wine from the barrel. —'Yes, sure,
I remember,' she said to me. 'At Tebidi there was the
bell and the bell tower that looked like the handle of a
saltcellar, and they rang the bell from the platform, and
there were two stone cats that purred on the gate of the
garden.' —I felt them here inside, all those things, as
she was saying them. Mara looked at me from head to
foot, all eyes, and said over and over again—'You're sure
big now!' And she also began to laugh and hit me here
on the head."

So Ieli, the horsekeeper, lost his bread, because just at
that moment a carriage suddenly came along, which

---

[10] *Tu* is the familiar form of address in Italian and was
considered a sign of intimacy. If an unmarried girl and a
young man addressed each other with *tu*, people thought
that they were at least engaged to be married, and as a
result the girl would have no other suitors.

hadn't been heard before, since it had been climbing step by step up the steep grade, and when it had reached the level it had begun to trot with a terrific cracking of whips and jingling of bells, as if the devil were driving it. The colts, frightened, scattered in a flash, as if there were an earthquake, and it took a lot of calling and shouting and ohee, ohee, ohee's! by Ieli and the boy before they could gather them around Bianca, who was listlessly trotting away, the bell on her neck.

As soon as Ieli had counted his animals, he noticed that Stellato was missing, and he thrust his hands into his hair, because at that spot the road ran along the ravine, and it was in the ravine that Stellato broke his back—a colt that was worth twelve *onze,* like twelve angels of paradise! Weeping and shouting, Ieli called the colt—ahoo! ahoo! ahoo!—for it was still dark. Stellato finally answered from the bottom of the ravine with a painful neighing, as if he could speak, poor animal!

"Oh, *mamma mia!*" Ieli and the boy were screaming. "Oh, how terrible, how terrible, *mamma mia!*"

The travelers who were going to the fiesta, hearing them cry like that in the darkness, asked what they had lost; and then, when they found out what it was all about, continued on their way.

Stellato was lying motionless where he had fallen, with his legs in the air, and while Ieli was feeling him all over, crying and speaking to him as if the colt could understand, the poor animal lifted his neck painfully and turned his head toward him, and you could hear the panting, broken by convulsions.

Ieli

"He must have broken something!" whined Ieli, desperate because he couldn't see a thing in the dark; and the colt, as inert as a stone, let his head fall down again heavily. Alfio, who had remained on the road to look after the herd, had been the first one to calm down and had taken his bread out of his sack.

Now the sky had grown whitish, and the mountains all around seemed to rise one by one, black and tall. From the curve in the highroad you could begin to see the town, with Monte Del Calvario and Monte Del Mulino A Vento outlined against the pale light of dawn; they were still hazy and speckled by white blotches of sheep, and as the oxen, grazing atop the mountain in the blue, moved here and there, it seemed that the profile of the mountain itself became animated and swarmed with life. From the bottom of the ravine the bell could no longer be heard; the travelers were rarer, and those few who passed were in a hurry to get to the fair. Poor Ieli didn't know which saint to turn to, in that solitude: Alfio, by himself, couldn't help him at all, so he slowly nibbled his piece of bread.

Finally, the factor was seen, coming on his mule, hurrying toward them, shouting and swearing in the distance as he saw the animals stopped on the road; so that Alfio ran up the hill as fast as his legs could carry him. But Ieli didn't move from the side of Stellato. The factor left the mule on the road and went down into the ravine and tried to help the colt get up, pulling him by the tail.

"Leave him alone!" said Ieli, white in the face as if

he had been the one to break his back. "Leave him alone! Don't you see that he can't move, poor animal?"

Stellato, in fact, at every movement and every effort they had him make, gave a death rattle, as if he were a Christian.[11] The factor vented his rage by kicking and beating Ieli and let go a stream of curses that burned the ears of all the saints and angels in paradise. Alfio, a little reassured by this time, had gone back to the road, in order not to leave the animals unguarded, and he kept trying to clear himself by saying:

"It isn't my fault. I was up front with Bianca."

"There's nothing we can do here," said the factor at last, when he realized that it was all a waste of time. "All we can get out of him is the hide, as long as it's good."

Ieli began shaking like a leaf when he saw the factor go and pull the shotgun from the saddle of the mule.

"Get out of the way, you good-for-nothing!" the factor howled at him. "I don't know who's stopping me from leaving you dead on the ground with that colt who was worth a lot more than you, in spite of the stinking baptism that thief of a priest gave you!"

Stellato, who couldn't move, turned only his head, his eyes wide and staring as if he had understood everything, and his hair curled in waves along his ribs and it seemed that a shiver ran under it. And so the factor killed Stellato on the spot to get the hide, at least, and Ieli seemed to feel inside himself the dull noise made by the shot fired at close range into the live flesh.

---

[11] In Sicily, a human being in general.

Ieli

"Now, if you want a piece of advice," the factor told him, "don't try to come to the master for the money he owes you, because he'd sure pay you, but good!"

The factor went away with Alfio, and with the other colts, who cropped grass from the edge of the road and didn't even turn to see where Stellato remained. And Stellato remained alone in the ravine, waiting for somebody to come and skin him, his eyes still wide open and his four legs stretched out—lucky he, who at last didn't suffer any more. Ieli, now that he had seen how the factor had aimed at the colt and fired the shot in cold blood while the poor animal turned his head painfully as if he were human, stopped crying and sat there on a stone, staring fixedly at Stellato until the men came to get the hide.

Now he could go wherever he pleased, to enjoy the fiesta or stay in the square all day, to see the rich men in the café, anything he liked, because he didn't have bread, or a roof over his head any more, and he had to look for a master, if anyone wanted him after the accident with Stellato.

That's the way the world goes: while Ieli, with his sack on his shoulder and his staff in his hand, went looking for a master, the band played gaily in the square, with plumes in their hats, in the middle of a crowd of white caps as thick as flies, and the rich men sat in the café enjoying it all. Everybody was dressed up, like the animals of the fair, and in a corner of the square there was a woman with a short skirt and flesh-colored stockings that made her legs look bare, and she was pounding a big drum in front of a large painted sheet on which you could see a massacre of Christians, with blood flowing in torrents; and in the crowd that was watching openmouthed, there was *massaro* Cola too, who knew Ieli from the time he was at Passanitello, and he said that he would find him a master, because Isidoro Macca was looking for a swineherd.

"But don't say anything about Stellato," *massaro* Cola warned him. "An accident like that can happen to anybody in this world; but it's better not to talk about it."

So they went in search of Macca, who was at the dance, and while *massaro* Cola went to talk to him, Ieli waited on the street, in the middle of the crowd that was looking in from the door of the shop. In the shabby room there were lots of people jumping around and enjoying themselves, all excited and red in the face, and making a terrific noise pounding their big shoes on the brick floor, and you couldn't even hear the *ron-ron* of the double bass; and as soon as one piece, costing a *grano,* was finished, they raised their finger as a sign that they wanted another, and the double-bass player, to keep a count, made an X on the wall with charcoal, and started all over again.

"Those people spend money without thinking," Ieli was saying to himself, "so they must have their pockets full, and they're not in difficulty like me, left without a master, since they sweat and wear themselves out jumping around as if they were paid for it!"

Massaro Cola came back saying that Macca didn't

need anybody. Then Ieli turned his back and went away dejected.

Mara lived near Saint Anthony's, where the houses climb up the mountain facing the valley of Canziria, which is all green with cactus, and has mill wheels foaming below in the torrent; but Ieli didn't have the courage to go over there now, after he hadn't even been wanted as a swineherd, and as he wandered around in the middle of the crowd that bumped and pushed him without paying any attention to him, he felt more alone than when he was with the colts on the desert lands of Passanitello, and he felt like crying.

He finally met *massaro* Agrippino, who was walking around in the square with his arms hanging down, enjoying the fiesta, and who began shouting after him: "Hey! Ieli! Hey!" And he took him home. Mara was all dressed up, with long earrings beating against her cheeks, and her ring-laden hands on her belly, waiting at the doorway for it to get dark, to go and see the fireworks.

"Oh!" said Mara. "You've come for the fiesta of Saint John too?"

Ieli didn't dare go in because he was badly dressed; but *massaro* Agrippino pushed him by the shoulders, telling him that they weren't seeing each other for the first time, and all of them knew he had come to the fair with his master's colts. Lia poured him a big glass of wine, and they took him along with the women and other friends of the neighborhood, to go and see how the town was all lit up.

When they got to the square, Ieli was openmouthed with wonder; it was all a sea of fire as when the stubbles are burning, because of the large number of rockets the faithful lit in front of the Saint, who, all black under the silver canopy, was enjoying it all from the entrance to Rosario.[12] The faithful were coming and going among the flames like so many devils, and there was even a woman with her clothes all loose and in disorder, her hair disheveled and her eyes bulging out of her head, who was lighting rockets too, and a priest with his gown flying in the air, without a hat, who seemed to be obsessed by devotion.

"That's the son of *massaro* Neri, the factor of Salonia; he spends more than ten *lire* for rockets!" said Lia, nodding toward a young man who was going around the square holding in his hands two rockets at a time, like candles, so that all the women devoured him with their eyes, and shouted to him: *Viva San Giovanni!*

"His father's rich and owns more than twenty head of cattle," added *massaro* Agrippino.

Mara also knew that he had carried the big banner in the procession, and had held it as straight as a pole—he was such a strong and good-looking young man.

Massaro Neri's son seemed to hear this talk and to light his rockets for Mara, whirling about her; in fact, after the fireworks he joined them and took them to the dance and to the *Cosmorama,* where you could see the old world and the new, and he paid for everyone, of course, even for Ieli, who walked behind the group like

---

[12] The name of a section of Vizzini.

a dog without a master to see *massaro* Neri's son dance with Mara, who twirled around and curtsied like a turtledove, prettily holding out one corner of her apron. *Massaro* Neri's son capered like a colt, so that Lia wept with joy, and *massaro* Agrippino nodded yes, yes, all was going well.

Finally, when they were tired, they walked here and there on the Promenade, carried along by the crowd as if they were in a raging river, and they went to see the illuminated pictures, in which Saint John's head was being cut off—a sight that would have moved even the Turks to pity[13]—and under the ax Saint John kicked like a wild buck. Close by, the band played under a big wooden umbrella that was all lit up, and in the square the crowd was so thick that never before had so many Christians been seen at a fair.

Mara walked arm in arm with *massaro* Neri's son, like a rich girl, and whispered in his ear and laughed and seemed to be having a lot of fun. Ieli was dead tired, and fell asleep sitting on the sidewalk until the first explosions of the fireworks woke him up. At that moment Mara was still at the side of *massaro* Neri's son, leaning against him with her two hands clasped on his shoulder, and in the light of the colored fireworks she looked all white and then all red. When the last rockets fled into the sky in one big bunch, *massaro* Neri's son,

---

[13] In Sicily and in other parts of Italy the word *Turco* ("Turk") often indicates a non-Christian in general and a man of cruel nature in particular.

whose face looked green, turned toward her and kissed her.

Ieli didn't say anything, but at that moment the whole fiesta, which he had enjoyed until then, changed to poison for him, and he again began to think of all his troubles, which he had forgotten—that he was without a master, and no longer knew what to do or where to go, and no longer had bread, or a roof over his head—in short, that it would be better to go and throw himself into the ravine, like Stellato, whom the dogs were eating by now.

In the meantime, around him people were gay. Mara and her girl friends skipped and sang along the stony little road while they were going back home.

"Good night! Good night!" the friends kept saying as they separated along the way.

Mara said good night, and seemed to be singing, there was so much happiness in her voice; and *massaro* Neri's son seemed to go completely wild and never want to leave her, while *massaro* Agrippino and Lia argued as they opened the door of the house. No one paid any attention to Ieli; only *massaro* Agrippino remembered that he was there, and asked him:

"And now where'll you go?"

"I don't know," said Ieli.

"Tomorrow come and see me and I'll help you find a job. Tonight, go back to the square where we were listening to the band; you'll find some room on a bench, and as for sleeping in the open, you must be used to it."

Ieli

He was used to it all right, but what hurt him most was that Mara didn't say anything to him, and left him just like that at the doorway, like a tramp; so that he told her about it the next day, as soon as he could find her alone in the house for a moment:

"Oh, Mara! How you forget your friends!"

"Oh, it's you, Ieli!" said Mara. "No, I haven't forgotten you. But I was so tired after the fireworks!"

"Do you love *massaro* Neri's son at least?" he asked, turning his staff over and over in his hands.

"What are you talking about?" answered Mara bluntly. "My mother's right in the next room and can hear everything."

Massaro Agrippino found him a job as shepherd at Salonia, where *massaro* Neri was the factor; but since Ieli was new to this kind of work, he had to be satisfied with a very poor salary.

Now he was busy tending his sheep, and learning how to make cheese, and *ricotta*,[14] and *caciocavallo*,[15] and all the other products of the herd; but when chattering in the courtyard in the evening with the other shepherds and peasants while the women shelled broad beans for the soup, if they started speaking of *massaro* Neri's son, who was going to marry *massaro* Agrippino's Mara, Ieli didn't say anything any more and didn't even dare open

---

[14] A type of cottage cheese made by heating the curd that is left after cheese has been extracted.

[15] A special kind of full-cream cheese made in southern Italy.

his mouth. Once, when the field watchman made fun of him by saying that Mara had dropped him after everyone had said that they were going to be husband and wife, Ieli, who was busy watching the pot in which the milk was boiling, answered, as he slowly and carefully stirred in the rennet:

"Mara's prettier now that she's grown up, she's like a rich young lady."

Since he was patient and a hard worker, he quickly learned everything about his job better than one who had been born to it, and since he was used to staying with animals, he loved his sheep as if they were his own children; the "disease," therefore, didn't cause such a slaughter at Salonia, and the herd prospered so that it was a pleasure for *massaro* Neri every time he came to the farm, and as a result, at the beginning of the following year, he decided to induce the owner to raise Ieli's salary, and so Ieli now got almost as much as he had been earning as horsekeeper. And it was money well spent, for Ieli never counted the miles and miles he covered looking for better pastures for his animals, and when the sheep gave birth or were sick he took them to the pasture in the saddlebags of his little donkey, and carried in his arms the lambs, who bleated in his face with their noses out of the sack, and suckled his ears.

In the famous snowstorm on Saint Lucy's night, more than three feet of snow fell in the Lago Morto at Salonia, and all around for miles and miles, as day came you couldn't see anything else in the whole countryside. —*Massaro* Neri would have been ruined that time, as

were so many others in the region, if Ieli hadn't gotten
up three or four times during the night to chase the
sheep around in the corral, so that the poor animals
shook the snow off and didn't get buried like so many
in the nearby herds—at least that's what *massaro* Agrippino said when he came to take a look at the little field
of broad beans he had at Salonia, and he also said that
the other story about *massaro* Neri's son marrying his
daughter Mara wasn't true at all, for Mara had anything
but that on her mind.

"But people said they were supposed to get married at
Christmas!" said Ieli.

"It's not true at all, they weren't supposed to marry
anybody! It's all just gossip of envious people who stick
their noses in somebody else's business," answered *massaro* Agrippino.

But, after *massaro* Agrippino had gone, the field
watchman, who knew all about it because he had heard
the talk in the square when he went to town on Sunday,
told how it really was: they weren't going to get married
because *massaro* Neri's son had found out that *massaro*
Agrippino's Mara was carrying on with Don Alfonso,
the rich young man, who had known Mara since she was
a little girl; and *massaro* Neri had said that he wanted
his son to be honorable like his father, and the only kind
of horns he wanted in his house were those of his oxen.[16]

---

[16] In Italy people say that cuckolds "wear horns." This
expression was already very common in Boccaccio and in the
writers of the Italian Renaissance and passed to English
Renaissance literature through their works. In our time
Italians apply it also to wives of unfaithful husbands.

Ieli was there too, seated with the others in a circle, having lunch, and at that moment was slicing bread. He didn't say anything, but he lost his appetite for the whole day.

While he was driving the sheep to pasture, he began to think of Mara again, when she was a little girl and they spent the whole day together and walked in the Valle Del Iacitano and on Poggio Alla Croce, and she watched him with her chin in the air as he climbed up to get the nests at the tops of the trees; and he also thought of Don Alfonso who used to come and see him from the nearby villa, and they would lie flat on their stomachs in the grass to tease the crickets in the nests, with a little twig. Sitting on the edge of a brook, his arms around his knees, for hours and hours he kept turning over in his mind all these things, and the high walnut trees at Tebidi, and the thick bushes of the valleys, and the slopes of the hills green with sumacs, and the gray olive trees that covered the valley like fog, and the red roof of the big house, and the bell tower, "that looked like the handle of a saltcellar" among the orange trees of the garden. —Here the countryside spread out before him barren, desolate, speckled with scorched grass, fading silently into the faraway suffocating heat.

In the spring, as soon as the broad-bean pods began to bend down with weight, Mara came to Salonia with her father and mother and the boy and the little donkey, to pick the beans, and they all came to sleep at the farm for the two or three days the harvest lasted. So Ieli saw the girl morning and evening, and they often sat side by side on the little wall of the sheepfold, talking together, while the boy counted the sheep.

"It's like being at Tebidi," said Mara, "when we were small, and used to be together on the little bridge of the path."

Ieli remembered it all too, although he didn't say anything, because he had always been sensible and a boy of few words.

When the harvest was over, the evening before she left Mara came to say good-by to the young man, while he was making *ricotta* and was intent on skimming the whey with the ladle.

"I'll say good-by now," she said, "because tomorrow we're going back to Vizzini."

"How did the broad beans go?"

"Bad! The rust ate them all up this year."

"We didn't have enough rain," said Ieli. "Just think, we had to kill even the ewe lambs because they didn't have anything to eat; all over Salonia there weren't even two inches of grass."

"But it doesn't make much difference to you. You always have your salary, good crops or bad!"

"Yes, it's true," he said, "but I hate to hand those poor animals over to the butcher."

"Remember when you came for the fiesta of Saint John, and you didn't have a master?"

"Yes, I remember."

"It was my father who found you a job here, with *massaro* Neri."

"And you, why didn't you marry *massaro* Neri's son?"

"Because it wasn't the will of God . . . My father's been unlucky," she went on after a while. "Since we went to Marineo everything has gone wrong, the broad beans, the wheat, that piece of vineyard we have up there. Then my brother had to go into the service, and we lost a mule that was worth forty *onze.*"

"I know," answered Ieli, "the bay mule!"

"Now that we've lost so many things, who'd want to marry me?"

Mara was breaking a little prune shoot to pieces while she was talking, her chin on her breast and her eyes low, and she nudged Ieli's elbow a little with her own, as if by accident. But Ieli didn't say anything, his eyes on the churn; so she went on:

"At Tebidi they used to say we were going to be husband and wife someday, remember?"

"Yes," said Ieli, and put the ladle down on the edge of the churn. "But I'm a poor shepherd and couldn't dream of marrying a *massaro*'s daughter, like you."

Mara remained silent for a little while, and then she said:

"If you love me, I'd be glad to marry you."

"Really?"

"Yes, really."

"And what will *massaro* Agrippino say?"

"My father says you know your job now, and you're not one of those who squander their salary but you make two pennies out of one, and you hardly eat in order not to use up the bread, so someday you'll have sheep of your own and you'll get rich."

"In that case," concluded Ieli, "I'll be glad to marry you too."

"Here!" Mara said to him after it became dark, and the sheep were quieting down little by little. "If you want a kiss now, I'll give it to you since we're going to be husband and wife."

Ieli took it meekly, and not knowing what to say, added:

"I've always loved you, even when you wanted to leave me for *massaro* Neri's son . . ." But he didn't have the heart to talk about the other one.

"See? We were meant for each other!" concluded Mara.

In fact, *massaro* Agrippino said yes, and Lia hurriedly put together a new jacket and a pair of velveteen pants for her son-in-law.

Mara was as beautiful and fresh as a rose, with a white mantilla that looked like the Easter Lamb, and an amber necklace that made her neck look white; so Ieli, going along the street at her side, walked straight and stiff, all dressed up in new wool and velveteen, and didn't dare blow his nose with his red silk handkerchief, not to call people's attention to him; but the neighbors and all those who knew the story of Don Alfonso laughed in his face. When Mara said "I will," and the priest, making a big sign of the cross, gave her to him as a wife, Ieli led her home, and he felt as if he had been given all the gold of the Madonna and all the land his eyes had seen.

"Now that we are husband and wife," he said to her when they got home, sitting opposite her and making himself very small, "now that we are husband and wife, I can tell you that I can't believe that you wanted me . . . when you could have had so many others better than I am . . . as beautiful as you are! . . ."

The poor man couldn't say anything else to her, and could hardly fit in his new clothes, so happy was he to see Mara arranging and touching everything and being the mistress of the house. So he didn't know how to tear himself away from the door to go back to Salonia; when Monday came, he lingered around as he arranged his bags, his cloak, and his umbrella of oilcloth on the packsaddle of the little donkey.

"You should come to Salonia too!" he said to his wife, who was watching him from the threshold. "You should come with me."

But the woman began to laugh, and answered that she wasn't born to be a shepherdess, and there was no reason for her to go to Salonia.

In fact, Mara wasn't born to be a shepherdess, and she wasn't used to the north wind of January when your hands stiffen on the staff and your fingernails seem to be falling out, and to the furious rainstorms when the water goes through to your bones, and to the suffocating dust of the roads when the sheep move along under the burning sun, and to the hard bed on the ground and to the moldy bread, and to the long silent and solitary days when in the scorched countryside you can see nothing but a rare sun-blackened peasant driving his little donkey silently ahead of him on the white, endless road. At least Ieli knew that Mara was warm under the covers, or spinning by the fire together with her neighbors, or that she was enjoying the sun on the balcony, while he was coming back from the pastures tired and thirsty, or drenched with rain, or when the wind drove the snow into his hut and put out the fire of sumac wood. Every month Mara went to get his salary from the master, and she was neither without eggs in the chicken coop, nor without oil in the lantern, nor without wine in the flask.

Twice a month Ieli went to see her, and she waited for him on the balcony with her spindle in her hand; then when he had tied the donkey in the stable and had taken off the saddlebags and put the feed in the manger, and had set the firewood in the shed in the yard, or put away whatever else he was carrying into the kitchen, Mara helped him hang his cloak on the nail and take off his drenched leggings in front of the fire, and poured him wine while the soup boiled gaily; and quiet and considerate like a good housewife she set the table, while she was talking to him of this and that, of the hen that was brooding, of the cloth she had on her loom, of the calf they were raising, without forgetting a single one of the little chores of the household, so that Ieli felt like a king there.

But on Saint Barbara's night he went home at an unusual hour, when all the lights were out in the little street, and the clock in the town was striking midnight. It was a night for wolves, and the wolf had gone into Ieli's house while he stayed out in the rain and wind for love of his salary and of the master's mare, who was sick and needed the farrier right away. He knocked and stormed at the door, calling aloud for Mara, while the water poured down on him from the roof gutter and came out at his heels. His wife finally came to open the door and began to give him a tongue-lashing as if she had been the one to run around the fields in that bad weather, and she had such a look on her face that he asked:

"What's wrong? What's the matter?"

"The matter is that you scared me coming at this hour! Do you think this is an hour for Christians? To-morrow I'll be sick."

"Go to bed, I'll light the fire myself."

"No, I've got to go and get some wood."

"I'll go."

"No, I say!"

When Mara came back with the wood in her arms, Ieli said:

"Why did you open the door to the courtyard? Wasn't there any more wood in the kitchen?"

"No, I went to get it from the shed."

She let herself be kissed, very coldly, and turned her head the other way.

"His wife lets him get drenched outside the door," said the neighbors, "when there's another bird inside!"

But Ieli didn't know that he was a cuckold, nor did

the others take the trouble to tell him, since he didn't seem to care at all, and had taken the woman as she was, after *massaro* Neri's son had jilted her because he knew the story of Don Alfonso. Instead, Ieli was happy and content in his disgrace, and grew as fat as a pig, "for horns are thin, but keep the house fat!"

Finally one day, the herd boy told him to his face, when they were wrangling over some cheese that had been stolen by shaving off a piece at a time:

"Now that Don Alfonso has taken your wife, you think you're his brother-in-law, and you've become so conceited that you think you're a crowned king, with those horns on your head."

The factor and the field watchman expected to see blood flow at these words; instead, Ieli kept quiet as if it were none of his business, and he had such an idiotic look on his face that the horns suited him very well.

It was getting close to Easter now, so the factor sent the farm hands to confession, hoping that for fear of God they wouldn't steal any more. Ieli also went, and coming out of the church he looked for the boy with whom he had had words, and threw his arms around his neck saying:

"The father confessor told me to forgive you; but I'm not angry with you about what you told me; and if you don't shave pieces of cheese off any more, I won't care at all about what you said to me when you were angry."

It was from that moment on that they called him Golden Horns, and the nickname stuck with him and all his family even after he washed those horns in blood.

Mara had gone to confession too, and came back from church all huddled up in her mantilla, her eyes low, so that she looked like Saint Mary Magdalene. When Ieli, waiting for her in silence on the balcony, saw her come like that, and it was clear that she had the Sacrament inside her, he, as pale as death, kept looking her over from head to foot, as if he were seeing her for the first time, or as if they had changed her, his Mara, and he didn't even dare lift his eyes to her while she spread out the tablecloth and put the bowls on the table, calmly and neatly as usual.

Then after having thought about it awhile, he asked her coldly:

"Is it true you're carrying on with Don Alfonso?"

Mara fixed her beautiful, limpid eyes on his face and made the sign of the cross:

"Why do you want to make me sin on this holy day?" she exclaimed.

"No! I still don't want to believe it . . . because Don Alfonso and I were always together when we were boys, and not a single day passed that he didn't come to Tebidi . . . just like two brothers. . . . Then he's rich and has money by the shovelful, and if he wanted women he could get married because he's got bread and everything else."

Mara was losing her temper and began to give him such a tongue-lashing that he didn't raise his nose from his plate any more.

Finally, so that the food they were eating didn't turn to poison, Mara changed the subject and asked if he had thought of having someone hoe the flax they had sown in the broad-bean field.

"Yes," answered Ieli, "and the flax will be good."

"In that case," said Mara, "this winter, I'll make you two new shirts to keep you warm."

In short, Ieli simply didn't understand what "cuckold" means, and didn't know what jealousy was; every new thing was slow getting into his head, and this one was so big that it really had a devil of a time getting in especially when he saw his Mara before him, so beautiful and white and neat, and she herself had wanted him, and he loved her so much, and had thought of her for such a long time, for so many years, since he was a boy, so that when they had told him she wanted to marry somebody else he hadn't felt like eating or drinking the whole day. —And even when he thought of Don Alfonso, he couldn't believe that such a dirty trick was possible; he still could see him at Tebidi, with his kind eyes and his smiling little mouth coming to bring sweets and white bread, so long ago—such a dirty trick! And since he hadn't seen him any more, for he was a poor shepherd who stayed in the country the whole year round, he always remembered him that way.

But the first time that, unfortunately, he saw Don Alfonso again, now a full-grown man, Ieli felt as if he had had a blow in the stomach. How big and handsome he had become! With that gold chain on his vest, and the velvet jacket, and that smooth beard that seemed to be of gold too. Not conceited either; in fact, he slapped Ieli on the shoulder calling him by his first name. He had come with the owner of the farm and a group of friends for a picnic in the country at shearing time; and unexpectedly Mara had come too, under the pretext that she was pregnant and had a craving for fresh *ricotta*.

It was a beautiful, warm day in the golden fields with the flowering hedges and the long green rows of vines. The sheep were gamboling and bleating with pleasure at feeling themselves freed from all that wool, and in the kitchen the women were making a big fire to cook all the things that the owner had brought for dinner. Meanwhile, the rich men who were waiting had gone into the shade under the carob trees, and were having someone play the tambourines and bagpipes, and those who wanted to, danced with the women of the farm.

Ieli, while he was shearing the sheep, felt something gnaw inside him, without knowing why, like a thorn, a driven nail, a pair of fine shears that worked around inside him bit by bit, worse than poison. The owner had ordered that they kill two kids, and the year-old wether, and some chickens and a turkey. In short, he wanted to do things in a big way, without stinting, so that he would make a good show in front of his friends; and while all those animals cried out in pain, and the kids screamed under the knife, Ieli felt his knees shake, and at times it seemed to him that the wool he was shearing and the grass, in which the sheep were gamboling, were aflame with blood.

"Don't go!" he said to Mara, when Don Alfonso was

calling her to come and dance with the others. "Don't go, Mara!"

"Why not?"

"I don't want you to go. Don't go!"

"Don't you hear them calling me?"

He said nothing more; he had become dark and gloomy like a gathering storm, while he was bent over the sheep he was shearing. Mara shrugged her shoulders and went to dance. She was flushed and gay, her black eyes looked like two stars, and when she laughed you could see her white teeth, and all the gold she was wearing beat and glistened on her cheeks and breast, and she looked just like the Madonna. All at once Ieli straightened up, the long shears in his fist, so white in the face, as white as his father, the cowherd, had once been, when he shook with fever by the fire in the hut. He looked at Don Alfonso—his fine curly beard, and the velvet jacket and the gold chain on his vest—who was taking Mara's hand and inviting her to dance; he saw him reach out with his arm, as if to press her to his chest, and she was letting him do it—then, God forgive him, he lost his head, and cut Don Alfonso's throat with a single stroke, just like a kid's.

Later, while they were leading him before the judge, bound, broken, without having dared offer the least resistance,

"What!" he said. "I shouldn't even have killed him? . . . But he'd taken Mara! . . ."

1880

ROSSO MALPELO

He was called Malpelo because he had red hair;[1] and he had red hair because he was a mean and bad boy, who promised to turn into a first-rate scoundrel. So everybody at the red-sand quarry called him Malpelo, and even his mother, having always heard that name, had almost forgotten his real one.

But then, she saw him only on Saturday nights, when he came back home with that little bit of money he had earned during the week; and since he was *malpelo* there was even the fear that he might keep some of that money for himself: his older sister, considering the doubt and to make sure she wasn't mistaken, gave him a good beating for a receipt.

The owner of the quarry, however, had said the money was just that much, and no more; and in all honesty, it was even too much for Malpelo, a little brat whom no one wanted around, and whom everybody avoided as if he were a mangy dog, giving him a kick whenever he was within reach.

[1] *Rosso Malpelo* is a nickname which combines "red-haired" (*Rosso*) and "evil-haired" (*Malpelo*). Sicilians believed that red-haired people had a malicious and evil disposition.

Rosso Malpelo

He was really an eyesore, surly, snarling, and wild. At noon, while the other quarrymen were gathered together eating their soup and having a little fun, he would go and huddle in a corner, his basket between his legs, to nibble his piece of dark bread, as animals like him do; and everyone called him names and threw stones at him, until the overseer sent him back to work with a kick. He grew fat there, with all those kicks, and let himself be loaded worse than the gray donkey, without daring to complain. He was always ragged and filthy with red sand, because his sister had gotten engaged and had anything on her mind but remembering to clean him up on Sundays. Nonetheless, his name was a household word all around Monserrato and Carvana, so that the quarry where he worked was called "Malpelo's quarry," which annoyed the owner very much. In short, they kept him purely out of charity and because his father, *mastro* Misciu, had died in that same quarry.

This is the way he had died. One Saturday he had wanted to finish a certain contract job on a pillar which had been left earlier to hold up a tunnel, and since the pillar was no longer needed, he had figured roughly with the owner that it would yield thirty-five or forty cart loads of sand. Instead, *mastro* Misciu had been digging for three days and there was still enough left for a half day's work on Monday. It had been a poor bargain, and only a fool like *mastro* Misciu could have let the owner take him in that way. This was just why they called him *mastro* Misciu, the Jackass, and he was the pack animal of the whole quarry. The poor devil let them talk, and all he wanted was to earn his bread with his hands instead of raising them against his companions and starting fights. Malpelo would make a face as if those abuses fell on his own shoulders, and small as he was, he had such a look in his eyes that the others said:

"Go on, you won't die in your bed like your father."

But not even his father died in his bed, though he was a good devil. Uncle Mommu, the cripple, had said he wouldn't have taken that pillar out for twenty *onze,* it was so dangerous; but on the other hand, everything is dangerous in the quarries, and if you pay attention to all the silly things people say, it's better to go and be a lawyer.

So on Saturday night *mastro* Misciu was still scraping away at his pillar; the Ave Maria had long since sounded and all his companions had lit their pipes and gone away after telling him to have a good time scratching the sand for love of the owner, and warning him not to die the death of a rat. Being used to jeers, he paid no attention, and answered only with the "ah! ah!" of the fine full strokes of his hoe, and muttered meanwhile:

"This is for the bread! This for the wine! This for Nunziata's dress!" And so he went on figuring how he'd spend the money from the job—the contract worker!

Outside the quarry, stars were swarming in the sky, and down below, the lantern smoked and turned like a spinning wheel. The big red pillar, gutted by the strokes of the hoe, twisted and bent itself into an arch, as if it had a stomach-ache and were saying "Oh me!" Malpelo was clearing off the ground and putting the pick, the empty sack, and the wine flask in a safe place. His father, poor man, who loved him, kept saying: "Get away!" or "Watch out! Watch out! If you see any stones or heavy sand fall from above, run!" All of a sudden, Boom! Malpelo, who had turned his back to put the tools in the basket, heard a hollow roar, the sound the traitor sand makes when it swells up and breaks open all at once—and the light went out.

The engineer who directed the quarry work was at the theater that evening, and wouldn't have changed his seat for a throne, when they came looking for him on account of Malpelo's father, who had died the death of a rat. All the women of Monserrato screamed and beat their breasts to announce the great misfortune that had befallen Santa, the only one, poor woman, who didn't say anything, and whose teeth chattered instead, as if she had the tertian fever. The engineer, when told the why and wherefore, three hours after the accident— by which time Misciu, the Jackass, must have already gotten to paradise for sure—went with ladders and ropes to make a hole in the sand, as if to relieve his conscience. Forty cart loads—what a joke! The Cripple said it would take at least a week to clear out the gallery. A mountain of sand had fallen, all fine and well burned by the lava; it was so good that you could have mixed it into mortar with your own hands and it would have taken a double amount of lime. There was enough to fill carts for weeks. The fine bargain of *mastro* Misciu, the Jackass!

Nobody paid any attention to the boy, who was

scratching his face and howling, like a real animal.

"Look!" someone said at last. "It's Malpelo! Now where did he come from? If he hadn't been 'Malpelo' he wouldn't have gotten off so easily . . ."

Malpelo didn't answer at all, didn't even cry; he was digging there in the sand with his nails; he was deep in the hole, so he hadn't been noticed. And when they came close with a lamp they saw such a distorted face, such ugly glassy eyes and foam at the mouth, that would frighten anybody; his nails were torn and were hanging from his bleeding hands. Then, when they wanted to take him away from there, they had quite a time; no longer able to scratch, he bit like a mad dog and they had to grab him by the hair to drag him away with brute force.

But after a few days he at last went back to the quarry, when his mother, sobbing, led him there by the hand, since there are times when you can't go looking here and there for bread to eat. He never wanted to leave that tunnel again, and dug furiously as if every basketful of sand were taken off his father's chest. Often, while digging, he stopped suddenly with his hoe in the air, his face surly and his eyes wild; and he seemed to be listening to something that his demon whispered in his ear from the other side of the mountain of fallen sand. In those days he was more wretched and mean than usual, so that he hardly ate, and threw his bread to the dog, as if it were not "the gift of God." The dog loved him, for dogs look only to the hand that feeds them, and beats them, perhaps. But the donkey, poor animal, crooked

and run-down, had to put up with all the raging mean-
ness of Malpelo, who beat him with the hoe handle
without pity, muttering:

"This way you'll die sooner!"

After the death of his father it seemed that the devil
had gotten into him; he worked like one of those ferocious oxen that are kept with an iron ring in the nose.
Knowing he was *malpelo,* he tried to live up to that
name as well as he could, and if an accident happened,
if a worker lost his tools, or a donkey broke a leg, or a
piece of the tunnel caved in, everyone always knew it
was his doing; and in fact, he took the beatings without
complaining, just like the donkeys, who arch their backs,
but go on doing things their own way. With the other
boys he was downright cruel, and it seemed that he
wanted to take vengeance on the weak for all the wrongs
he imagined the others had done to him and his father.
He certainly felt a strange pleasure in remembering one
by one all the ill-treatment and the abuses they had made
his father bear, and the way they had let him die. And
when he was alone he muttered:

"That's the way they treat me too! They called my
father the Jackass, just because he didn't act the way
they do!"

And once, as the owner went by, he followed him
with a surly look:

"He was the one, for thirty-five *tarì!*"

And another time, behind the Cripple:

"That one too! And he laughed! I heard him that
night!"

Out of refined cruelty he seemed to have made himself guardian of a poor little boy, who had come to work in the quarry a short time before, and who, having broken his thighbone in a fall from a scaffold, couldn't work as a bricklayer's helper any more. When he carried his basketful of sand on his shoulder, the poor little fellow hobbled in such a way that they had given him the name Frog; but working underground, froglike as he was, he managed to earn his bread. Malpelo gave him some of his bread too, to be able to have the fun of abusing him, said the others.

In fact, he did torment him in a hundred ways. He beat him without reason and without mercy, and if Frog didn't defend himself he beat him harder, with still more fury, saying:

"There, jackass! A jackass, that's what you are! If you're not game enough to defend yourself from me who doesn't have anything against you, you'll let just anybody smash your face!"

Or if Frog dried off the blood that ran out of his mouth and nose:

"If you feel how blows hurt, you'll learn to give some yourself!"

When he drove a loaded donkey up the steep ramp of the gallery, and he saw him point his hoofs, all worn out, sagging under the weight, panting, his eyes lifeless, he beat him with the hoe handle without mercy, and the blows sounded hollow on the shins and the bare ribs. At times the animal bent in two from the beatings, but without an ounce of strength left he couldn't go a step farther and fell on his knees; one of the donkeys had fallen so many times that he had two big sores on his legs. Malpelo used to say to Frog:

"The donkey must be beaten, because he can't beat us; if he could, he'd smash us under his hoofs and rip our flesh off with his teeth."

Or: "If you happen to give blows, be sure to make them as hard as you can; that way the others will think a lot more of you, and you'll have less people trying to knock you around."

Working with pick or hoe, he swung his arms furiously, like one who had something against the sand; he beat and beat with clenched teeth, and with the *ah! ah!* of his father.

"The sand's a traitor," he said to Frog in a whisper. "It's like all the others, who'll smash your face if you're weaker, but if you're stronger, or if you go with a group, like the Cripple, then it'll give in. My father used to beat it all the time, and he beat nothing but the sand, that's why they called him the Jackass, and the sand set its trap and ate him up, because it was stronger than he was."

Every time Frog got a job that was too heavy for him, and the boy whined like a little girl, Malpelo hit him on the back and scolded him:

"Shut up, chicken!"

And if Frog kept it up, he would give him a hand, saying with a certain pride:

"Let me do it; I'm stronger than you are."

Or he would give him his half onion, and would be

satisfied with eating dry bread, and would shrug his shoulders, adding:

"I'm used to it."

He was used to everything: to slaps on the head, to kicks, to blows from the shovel handle or the packsaddle strap, to being insulted and jeered at by everybody, to sleeping on stones, his arms and his back broken by fourteen hours of work; he was used to fasting too, when the boss punished him by taking away his bread or his soup. He said that the boss had never taken away his share of blows; but blows didn't cost anything. He, however, didn't complain, and got his revenge on the sly, behind their backs, with tricks that seemed to have been planned by the devil; and so he always took the punishment, even when he wasn't the guilty one. True enough, if he hadn't done it, he was capable of doing it; and he never tried to offer excuses; it would have been useless anyway. Sometimes when Frog was frightened and begged him, crying, to tell the truth and clear himself, he would repeat:

"What for? I'm *malpelo!*"

And no one knew whether that continual bending of the head and shoulders was a result of strong pride or desperate resignation, and you couldn't even tell if he was wild or timid. One thing was certain: not even his mother had ever had a caress from him, and so she never gave him any.

On Saturday nights, as soon as he came home, with that ugly face filthy with freckles and red sand, and those rags hanging down sadly all over him, his sister grabbed the broomstick, as she noticed him in such a mess at the door;—it would have chased her fiancé away if he had seen what kind of people were to become his in-laws. His mother was always out visiting this neighbor or that, and so Malpelo would go and curl up on his straw mattress, like a sick dog. On Sundays, when all the other boys of the neighborhood put on their clean shirts to go to Mass or to romp in the yard, he seemed to enjoy himself only by wandering along the paths in the vegetable fields, chasing lizards and other poor animals that hadn't done him any harm, or breaking through the cactus hedges. But then, he didn't like other children jeering and throwing stones at him.

Mastro Misciu's widow was desperate about having that ruffian, as everyone called him, for a son, and he really had become like those dogs that, having kicks and stones constantly thrown at them by everybody, end up by putting their tails between their legs and running away from the first living soul they see, growing hungry, hairless, and wild, like wolves. At least, underground in the sand quarry, ugly, ragged, and filthy as he was, they no longer jeered at him, and he seemed made just for that kind of work even to the color of his hair and to those mean cat eyes that squinted if they saw the sun. There are donkeys like that, working in the quarries for years and years without ever coming out; they are lowered with ropes into those galleries whose entrance is a vertical shaft, and stay there as long as they live. They are old donkeys, it is true, bought for twelve or thirteen *lire* when they are about to be taken to the Plaia[2] to be slaughtered; but for the work they have to do down below they are still good. And Malpelo, certainly, was not worth any more; and if he came out of the quarry on Saturday nights, it was because he had hands to help himself up the rope, and because he had to take the week's pay to his mother.

No doubt he would rather have been a bricklayer's helper, like Frog, singing as he worked on the scaffolds, high up in the blue of the sky, with the sun on his back —or a cart driver, like Gàspare, who came to get the sand of the quarry, rocking himself sleepily on the shafts of his cart, his pipe in his mouth, and going the whole day along the beautiful roads of the countryside;—or better yet, he would have liked to be a farmer, who spends his life in the green of the fields, under the thick carob trees, with the blue sea there below and the singing of the birds overhead. But his father had been a quarryman and Malpelo had been born to this kind of work.

And thinking of all this he would tell Frog the story of the pillar that had fallen on his father, and that still yielded fine, burned sand which the cart driver came to load, with his pipe in his mouth, rocking himself on the shafts; and he said that when they finished digging they'd find the body of his father, who should still be wearing a pair of almost new fustian pants. Frog was afraid, but not *he*. He was thinking that he had always

---

[2] *Plaia* is Sicilian for "beach." Here it refers to a specific place near Catania where cattle were slaughtered.

been there, from the time he was a baby, and he had always seen that black hole which sank far under the ground, where his father used to lead him by the hand. Then he would stretch out his arms to the right and to the left, describing how the intricate maze of tunnels spread out endlessly under their feet, on this side and that, as far as they could see the black and desolate *sciara*,[3] spotted with scorched broom scrub; and how so many men had been swallowed up, either crushed to death or lost in the darkness, and they have walked for years and are still walking, without being able to find the light of the shaft by which they went in, and without being able to hear the desperate cries of their children who are looking for them in vain.

But once when they were filling the baskets and one of *mastro* Misciu's shoes was found, Malpelo was seized with such a fit of shaking that they had to pull him out into the open with ropes, just like a donkey that is about to die. However, they couldn't find the almost new pants, or the rest of *mastro* Misciu, though the older men said that that should be the very spot where the pillar had fallen on him; and some of the workers, new to quarry work, remarked curiously how capricious the sand was, that it had knocked the Jackass all over, his shoes in one place and his feet in another.

After that shoe had been found, Malpelo was seized with such fear of also seeing his father's naked foot come

---

[3] The name of the barren lava beds around Mount Etna. The word *sciara* is of Arabic origin and was brought to Sicily by Arab immigrants.

out of the sand that he never wanted to strike there with the hoe again;—they could hit him on his head with the hoe! He went to work in another part of the tunnel and never wanted to go back to that place again. Two or three days later, in fact, they uncovered the body of *mastro* Misciu with his pants on, lying on his face as if he were embalmed. Uncle Mommu observed that he must have suffered a lot in dying, because the pillar had bent right over him and had buried him alive; one could see even now that *mastro* Jackass had tried instinctively to free himself, digging in the sand, and his hands were torn and his nails broken.

"Just like his son Malpelo!" the Cripple kept repeating. "He was digging here while his son was digging out there."

But they didn't say anything to the boy because they knew he was malicious and vengeful.

The cart driver carried off *mastro* Misciu's body the same way he did the fallen sand or the dead donkeys, but this time, besides the stench of a carcass, he carried a friend, and *baptized flesh*. The widow made the pants and the shirt smaller for Malpelo, who was thus dressed in almost new clothes for the first time. Only the shoes had been put aside for him until he would be big enough, since you can't make shoes smaller, and his sister's fiancé hadn't wanted the dead man's shoes.

Malpelo stroked those almost new fustian pants on his legs; to him they seemed soft and smooth like his father's hands that used to caress his hair, though they had been so rough and callous. As for the shoes, he kept them hung on a nail above his straw mattress, as if they were the pope's slippers, and on Sundays he took them in his hands, shined them and tried them on; then he put them on the ground, one beside the other, and sat there looking at them for hours, his elbows on his knees and his chin in his hands, turning over God knows what ideas in that warped brain of his.

He had some strange ideas, that Malpelo! Since he had also inherited his father's pick and hoe, he used them, though they were too heavy for a boy of his age; and when he was asked if he wanted to sell them and was told he would be paid as if they were new, he answered no. His father had made the handles so smooth and shiny with his own hands, and Malpelo couldn't have made any others smoother and shinier if he had worked with them for hundreds of years.

At that time the gray donkey died of hardship and old age; and the cart driver went to throw him far out in the *sciara*.

"That's the way it is," muttered Malpelo. "Tools that can't be used any more are thrown far away."

He went to see the Gray's carcass at the bottom of the ravine, and dragged Frog along too, though he didn't want to go. Malpelo told him that in this world you have to get used to looking everything in the face, good or bad, and with the eager curiosity of a little brat, he watched the dogs that ran up from all the nearby farms to fight over the flesh of the Gray. When the boys came into sight, the dogs bolted yelping, and circled around howling on the steep slopes opposite, but Rosso didn't let Frog chase them away with stones.

"See that black bitch that's not afraid of your stones?" he said. "She's not afraid because she's hungrier than the others. See those ribs of the Gray? Now he doesn't suffer any more."

The gray donkey was lying there, calm, his four legs stretched out, and was letting the dogs enjoy themselves emptying out his deep eyeholes and stripping his white bones. The teeth that were tearing his entrails couldn't make him move an inch, as he did when people hit him on the back with a shovel to put a little life in him while he was going up the steep path.

"That's how things go! The Gray has had blows from the hoe too, and harness sores; when he bent under the weight or didn't have any breath to go ahead, he had such a look in his eyes too, as they beat him, that he seemed to say: No more! No more! But now the dogs are eating his eyes and he laughs at the blows and harness sores, with that stripped mouth of his that's nothing but teeth. But it would have been better for him if he'd never been born."

The *sciara* spread out melancholy and deserted, as far as the eye could see, rising and falling in peaks and ravines, black and wrinkled, without a cricket ever chirping or a bird coming to sing there. You could hear nothing, not even the pick strokes of the men working underground. Malpelo used to repeat that the earth there below was all hollow from the tunnels, everywhere, toward the mountain and toward the valley; in fact, once a miner went in when he was young and came out with gray hair; and another, whose candle had gone out, called in vain for help for years and years.

"He alone hears his own cries!" he said, and at that thought, though his heart was harder than the *sciara,* he started. "The boss often sends me far in, where the others are afraid to go. But I'm 'Malpelo,' and if I never come back, nobody will look for me."

Yet, during the beautiful summer nights, the stars shone brightly on the *sciara* too, and the countryside all around was as black as the lava, but Malpelo, tired after the long day's work, lay down on his sack with his face toward the sky, to enjoy that silence and that glittering fiesta high above; on the other hand, he hated the moonlit nights, when the sea swarms with sparks and the countryside takes form dimly here and there, for then the *sciara* seems more barren and desolate than ever.

"For us who are made to live underground," thought Malpelo, "it should always be dark, everywhere."

The owl screeched on the *sciara* and fluttered around in all directions.

"Even the owl smells the dead who are here underground, and is frantic because it can't find them."

Frog was afraid of owls and bats, but Rosso scolded him, because if you have to be alone you must not be afraid of anything; and not even the gray donkey was afraid of the dogs that were stripping his bones, now that his flesh could no longer feel the pain of being eaten.

"You were used to working on roofs like a cat," he

said to him, "and that was something altogether different. But now that you have to live underground like a rat, you mustn't be afraid of rats any more, or of bats, which are old rats with wings; and they like to keep company with the dead."

Frog, instead, took great pleasure in explaining to him why the stars were up there; and he said that up there was paradise where dead people go if they've been good, and if they haven't given their parents trouble.

"Who told you?" asked Malpelo, and Frog answered that his mother had told him.

Then Malpelo scratched his head, smiled and made a scornful gesture like a malicious brat who knows it all, and said:

"Your mother tells you that because you should wear a skirt instead of pants."

And after thinking it over awhile:

"My father was good and didn't do anything wrong to anybody, so they called him the Jackass. But he's there below, and they've even found his tools and his shoes, and these pants I've got on."

Not long after, Frog, whose health had been failing for some time, got so sick that every evening they had to take him out of the quarry on a donkey, stretched out between the baskets and shaking like a wet chicken. One of the workers said that the boy would never harden to that job, and that you have to be born to it if you want to work in a mine without leaving your hide there. Then Malpelo felt proud that he had been born to it and stayed so healthy and strong in that bad air, with all those hardships. He loaded Frog on his shoulders and encouraged him in his own way, scolding and hitting him.

But once, while Malpelo was hitting him on the back, Frog began to spit blood; frightened then, Malpelo looked anxiously in his nose and inside his mouth, to see what he had done to him, and swore that the way he had beaten him couldn't really have hurt him very much, and to show what he meant he punched himself hard on his chest and on his back with a stone; as a matter of fact, a worker who happened to be there gave him a terrific kick between the shoulders—a kick that resounded as if it had hit a drum; yet Malpelo didn't budge, and only after the worker had gone away he added:

"See? He didn't hurt me at all! And he hit harder than I did, I swear it!"

Meanwhile, Frog didn't get any better and kept on spitting blood and having fever every day. So Malpelo took some money from his week's pay, to buy wine and hot soup for Frog, and gave him his almost new pants, which covered him better. But Frog always coughed and sometimes seemed to be choking; and at night there was no way to overcome the chills of the fever, neither with sacks, nor by covering him with straw, nor by putting him in front of the fire. Malpelo stayed there quiet and motionless, bent over him, his hands on his knees, staring at him with those ugly eyes wide open as if he wanted to paint his picture; and when he heard him moan softly and saw his wasted face and lifeless eyes—just like those of the gray donkey as he panted all worn out under the load going up the steep path—he muttered:

"It's better for you to die soon! If you have to suffer like this, it's better for you to die!"

The boss said Malpelo was capable of smashing the boy's head in, and he'd have to be watched.

Finally one Monday, Frog didn't come to the quarry any more, and the boss washed his hands of him, because in the state he was in by now he was more trouble than anything else. Malpelo found out where he lived, and on Saturday went to see him. Poor Frog already had one foot in the grave; his mother cried and was in despair as if her boy were one of those who earned ten *lire* a week.

This Malpelo couldn't understand, and he asked Frog why his mother screamed like that, when for two months he hadn't even earned what he had eaten. But poor Frog didn't pay any attention to him; he seemed busy counting the rafters in the ceiling. Then Rosso got the idea into his head that Frog's mother screamed like that because her boy had always been weak and sickly and she had kept him like one of those babies who are never weaned. He, instead, had always been healthy and strong, and he was *malpelo,* and his mother had never cried for him because she had never been afraid of losing him.

Shortly after, at the quarry they said that Frog was dead, and Malpelo thought that now the owl was screeching for him too at night, and went back to see the stripped bones of the Gray, in the ravine where he used to go with Frog. Now nothing more was left of the Gray than a jumble of bones, and it would be the same with Frog. His mother would dry her tears, for Malpelo's mother had dried hers too after *mastro* Misciu's death, and now she was married again and had gone to live at Cifali with her married daughter and they had locked the door of the house. From now on, if he was beaten, it didn't matter to them at all, and not even to him, for when he would become like the Gray or like Frog, he wouldn't feel anything any more.

About that time a man came to work in the quarry, who had never been seen there before and kept himself hidden as much as he could; the other workers said among themselves that he had escaped from prison, and if he was caught he would be taken back and locked up for years and years. Malpelo found out then, that prison was a place where they put crooks and ruffians like himself, and they kept them always locked up in it and watched them.

From that moment he felt a morbid curiosity about that man who had known what prison was like and had escaped. After a few weeks, however, the fugitive stated flatly that he was tired of that lousy life of a gopher and that he would rather stay in prison for the rest of his life, because in comparison prison was paradise, and he would be glad to go back there on his own two feet.

"Then why don't all those who work in the quarry have themselves put in prison?" asked Malpelo.

"Because they're not *malpelo* like you!" answered the

Cripple. "But don't worry, you'll get there and you'll leave your bones there."

Instead, Malpelo left his bones in the quarry, like his father, but in a different way. One day they had to explore a passage that was supposed to connect with the great shaft on the left, toward the valley, and if all went well, a good half of the labor of taking out the sand could be saved. On the other hand, however, there was the danger of getting lost and never coming back. So no man with a family wanted to take a chance, nor would he let his own flesh and blood run such a risk for all the gold in the world. But as for Malpelo, he didn't even have anyone who would want to take all the gold in the world for his hide, if it was really worth that much: so they thought of him.

As he left then, he remembered the miner who got lost years and years ago, and who still walks and walks in the dark, crying for help, and nobody can hear him. But he didn't say anything. After all, what good would it have done? He took his father's tools, the pick, the hoe, the lantern, the sack of bread, the flask of wine, and started out:—and he has never been heard of since.

So even Malpelo's bones were lost, and the boys of the quarry lower their voices when they speak of him in the gallery, for they are afraid of seeing him appear before them, with his red hair and his ugly gray eyes.

1880

GRAMIGNA'S MISTRESS

To Salvatore Farina[1]

Dear Farina, here is not a story but the sketch of a story. It will at least have the merit of being very short and of being factual—a human document, as they say nowadays—interesting perhaps for you, and for all those who study the great book of the human heart. I shall repeat it to you just as I picked it up along the paths in the countryside, with nearly the same simple and picturesque words that characterize popular narration, and you will certainly prefer to find yourself face to face with the naked and unadulterated fact, without having to look for it between the lines of the book, through the lens of the writer.

The simple human fact will always make one think; it will always have the force of what *has really been,* of true tears, of the fevers and sensations that have passed through the flesh. The mysterious process by which passions tie themselves together, intertwine, mature, develop in their subterranean journey, in their meanderings that often seem contradictory, will still constitute

---

[1] Salvatore Farina (1846–1918) was a contemporary of Verga and a prolific writer of novels and short stories.

for a long time the powerful attraction of that psychological phenomenon which forms the subject of a story, and which modern analysis endeavors to follow with scientific precision.

Of this story that I'm relating to you today, I shall tell you only the point of departure and that of arrival, and for you it will suffice—and some day perhaps it will suffice for everyone.

We renew the artistic process to which we owe so many glorious monuments, with a different method, more attentive to details and more intimate. We willingly sacrifice the effect of the denouement to the logical, necessary development of passions and facts leading to the denouement, which is thus rendered less unforeseen, less dramatic perhaps, but not less fatal. We are more modest, if not more humble; but the demonstration of this obscure tie between causes and effects will certainly not be less useful to the art of the future. Shall we ever reach such perfection in the study of passions that it will become useless to continue in this study of the inner man? Will the science of the human heart, which will be the fruit of the new art, develop so much and so generally all the powers of the imagination that in the future the only novels written will be *faits divers*?

When in the novel the affinity and cohesion of its every part will be so complete that the creative process will remain a mystery, like the development of human passions, and the harmony of its elements will be so perfect, the sincerity of its reality so evident, its manner of and its reason for existing so necessary, that the hand

of the artist will remain absolutely invisible, then it will
have the imprint of an actual happening; the work of
art will seem *to have made itself,* to have matured and
come into being spontaneously, like a fact of nature,
without retaining any point of contact with its author,
any stain of the original sin.

Several years ago, down there along the Simeto,[2] they
were chasing a bandit, a certain Gramigna, if I'm not
mistaken, a name as cursed as the grass that bears it;[3]
from one end of the province to the other he had left
behind him the terror of his fame. *Carabinieri,* soldiers,
and cavalrymen had been after him for two months,
without having been able to lay their claws on him; he
was alone but he was worth ten, and the evil plant
threatened to multiply. On top of this, harvest time was
getting close, all the year's crops in the hands of God,
because the owners didn't risk leaving the village, for
fear of Gramigna; so the complaints were general.

The prefect[4] sent for all those gentlemen of the police
department, the *carabinieri,* and the soldiers; patrols and
squads were immediately in motion, sentries were placed
along every ditch and behind every wall; they drove him
before them like an evil beast, over the whole province,
by day, by night, on foot, on horseback, and by telegraph.
Gramigna slipped through their fingers, or answered
with gunshots, if they came a little too close on his heels.

[2] A river that crosses the Plain of Catania.

[3] *Gramigna* is the Italian for crab grass.

[4] A high officer appointed by the government to administer the affairs of a province.

In the fields, in the villages, on the farms, under the tavern boughs,[5] wherever people met, they spoke only of him, of Gramigna, of that relentless chase, of that desperate flight. The *carabinieri*'s horses dropped dead tired; the soldiers, exhausted, threw themselves on the ground in every stable; the patrols slept on their feet; he alone, Gramigna, was never tired, never slept, always fought, climbed on the cliffs, slipped through the wheat, ran on all fours in the thick of the cactuses, slunk like a wolf down the beds of dry creeks. For two hundred miles around, ran the legend of his deeds, of his courage, of his strength, of that desperate struggle, he alone against a thousand, tired, hungry, burning with thirst, in the immense burnt plain, under the June sun.

Peppa, one of the most beautiful girls of Licodia, was at that time to marry Finu, called "Tallow Candle," who had land under the sun and a bay mule in his stable, and was a young man as big and beautiful as the sun and carried the banner of Saint Margaret without bending his back, as straight as if he were a pillar.

Peppa's mother wept with joy at the good fortune that had befallen her daughter and spent her time turning and turning the bride's trousseau in the chest, "all white stuff, four of everything" like a queen's, and earrings that reached down to her shoulders, and gold rings for each of her ten fingers: she had so much gold that not even Saint Margaret could have had more, and they

---

[5] In the villages and in the country, a bough was used as the sign of an *osteria,* a kind of tavern where people would go to drink wine and sometimes to eat.

were to be married on Saint Margaret's day, in fact, which came in June, after the mowing of the hay. "Tallow Candle," on his way back from the fields each evening, left his mule at Peppa's doorway, and came to tell her that the wheat was a joy to look at, if only Gramigna wouldn't set it on fire, and that the wicker mat by the bed wouldn't be large enough to hold all the grain of the harvest, and that he couldn't wait to take his bride home on the back of his bay mule. But one fine day Peppa told him:

"Never mind your mule, because I don't want to get married."

Imagine the commotion! The old woman tore her hair, and "Tallow Candle" remained openmouthed.

All of a sudden, out of the blue, Peppa had lost her head over Gramigna, without even knowing him. That one, that one was a man!

"What do you know about him?"

"Where did you see him?"

Nothing. Peppa didn't even answer, her head low, her face hard, without pity for her mother, who acted like a crazy woman with her gray hair in the wind and looked like a witch.

"Ah, that devil has come this far to bewitch my daughter!"

The women who had envied Peppa the prosperous wheat, the bay mule, and the handsome young man who carried the banner of Saint Margaret without bending his back, were telling all kinds of ugly stories—that Gramigna came to see the girl in the kitchen at night, and that they had seen him hidden under her bed. The poor mother kept a lamp lit for the souls in Purgatory, and even the priest had gone with his stole to Peppa's house to try to touch her heart, in order to chase out that devil of a Gramigna who had taken possession of it.

But she continued to say that she didn't even know that Christian by sight; yet she was always thinking of him, she saw him in her dreams at night, and in the morning she got up with her lips burning, and felt as thirsty as he was.

Then the old woman locked her in the house, not to let her hear anybody talk about Gramigna any more, and plugged up all the cracks of the door with pictures of saints. Peppa listened from behind the holy pictures to what they were saying in the street, and turned pale and red, as if the devil were blowing all of hell into her face.

Finally it was learned that Gramigna had been traced to the cactuses of Palagonia.

"He kept shooting for two hours!" they said. "There's one *carabiniere* dead and more than three soldiers wounded. But they poured such a hail of bullets on him that this time they found a pool of blood where he had been."

One night Peppa made the sign of the cross before the old woman's bed and fled through the window.

Gramigna was in the cactuses of Palagonia—they hadn't been able to root him out of that rabbit fortress, his clothes torn, bleeding, pale after two days without food, burning with fever, and his rifle ready.

As he saw her come, determined, through the dense bushes, in the hazy light of dawn, he thought for a minute if he should pull the trigger.

"What do you want?" he asked her. "What are you coming here for?"

She didn't answer, staring at him.

"Go away!" he said. "Go away, while Christ is on your side!"

"I can't go back home any more now," she answered; "the road is full of soldiers."

"What do I care? Go away!"

And he aimed his gun at her. Since she didn't move, Gramigna, amazed, went up to her with his fists clenched:

"Well? . . . Are you crazy? . . . Or are you a spy?"

"No," she said. "No!"

"Good; if that's the way it is, go and get me a flask of water down there in the creek."

Peppa went without saying anything, and when Gramigna heard the shots he broke into vicious laughter, and said to himself:

"Those were meant for me."

But shortly after, he saw the girl come back, bleeding, her clothes torn, with the flask in her hand. Burning with thirst, he jumped at her, and when he had drunk enough to be out of breath, he said at last:

"You want to come with me?"

Yes, she nodded avidly, yes.

And she followed him in the valleys and the mountains, hungry, half-naked, often running to find him a flask of water or a piece of bread at the risk of her life. When she came back empty-handed, through the bullets, her lover, devoured by hunger and thirst, would beat her.

One night the moon was shining and you could hear the dogs barking far-off on the plain. Gramigna leaped to his feet all at once and said to her:

"You stay here, or I swear to God, I'll kill you!"

She was standing up against the cliff, at the bottom of the ravine, while he went running through the cactuses. But the others, more cunning, came toward him from that very direction.

"Stop! Stop!"

And bullets fell like hail. Peppa, who trembled only for him, saw him come back wounded, hardly able to drag himself along, and he threw himself on his knees to reload the gun.

"It's all over!" he said. "Now they'll get me." And he was foaming at the mouth and his eyes were shining like those of a wolf.

As soon as he fell on the dry branches like a bundle of wood, the soldiers were on him all at once.

The day after, they dragged him through the streets of the village on a cart, bleeding, his clothes torn. People crowded around to see him—and his mistress too, handcuffed like a thief, she who had as much gold as Saint Margaret!

Peppa's poor mother had to sell "all the white stuff" of the trousseau, and the gold earrings and the rings for the ten fingers, in order to pay her daughter's lawyers, and to be able to drag her back home, poor, sick, in shame, and carrying the son of Gramigna in her arms. In the village no one ever saw her again. She hid herself away in the kitchen like a wild animal, and came out only when her old mother died of hardship and misery, and the house had to be sold.

Then, at night, she went away from the town, leaving her son at the orphanage, without even turning back, and she came to the city where they had told her that Gramigna was in prison. She wandered around that big gloomy building, looking at the bars, and trying to find out where he was, with the guards at her heels, insulting and chasing her at every step.

She finally learned that her lover was no longer there; they had taken him away, beyond the sea, handcuffed and with his sack tied at his neck. What could she do? She remained where she was, to earn her bread by doing little jobs for the soldiers, for the jailers, as if she herself were a part of that big gloomy, silent building. Toward the *carabinieri,* then, who had caught Gramigna in the thick of the cactuses, she felt a kind of respectful tenderness, like the admiration for brute strength, and she was always around the barracks, sweeping the dormitories and shining boots, so that they called her "the rag of the barracks." Only when she saw them load their guns and leave on a risky assignment, did she grow pale and think of Gramigna.

1880

WAR BETWEEN SAINTS

All of a sudden, while Saint Rocco was peacefully going his own way under the canopy, with the dogs on a leash,[1] a great number of candles burning all around, and the band, the procession, the crush of the faithful, there was pandemonium, a hurry-scurry, a devil of a row: priests running away with their gowns flying in the air, trumpets and clarinets hitting you in the face, women screaming, blood flowing in rivulets, and cudgel blows raining down like rotten pears, even under the nose of blessed Saint Rocco himself. The magistrate, the mayor, and the *carabinieri* rushed to the spot: broken bones were carried to the hospital, the worst rioters went to jail for the night, the Saint went back to church at a run rather than at procession pace, and the fiesta ended like a punchinello farce.

All this because of the envy of those in Saint Paschal's district;[2] for that year the faithful of Saint Rocco had

---

[1] St. Rocco devoted his life to caring for people affected by the plague; he caught the disease himself and retired to solitude, where he was discovered by a dog and cured by its owner. For this reason he is traditionally pictured in the company of a dog or dogs.

[2] In the present story districts are the equivalent of parish districts: each one of them has a patron saint, who, in the minds of the townsfolk, becomes identified with the district itself, and therefore the people of the district identify themselves with him.

spent a fortune to do things in a big way: the band had come from the city, more than two thousand squibs had been fired off, and there was even a new banner, all embroidered with gold, which weighed more than a quintal—they said—and in the middle of the crowd it really looked like a "golden foam." All this got terribly on the nerves of Saint Paschal's faithful, so that finally one of them lost his patience and began to shout, pale with rage: *"Viva San Pasquale!"* [3] Then cudgel blows had begun.

For to go and say *Viva San Pasquale* in the very face of Saint Rocco in person is just letting yourself in for it —the same as if someone should come and spit in your house or amuse himself pinching the woman on your arm. In such a case you don't give a damn for either heaven or hell, and you trample under foot even what little respect you have for the other saints, who, when you come to think of it, are all one family. If you are in church, the benches go up in the air, in processions pieces of candles rain down like bats, and at the table the soup bowls begin to fly.

"Damn it!" howled Nino, all pounded and bruised. "Let's see who's got the courage to shout *Viva San Pasquale* again!"

"I do!" fumed Turi, the tanner, who was to become Nino's brother-in-law, and was mad because of a punch he had gotten in the row, which had half blinded him. *"Viva San Pasquale,* to the death!"

"For heaven's sake! For heaven's sake!" screamed his

[3] "Long live Saint Paschal!"

sister Saridda, throwing herself between her brother and her fiancé, for the three of them had been walking together in peace and harmony until that moment.

Nino, the fiancé, was bellowing in mockery:

"Viva i miei stivali! Viva San Stivale!" [4]

"There!" howled Turi, foaming at the mouth, his eye swollen and livid as an eggplant. "There, for Saint Rocco, you with your boots! Take that!"

So they exchanged punches that would have felled an ox, until their friends succeeded in parting them with cuffs and kicks. Saridda herself had warmed up and screamed *"Viva San Pasquale,"* so that she almost came to blows with her fiancé, as if they were already husband and wife.

On such occasions parents fight with their children, and wives leave their husbands, if unfortunately a woman from Saint Paschal's district has married a man from Saint Rocco's.

"I don't want to hear of that Christian again!" Saridda, with her fists on her hips, yelled to the women neighbors who asked her why the engagement had gone up in smoke. "Not even if they give him to me dressed in gold, do you hear!"

"As far as I'm concerned, Saridda can grow moldy!" said Nino at the tavern while they were washing his face, all filthy with blood. "They're a bunch of bums and loafers, in that tanners' district! When I got it into

---

[4] "Long live my boots! Long live Saint Boot!" The insult is based on the phonic resemblance of the words Pasquale and *stivale* ("boot").

my head to go there to look for a girl, I must have been drunk."

"Since this is the way things are," had concluded the mayor, "and one can't carry a saint to the square without cudgel blows—which is absolutely indecent—I don't want any more fiestas or 'Forty Hours,'[5] and if they come out with a piece of candle, even a piece of candle, I'll throw them all in jail."

It had become a serious business, for the bishop had granted the canons of Saint Paschal the privilege of wearing the mozzetta, and the people of Saint Rocco, whose priests did not wear mozzettas, had even gone to Rome to raise hell at the feet of the Holy Father, with documents in hand, on legal paper and everything; but it had all been in vain, because their foes of the lower district—everyone remembered when they couldn't even afford to wear shoes—had become as rich as pigs with this new tanning industry, and you know that in this world justice can be bought and sold like Judas' soul.

In Saint Paschal's district they were waiting for the bishop's delegate, who was a sensible man, and wore two half-pound silver buckles on his shoes—said those who had seen him—and was coming to bring the mozzettas to the canons. So they had engaged a band, which had to go and meet the delegate three miles out of town, and people said that in the evening there were

---

[5] A religious service during which the Sacrament is exposed to view on the high altar for forty hours.

to be fireworks in the square, with a great big *Viva San Pasquale* in huge letters.

And the inhabitants of the upper district were in great turmoil; some of the more excited ones began to peel pear- or cherry-wood cudgels as big as door bolts, and muttered:

"If there's going to be music, somebody's got to beat the time!"

The bishop's delegate was running a great risk of ending his triumphal entry with broken bones. But the shrewd reverend let the band wait for him out of town, and came slowly and quietly on foot, by short cuts to the parish house, where he called a meeting of all the big shots of the two sides.

As those gentlemen found themselves face to face, after fighting such a long time, they began to look one another straight in the eyes, as if they felt a great compulsion to gouge them out, and it took the full authority of the reverend, who for the occasion was wearing his new cloth cloak, to have the ice cream and the refreshments served without trouble.

"That's good!" said the mayor approvingly, his nose in his glass. "If you want me in the interest of peace, you'll always find me ready."

The delegate said, in fact, that he had come for the reconciliation, with the olive branch in his mouth, just like Noah's dove; and while giving his little sermon, he kept on distributing smiles and handshakes, and kept saying:

"You gentlemen will do me the honor of coming to

the sacristy to have chocolate on the day of the fiesta."

"Let's leave the fiesta alone," said the vice-magistrate, "or there'll be more trouble."

"There'll be trouble with all these abuses going on; a man isn't even free to enjoy himself as he likes with his own money!" exclaimed Bruno, the cartwright.

"I wash my hands of it. The government orders are clear. If you have the fiesta, I'll send for the *carabinieri*. I want order."

"Order is *my* problem," declared the mayor, tapping the floor with his umbrella and looking around.

"Fine! As if we didn't know that the man who prompts you in the Council is your brother-in-law Bruno!" retorted the vice-magistrate.

"And you oppose everything just out of spite, because you can't get over that fine for the laundry!" [6]

"Gentlemen! Gentlemen!" the delegate kept pleading. "This way we won't make any progress."

"We'll make a revolution, we will!" howled Bruno, his hands in the air.

Fortunately the parish priest had hastily put away the glasses and the cups, and the sexton had run off at breakneck speed to dismiss the band, which, having heard of the delegate's arrival, was rushing over to welcome him, blowing into their horns and tubas.

"This way we won't make any progress!" muttered the delegate; and he was also annoyed because the harvest was already ripe over there on his lands, while

---

[6] A reference to an infraction of a law forbidding hanging one's laundry out on the street.

he stayed here wasting his time with Bruno and the vice-magistrate, who were ready to eat each other up.

"What's this story about the fine for the laundry?"

"The usual abuses. Now you can't even hang a pocket handkerchief in the window without having them pin a fine on you. The wife of the vice-magistrate, confident because her husband was in office (until now there had always been a little respect for people in authority), used to hang her week's laundry out on the terrace—you know . . . her few things! . . . But now, with the new law, it's a mortal sin, and even dogs and chickens and all the other animals that up until now, if I may say so, kept the streets clean, are forbidden. With the first rain we'll have the filth up to our necks, God help us."

In order to pacify the people, the delegate sat nailed in the confessional from morning till night, like an owl, and all the women wanted to be confessed by him; he could give plenary absolution for all sorts of sins, just as if he were the bishop himself.

"Father!" said Saridda, her nose against the grating of the confessional. "Nino makes me sin in church every Sunday."

"How, my daughter?"

"That Christian was supposed to become my husband, before all this talk began in town; but now that the engagement is broken off, he plants himself by the high altar and looks at me and laughs with his friends, during the whole Mass."

And when the reverend was trying to touch Nino's heart:

"She's the one who turns her back on me every time she sees me, as if I were damned to hell," answered the farmer.

Instead, if Saridda happened to pass through the square on Sundays, he pretended to be hand and glove with the Sergeant or with another big shot, and wouldn't even notice her.

Saridda was very busy making little lanterns of colored paper which she lined up on the window sill, right under his nose, with the pretext of putting them there to dry.

Once when they happened to be together at a baptism, they didn't even say "hello" to each other, as if they had never met before; and as a matter of fact, Saridda even began to flirt with the baby girl's godfather.

"A fine sort of a godfather!" sneered Nino. "A baby girl's godfather! When a baby girl's born even the rafters of the roof give way!"

And Saridda, pretending to be talking to the mother:

"Things aren't always as bad as they look. Sometimes, when you think you have lost a treasure, you should thank God and Saint Paschal; since before you can really know a person, 'you've got to eat seven *salme*[7] of salt. . . .' That's right, you've got to take trouble as

---

[7] The *salma* was a Sicilian measure containing 275.1 liters, or 606 lbs. in weight. To eat large amounts of salt is an old Italian metaphor meaning to gain experience through a long—in this case, extremely long—period of time.

it comes; what's bad is to fret over things that aren't worth it. 'When one Pope dies they make another.'"

The crier's drum was sounding in the square.

"The mayor says we'll have the fiesta," they whispered in the crowd.

"I'll fight until the end of time! I can become poor and have nothing but the shirt on my back, just like Job, but I won't pay the five *lire* fine even if I have to put it in my will!"

"Hell! What kind of a fiesta do they want to make, if we're all going to die of starvation this year?" exclaimed Nino.

Not a drop of rain had fallen since March, and the yellowish wheat fields, that crackled like tinder, were dying of thirst. Instead Bruno, the cartwright, said that as soon as Saint Paschal should come out in procession, it would rain for sure. But what did he care about rain, since he was a cartwright, and what did all the tanners of his side care? . . .

In fact, they did carry Saint Paschal in procession, to the east and to the west, and they held him high on the hill to bless the fields, one sultry, cloudy day in May—one of those days when the farmers tear their hair in front of their burnt fields, and the wheatears bend down just as if they were dying.

"Damned Saint Paschal!" shouted Nino, spitting in the air and running through the wheat field like a madman. "You've ruined me, Saint Paschal, you thief! All you've left me is a sickle to cut my throat with!"

War Between Saints

In the upper district there was misery: it was one of those long years when the famine begins in June, and the women, with stunned eyes, stand idle and disheveled at the doorways.

Saridda, when she heard that Nino's mule was to be sold in the square to pay the rent for his land, which hadn't yielded anything, felt her anger blow over in a minute, and quickly sent her brother Turi to help him with the little money they had put aside.

Nino was standing in a corner of the square, his eyes staring absently and his hands in his pockets, while they were selling his mule, all decked out and with a new halter.

"I don't want anything," he answered with a surly face. "I still have my arms, thank God! What a fine saint, that Saint Paschal, eh!"

Not to begin a fight, Turi turned his back on him and left. But the truth of the matter was that the people were exasperated, now that they had carried Saint Paschal in procession to the east and to the west with that fine result. The worst of it was that many in the district of Saint Rocco had gone so far as to walk in the procession too, beating themselves like donkeys and wearing crowns of thorns, for love of the wheat fields. And now they gave vent to their rage with foul language, so much so that the bishop's delegate had to take off on foot and without the band, just as he had come.

The vice-magistrate, to revenge himself on the cartwright, kept sending telegrams saying that the people were excited and the public order jeopardized; so that one day the news spread that the soldiers had arrived during the night, and everyone could go and see them at the stables.

But others said: "They've come on account of the cholera. Down there in the city people're dying like flies."

The druggist bolted the door of his shop, and the doctor was the first to run away, for fear of having his brains knocked out.

"It won't be anything serious," said the few who remained in town because they couldn't flee here and there into the country. "Blessed Saint Rocco will watch over his town, and the first man we see around at night, we'll get his hide." [8]

Even those of the lower district had run barefoot to the church of Saint Rocco. But soon afterward people with cholera began to be more frequent, just like the big drops that precede a cloudburst—and of one they said that he was a pig and had killed himself by stuffing his stomach with prickly pears, and of another that he had come back from the fields late at night. In short, the cholera was there for sure, in spite of the watch and in spite of Saint Rocco, and even though an old woman in the odor of sanctity dreamed that Saint Rocco himself said to her:

---

[8] Sicilian peasants used to believe that cholera was fostered and spread by the night air. It was thought that malicious persons walked about after nightfall in order to catch the germs and then infect others.

"Don't be afraid of the cholera; I'll take care of it; I'm not like that good-for-nothing Saint Paschal."

Nino and Turi hadn't met since that business about the mule; but as soon as the farmer heard that brother and sister were both sick, he ran to their house and found Saridda with her face black and distorted at the back of the poor room, beside her brother, who was better but was tearing his hair and didn't know what to do.

"Ah, Saint Rocco, you thief!" Nino began to lament. "I didn't expect this from you! Oh, Saridda, don't you know me any more? It's Nino, your old friend."

Saridda looked at him with such sunken eyes that you needed a lantern to find them, while Nino's eyes were two fountains.

"Ah, Saint Rocco!" said he. "This is a dirtier trick than Saint Paschal played on us!"

But Saridda recovered, and standing at the doorway, her face as yellow as beeswax and her head wrapped in a kerchief, she would say to him:

"Saint Rocco has worked a miracle for me, and you too must come and bring him a candle for his fiesta."

Nino, his heart full, nodded yes; but in the meantime he had caught the disease himself, and was at the point of death. Saridda scratched her face then, and said that she wanted to die with him, and that she would cut off her hair and put it in his coffin, for no one would see her face again as long as she lived.

"No! No!" answered Nino, his face wasted away.

"Your hair will grow again; I'll be the one who won't see you again because I'll be dead."

"A fine miracle Saint Rocco's worked for you!" said Turi to console him.

And when the two of them were convalescent and were warming themselves in the sun, their shoulders against the wall and their faces long, they kept throwing Saint Rocco and Saint Paschal into each other's face.

Once Bruno, the cartwright, passed by; he was coming back from out of town after the cholera was over. He said:

"We want to have a big fiesta to thank Saint Paschal for saving all of us from the cholera. From now on there won't be any more troublemakers or opposition, now that the vice-magistrate is dead and has put his lawsuit in his will."

"Yes, we'll have a fiesta for those who are dead!" sneered Nino.

"And you? Do you think it was Saint Rocco who kept you alive?"

"Why don't you stop it!" broke in Saridda. "Or we'll need another cholera to make peace!"

1880

STINKPOT

Now it's "Stinkpot's" turn; he is quite a character too and looks very good among all those animals at the fair, and everyone going by says nasty things to him. He really deserved that ugly name,[1] for his pot was full every day, thanks to God and to his wife, and he ate and drank better than a crowned king, at the expense of Don Liborio.

If a man has never had that damned vice of jealousy and has always taken whatever came—Saint Isidore help and save us![2]—and then suddenly gets it into his head to do mad things, jail is just where he belongs.

He had wanted to marry Venera at any price, though she had neither king nor kingdom, and he, himself, could count only on his two hands to earn his bread. In vain his mother kept saying to him:

"Leave Venera alone; she's not for you; she wears her mantilla halfway back on her head and shows her feet when she walks down the street." —Old people know

---

[1] The nickname "Stinkpot" is used here as a popular synonym of cuckold.

[2] Saint Isidore, the Laborer, who is considered the patron saint of farmers and peasants.

better than we do, and we should listen to them, for our own good.[3]

But he couldn't get out of his head that little shoe, and those bewitching eyes that hunted for a husband from under the mantilla: so he married her and didn't want to hear any more, and his mother had to leave the house where she had lived for thirty years, because mother and daughter-in-law together are just like cat and dog. The daughter-in-law, with that sweet little mouth of hers, said so much and behaved in such a way that the poor grumbling old woman had to move out and go and die in a hovel; between husband and wife there were fights and brawls every time the month's rent for that hovel had to be paid. When finally the poor old woman's sufferings ended, and he ran there as soon as he heard that they had brought her the Sacrament, he couldn't even receive her blessing nor could he get the last word out of her mouth, for her lips had already been glued together by death and her face was distorted —in the corner of the little house where it was beginning to get dark. Only her eyes were alive and seemed to want to say so many things to him.

"Eh? . . . Eh? . . ."

Those who don't respect their parents cause their own ruin and come to a bad end.

The poor old woman died with the sad knowledge that her son's wife had turned out to be so bad; God had

---

[3] This is a proverbial expression, here said with tongue in cheek.

done her the favor of letting her take to the other world all that she had on her breast against her daughter-in-law, and she knew how it would have made her son's heart bleed.

As soon as Venera had become the mistress of the house, with no one to bridle her, she had carried on in such a manner that by now nobody called her husband anything but that ugly name, and when he himself happened to hear it and dared to complain to his wife:

"And you, you believe it?" said she. That was all. And he was happy as a king.

He was made that way, poor man, and so far he wasn't doing anybody any harm. If you had him see it with his own eyes, he would say it wasn't true, Good Saint Lucy be blessed! [4] Why fret? There was peace, the house was full, and there was health on top of it all, for Don Liborio was a doctor; what else could you want, good God?

He and Don Liborio did everything together: they shared the crops of a few fields, they had some thirty sheep and rented pasture land together; and whenever they went to the notary, Don Liborio gave his name as guarantee. "Stinkpot" brought him the first broad beans and the first peas, he chopped wood for his kitchen and pressed his grapes in the warehouse; in return he wasn't short of anything—neither of wheat on the wicker mat, nor of wine in the barrel, nor of oil in the jar. His wife, white and red as an apple, displayed new shoes and silk

---

[4] According to the legend, Saint Lucy's eyes were gouged out; hence she became the patron saint of eyesight.

handkerchiefs. Don Liborio didn't charge for his visits and had even been the godfather for one of the little boys. In short, they were one household; he called Don Liborio *signor compare,*[5] and worked conscientiously. As far as that was concerned, no one could say anything against "Stinkpot." He did all he could to make the business prosper and therefore the *signor compare* had his advantages too, and so everybody was happy.

Now it happened that this heavenly peace was turned into a devil of a row all of a sudden, in one day, in one moment—when the other farmers who worked on the fallow land, chatting in the shade one afternoon, just by chance began to talk about the life that he and his wife were leading, without noticing that "Stinkpot" had thrown himself down to sleep behind the hedge, and no one had seen him. —That's why people say: "When you eat, close your door, and when you talk, look around."

This time it really seemed as if the devil had come to tease "Stinkpot" while he was asleep, and to blow into his ears all the foul things they were saying about him, and to drive them into his heart with a nail.

"And look at that cuckold, that 'Stinkpot,' " they were saying, "who's gobbling up half of Don Liborio!" — "He sits in the manure and eats and drinks there!" —". . . and gets fat as a pig!"

---

[5] In southern Italy *compare*—literally "godfather"—is the equivalent of "friend," but it is so widely used as to have become meaningless in most instances. In the present context it combines "godfather" and "friend," and is ironically emphatic.

Stinkpot

What happened then? What went through "Stinkpot's" head? He suddenly got up without saying anything and in a blind fury, began to run toward the town as if he had been bitten by a tarantula, and even the grass and the stones seemed red as blood to him.

On the threshold of his house, he met Don Liborio who was peacefully going away, fanning himself with his straw hat.

"Listen, *signor compare,*" he said to him, "if I see you in my house again, I swear to God, I'll knock your brains out!"

Don Liborio looked him in the eye as if he were speaking Greek, and thought he had gone out of his mind in all that heat, for one just couldn't imagine that all at once "Stinkpot" should get it into his head to be jealous, after keeping his eyes shut for such a long time and being the best-natured man and husband in the world.

"What's the matter with you today, *compare?*" he asked him.

"The matter is that if I see you in my house again, I swear to God, I'll knock your brains out!"

Don Liborio shrugged his shoulders and went away, laughing. And "Stinkpot" walked into his house, his eyes wild, and repeated to his wife:

"If I see the *signor compare* here again, I swear to God, I'll knock his brains out!"

Venera stuck her fists on her hips and began to abuse him saying all sorts of foul things. He, standing against the wall, kept nodding yes, like an ox that is trying to chase a fly away and doesn't want to listen to reason.

The children screamed, seeing such a strange situation. Finally his wife took the door bolt and drove him out to get him out of her sight, telling him that in her own house she was the boss and could do whatever she pleased.

"Stinkpot" couldn't work in the fallow land any more; he was always thinking of the same thing and had so sour and twisted a face as had never been seen on him before. One Saturday evening before nightfall, he planted his hoe in the furrow and left without even getting his week's pay. His wife, seeing him arrive without money, and two hours earlier than usual on top of it, began to give him a tongue-lashing again, and then wanted to send him to the square to buy salted anchovies, because she felt a tickling in her throat. But he didn't want to move and stayed there, holding on his knees the baby girl who, poor thing, didn't dare move and kept whimpering because her father scared her with that face of his. That evening Venera was angry and at her wit's end, and the black hen, perched on the ladder, never stopped clucking, as when something bad is going to happen.

Don Liborio used to come after making his calls and before going to the café to play a game of cards. And that evening Venera said that she wanted him to take her pulse, for she had felt feverish all day because of that tickling in her throat. "Stinkpot," *he* kept quiet and didn't even move from his place. But as one heard the leisurely steps of the Doctor, who was coming very slowly up the path, a little tired from his calls, puffing from the heat and fanning himself with his straw hat, "Stinkpot" got the door bolt with which his wife drove him out of the house when he was in her way, and lay in wait behind the door. Unfortunately Venera didn't notice him, because at that moment she had gone to the kitchen to put an armful of firewood under the boiling kettle. As Don Liborio set foot in the room, his *compare* lifted the bolt and hit him on the back of the neck with such a blow that he killed him like an ox, and there was no need of a doctor or a druggist.

This was how "Stinkpot" ended up in jail.

1880

PART TWO

MALARIA

You'd think you could touch it with your hands—as if it came from the rich smoky earth, there, everywhere, all around the mountains that close it in, from Agnone to the snowcapped Etna [1]—stagnating on the plain like the heavy suffocating heat of July. There rise and set the red-hot sun, and the colorless moon, and the Puddara [2] that seems to sail through an evaporating sea, and the birds and the white daisies of spring, and the scorched summer; and there pass by the wild ducks, in long black files through the autumn clouds, and the river that glistens as if it were metal, between the wide and desolate banks, white, chipped, strewn with pebbles; and down below, like a pond, the Lake of Lentini, [3] with its flat shores, without a boat, without a tree on its edge, smooth and still. By the water, oxen graze listlessly, few and far between, covered with mud up to the chest, their hair coarse and shaggy. When the herd's bell resounds in the great silence, the wagtails fly away si-

---

1. The author is giving the geographical limits of the Plain of Catania, a Sicilian region that was infested with malaria until recently. Agnone is a village on the southern border of this region and Mount Etna is on the northern extremity.

2. See p. 39, n. 9.

3. The Lake of Lentini, which fostered malaria with its stagnant waters, was drained some years ago.

lently, and the herdsman himself, he, too, yellow with fever and white with dust, opens his swollen lids for an instant, lifting his head in the shade of the dry rushes.

Malaria gets into your bones with the bread you eat, and when you open your mouth to speak, as you walk on the roads that suffocate you with dust and sun, and you feel your knees give way, or you sink down on the saddle as your mule ambles along with its head low. In vain Lentini, and Francofonte, and Paternò[4] try to climb like stray sheep up the first hills that break loose from the plain, and surround themselves with orange groves, vineyards, evergreen vegetable fields; malaria snatches up the villagers in the deserted streets and nails them in front of the doors of their houses plasterless from the sun, and they shake with fever under their overcoats and under all the bed blankets piled upon their shoulders.

Down there, on the plain, the houses are rare and melancholy-looking: alongside the sun-eaten roads, between two piles of smoking manure, leaning on the crumbling sheds where the change horses tied to the empty manger wait with lifeless eyes; —or by the shore of the lake, the decrepit tavern bough hung over the doorway,[5] the ugly empty rooms, and the tavern-keeper dozing squatted on the doorstep, his head wrapped in a

---

4. Three small towns, the first two on the hills to the south of the Plain of Catania, and Paternò to the north on the lower slopes of Mount Etna.

5. See p. 89, n. 5.

kerchief, gazing out over the deserted countryside every time he wakes up, to see if a thirsty traveler is coming; —or like boxes of white wood, plumed by four scrawny, gray eucalyptus trees, alongside the railroad that cuts the plain in two like a hatchet blow, where the locomotive flies by whistling like an autumn wind, and at night there are bursts of fiery sparks; —or finally here and there, at the boundaries of the farms marked by roughly squared pillars, the roofs propped up from outside, the shutters broken down, in front of the cracked yard, in the shade of the tall straw ricks where the chickens sleep with their heads under their wings, and the donkey lets his head droop, his mouth still full of straw, and the dog leaps up suspiciously and barks hoarsely at the stone that falls from the plaster, at the lizard that slides by, at the leaf that moves in the inert countryside.

In the evening, as soon as the sun goes down, sunburned men with shabby straw hats and wide canvas pants appear in the doorways, yawning and stretching their arms; and half-naked women with blackened shoulders, nursing babies that are already so pale and wasted that one can't understand how they will get big and dark and how they will romp on the grass when winter is back and the yard becomes green once again, and the sky blue, and all around, the countryside laughs in the sun. And one can't understand either where they live, or why they live there, all those people who hurry off to Mass on Sundays, to the lonely little churches hemmed in by cactus hedges, from ten miles around, as far as you can hear the ringing of the little shrill bells over the plain that never ends.

However, where there is malaria the land is blessed by God. In June the ears of wheat fall to the ground from their weight, and the furrows smoke as if they had blood in their veins as soon as the plowshare goes into them in November. Then those who sow and those who reap must also fall like ripe ears, for the Lord has said: "In the sweat of thy brow shalt thou eat bread." When the sweat of the fever leaves someone stiff on the corn-husk mattress, and there is no need for quinine or for eucalyptus tea any more, they load him on the hay cart, or on the donkey's packsaddle, or on a ladder, any way they can, with a sack over his face, and they go to lay him by the lonely little church, under the spiny cactuses whose fruit for that reason no one eats. The women cry together in a group, and the men look on, smoking.

This was the way they had carried off the field watchman of Valsavoia, whose name was *massaro* Croce, who had been swallowing quinine and eucalyptus tea for thirty years. In spring he was better, but in autumn, when the wild ducks passed by again, he put his kerchief on his head and didn't show himself at the doorway more than once every other day; and he was down to skin and bones, and had a belly as big as a drum, so that they called him the Toad, also because of his rude and wild behavior, and because his eyes had become colorless and bulged out of his head. Before he died, he kept saying:

"Don't worry, the master'll take care of my children!"

And the last night, with those ugly stunned eyes he looked in the face one by one those who stood around his bed and who put the candle near his nose. Uncle Menico, the goatherd, who knew about these things, said that his liver must have been as hard as a rock and must have weighed one and a half *rotolo*.[6] And somebody added:

"Now he doesn't give a damn! He's grown fat and made himself rich at his master's expense and his children don't need anybody! You think he caught all that malaria and took all that quinine for thirty years just because he loved the master?"

Carmine, the tavern-keeper by the lake, had lost all five of his children in the same way, one after the other, three boys and two girls. With the girls one could take it! But the boys died just when they had grown up and were old enough to earn their bread. By now he knew how it was, and as the fever overpowered the boy after having tormented him for two or three years, he didn't spend another cent, nor for quinine nor for herb teas, but drew off some good wine and made all the fish ragouts he knew, to stimulate the sick boy's appetite. In the morning he would get his boat and go fishing, and

6. A Sicilian measure of weight, which was equivalent to about 800 grams.

come back loaded with mullets, and eels as big as your
arm, and then standing before his son's bed, with tears
in his eyes, he would say:

"Here! Eat this!"

Nanni, the cart driver, took the rest to sell it in town.

"The lake gives and the lake takes away!" said Nanni,
seeing Carmine cry in secret. "What can you do about it,
brother?"

The lake had given him a good profit. And at
Christmastime, when eels sell at a good price, they had gay
dinners before the fire in the house on the shore of the
lake—macaroni, sausages, everything you could think
of—while outside the wind howled like a cold and hungry wolf. In such a way, those who remained consoled
themselves for their dead. But little by little they were
thinning out so that the mother grew bent like a hook
from heartaches, and the father, who was big and fat,
was always at the doorway so as not to see those ugly
empty rooms where his children used to sing and work.
The last one absolutely didn't want to die, and cried
and was desperate when the fever came over him and
even went to throw himself into the lake out of fear of
death. But his father, who knew how to swim, fished
him out and scolded him saying that the cold bath would
bring back the fever worse than before.

"Ah!" sobbed the boy, thrusting his hands into his
hair. "There's no more hope for me! There's no more
hope for me!"

"Just like his sister Agatha, who didn't want to die
because she was engaged!" remarked Carmine to his

wife, who was sitting by the bed; and she, who was bent just like a hook and for some time now hadn't been crying any more, nodded in agreement.

She, reduced to that state, and her husband, big and fat, had tough hides, and remained there alone to watch the house.

Malaria doesn't strike everybody down. Sometimes you can live with it for a hundred years, like Cirino, the Idiot, who had neither king nor kingdom, neither ways nor means, neither mother nor father, neither a house to sleep in nor bread to eat, and everyone for forty miles around knew him, since he went from one farm to another, helping to feed the oxen, to carry the manure, to skin the dead animals, to do the lowest jobs, and he got kicks and a piece of bread; he slept in the ditches, on the embankments of the fields, behind the hedges, in the sheds by the stables; and lived on charity, wandering around like a dog without a master, barefoot and shirtless, the two ends of a pair of shorts tied with a little rope around his thin black legs; and yellow as saffron, he kept singing at the top of his lungs, under the sun that hammered down on his bare head. He didn't take quinine or medicine any more, nor did he catch the fever. A hundred times they had picked him up when they found him lying flat across the road, as if he were dead; at last malaria had left him, because it didn't know what to do with him any more. After it had eaten his brain and the meat from his legs, and had all gone into his belly that was swollen like a water bag, it had left him as happy as a king, singing in the sun better than a lark. The Idiot usually liked to stay in front of the stable of Valsavoia, because people passed by there, and he ran after them for miles, shouting "Oo-ooh! Oo-ooh!" till they threw him a couple of cents. The tavern-keeper took the cents and let him sleep under the shed, on the horses' straw, and when the horses began kicking one another Cirino ran to wake up the master shouting, "Oo-ooh!"; and in the morning he groomed and fed them.

Later he became interested in the railroad they built nearby. The cart drivers and the travelers were now rarer on the road, and the Idiot didn't know what to think, looking in the air for hours watching the swallows fly, and he blinked his eyes in the sun to figure it out. The first time he saw all those people packed in the big cars that passed through the station, he seemed to guess. And from then on he waited for the train every day, never a minute off as if he had a clock in his head; and while it fled in front of him, throwing its smoke and uproar in his face, he would run after it with his arms in the air, shouting with an angry and threatening voice: "Oo-ooh! Oo-ooh! . . ."

The tavern-keeper, each time that from the distance he saw the train pass, puffing through the malaria, didn't say anything either, but spat all his disgust toward it, shaking his head before the deserted shed and the empty pitchers. In the past, business had gone so well that he had taken four wives, one after the other, so that they called him "Wife-killer" and said that he had become hardened to it, and he would have been ready to take the fifth if the daughter of *massaro* Turi Orichiazza hadn't sent him this answer: "God forbid! Not even if he were made of gold, that Christian! He eats up people like a crocodile!" But it wasn't true that he was hardened to it, for when Santa died, and she was the third, he didn't have a mouthful of bread or a sip of water till lunchtime, and he really cried behind the tavern counter.

"This time I want to get one who's used to malaria," he had said after that happened. "I don't want to feel miserable like this any more."

Malaria killed his wives, one by one, but left him just the same, old and wrinkled, and you wouldn't have imagined how that man also had a murder on his conscience,[7] even though he was about to take his fourth wife. And yet, he looked, each time, for a young and appetizing wife, because without a wife a tavern can't go, and this was why customers had become fewer. Now the only one left was Mommu, the flagman from the nearby railroad, a man who never said a word, and who came between trains to drink his glass, sitting down on the little bench by the doorway, with his shoes

7. During the last century, in the interior of Sicily it was not unusual for a man to take the law into his own hands and kill someone. These murders were generally committed either to vindicate family honor or because of long-standing feuds.

in his hand to let his feet rest. "Malaria doesn't get these people!" thought "Wife-killer," without opening his mouth himself, because if malaria had made them fall like flies there wouldn't have been anyone left to make that railroad over there go. Since he had gotten rid of the one man who poisoned his existence, the poor devil had only two enemies in the world: the railroad that stole his customers, and malaria that took away his wives.

All the others on the plain, as far as the eye could see, felt a moment of happiness, even if they had someone in bed leaving this world little by little, or if the fever knocked them down at the doorway, their kerchiefs on their heads and their cloaks on their shoulders. They got some enjoyment from looking at the wheat that came up prosperous and green like velvet, or at the full-grown grain that moved in waves like a sea, and they listened to the long monotonous song of the reapers, who were spread out like a row of soldiers, and on every path you could hear the bagpipes, behind which swarms of peasants came from Calabria for the harvest, dusty, bent under their heavy knapsacks, the men in front and the women behind, limping and looking with tired burnt faces at the road that stretched before them. And on the edge of every ditch, behind every bush of aloes, in the hour when the evening drifts down like a gray veil, the watchman's pipe whistled among the ripe ears of wheat which were hushed and still as the wind fell away, they too filled by the silence of night.

"That's it!" thought "Wife-killer." "If all those people

manage not to leave their hides here and get back home, they'll get back with money in their pockets."

But not he, no! He wasn't waiting for the harvest or for anything else, and didn't have the heart to sing. The evening drifted down very sad in the empty stable and in the dark tavern. At that hour the train passed whistling in the distance, and Mommu was next to his little flagman shanty with the flag in his hand; but even up there, after the train had vanished in the darkness, you could hear Cirino the Idiot who ran after it howling "Oo-ooh! . . ." And "Wife-killer," in the doorway of the dark and deserted tavern, was thinking that for those people there was no malaria.

Finally, when he couldn't pay the rent for the tavern and the stable any more, the owner evicted him, after he had been there fifty-seven years, and "Wife-killer" too was forced to look for a job on the railroad, and to hold the flag in his hand when the train passed by.

Then, tired of running up and down the tracks all day, worn out with ailments and old age, he saw the long line of cars crammed with people pass by twice a day: the gay groups of hunters who scattered out over the plain; at times a peasant boy playing a harmonica with his head bowed, huddled up on a third-class bench; the beautiful rich women looking out of the windows, their heads wrapped in veils; the silver and the tarnished steel of the bags and suitcases shining under the polished lamps; the high backs of the seats stuffed and overlayed with lace. Ah, how good it must have been to travel in there, taking a little nap! It was as if a piece of the city were rolling by in front of you, with all the lights of the streets and the sparkling stores. Then the train became lost in the vast evening fog, and the poor man, taking his shoes off for a moment and sitting on the bench, muttered:

"Ah! for those people there just isn't malaria!"

1881

THE ORPHANS

The little girl appeared at the door, twisting one corner of her apron with her fingers, and said:

"I'm here."

Then, since nobody paid any attention to her, she began to look hesitatingly at one and then another of the women who were kneading the dough, and went on:

"They told me, 'Go to Sidora's.'"

"Come here, come here," shouted Sidora, red as a tomato as she stood before the oven. "Wait, I'll make you a nice big bun."

"If they've sent the child away, that means they're about to bring Nunzia the viaticum," observed the woman from Licodia.

One of the women who were helping to knead the dough turned her head, still working with her fists in the kneading trough, her arms bare up to the elbow, and asked the child:

"How's your stepmother?"

The child, who didn't know the woman, looked at her with her big eyes wide open, and then lowering her head again and working feverishly with the corners of her apron, mumbled in a whisper:

"She's in bed."

The Orphans

"Haven't you heard that the Sacrament is there?" answered the one from Licodia. "Now the women neighbors have begun to scream and lament at the door."

"When I've finished putting the bread in the oven," said Sidora, "I'll run over for a minute myself, to see if they need anything. Meno'll lose his right hand if this wife of his dies too."

"Some men aren't lucky with wives, just as some people don't have any luck with animals. They lose as many as they get. Look at Angela!"

"Last night," added the woman from Licodia, "I saw Meno at his doorway; he'd come back from the vineyard before the Ave Maria and he was blowing his nose in his handkerchief."

"But," added the woman who was kneading the dough, "he's really a good hand at killing off wives. In less than three years he's already eaten up two of *curatolo* Nino's daughters, one after the other! Wait a while and he'll eat up the third too, and he'll swallow up all of *curatolo* Nino's property."

"But is this child Nunzia's daughter or the first wife's?"

"She's the first wife's daughter. But the second one loved her just as if she were her real mother because the little orphan was also her niece."

The little girl, hearing the talk about her, began to cry very softly in a corner to relieve her heavy heart, which she had kept in check by playing with her apron.

"Come here, come here," Sidora went on. "The bun

is nice and ready. There, there, don't cry, your mamma's in heaven."

Then the child dried her eyes with her clenched fists, because she saw Sidora turn to open the oven.

"Poor Nunzia!" said a neighbor appearing at the doorway. "Now the undertakers are going there. They passed by here a moment ago."

"Keep away, keep away! I'm a daughter of Mary!" exclaimed the women, making the sign of the cross.[1]

Sidora took the bun from the oven, brushed the ashes off, and handed it nice and hot to the child, who took it in her apron and began to go away very slowly, blowing on it.

"Where are you going?" Sidora called after her. "Stay here. At home there's the big black bogeyman who carries people away."

The little orphan listened very gravely, opening her eyes wide. Then with her obstinate singsong she went on:

"I'm going to take it to mamma."

"Your mamma isn't there any more. Stay here," a neighbor repeated. "Eat the bun yourself."

Then the little girl squatted down on the doorstep, all sad, the bun in her hands, without taking a bite.

All of a sudden, seeing her father come, she got up happy and ran toward him. Meno came in without saying anything and sat down in a corner with his hands

---

1. Hearing the undertakers mentioned, the women utter these words and make the sign of the cross as if to conjure death away.

hanging between his knees, his face long and his lips as white as paper, because since the day before, he hadn't put a piece of bread in his mouth, he was so broken-hearted. He looked at the women as if to say: "Poor me!"

The women, seeing the black kerchief[2] around his neck, made a circle around him, their hands covered with flour, and chimed in to sympathize with him.

"Don't talk to me about it, Sidora!" he repeated, shaking his head and heaving his shoulders. "This is a thorn that'll never leave my heart! She was a real saint, that woman! You'll have to admit I didn't deserve her. She was so sick, and still until yesterday she'd been getting out of bed to go feed the colt that's just been weaned. And she didn't want me to call the doctor in order not to spend money and buy medicine. I'll never find another wife like that, believe me! Let me cry, I've got reason!"

And he went on shaking his head and heaving his shoulders, as if his misfortune weighed very heavily on him.

"As for finding yourself another wife," added the woman from Licodia to encourage him, "all you've got to do is look for one."

"No! No!" Meno kept repeating with his head low like a mule. "I'll never find another wife like that. This time I'll stay single! Believe me!"

---

2. A sign of recent death in the immediate family. In Sicily people are still very strict in observing the custom of wearing black during the period of mourning, which may last a year or longer.

Sidora cut him off shouting: "Don't say such things, it's not right! You've got to look for another wife, for the sake of this little orphan at least; otherwise who'll take care of her when you go to the fields? Do you want to leave her in the street?"

"You find me another wife like that one! She didn't wash herself so she wouldn't dirty the water; and at home she waited on me better than a servant, so affectionate and faithful that she wouldn't even have taken a handful of broad beans for the wicker mat, and she never opened her mouth to say 'Give me!' And on top of all this, she'd brought a good dowry, stuff that was worth as much as gold! And I have to give it all back because we didn't have any children! The sacristan told me so just now when he came with the holy water. And how she loved that little girl, who reminded her of her poor sister! Another one who wasn't her aunt wouldn't treat this little orphan right."

"If you'd take *curatolo* Nino's third daughter, everything would work out fine, both for the orphan and for the dowry," observed the woman from Licodia.

"That's what I say. But don't talk to me about it; my mouth's still as bitter as gall."

"This isn't the time to talk about such things," agreed Sidora. "Have a bite to eat instead, Meno; you don't look good at all."

"No! No!" Meno kept repeating. "Don't talk about eating; I've got a lump in my throat."

On a stool in front of him Sidora set hot bread, black olives, a piece of *pecorino* [3] cheese, and the flask of wine.

---

3. A type of cheese made from sheep's milk.

The Orphans

And the poor man began to nibble very slowly, continuing to mutter with a long face.

"Bread," he observed moved almost to tears, "nobody knows how to make bread the way the good soul used to make it. It seemed to be made out of pure meal, no less! And with a handful of wild fennel she'd cook you a soup that made you smack your lips. Now I'll have to buy bread at the store from that thief, *mastro* Puddo; and I won't find any more hot soup every time I come back home soaking wet. And I'll have to go to bed with a cold stomach. Just the other night I was staying up with her after having hoed and grubbed on the slope all day, and sitting by the bed I heard myself snore, I was so tired, and the good soul said to me, 'Go have some soup. I kept it warm for you in the fireplace.' And she was always thinking about me, about the house, about the things that had to be done, about this and about that, and she never stopped talking to me and giving me her last advice, like somebody who's going on a long trip, and while I was half asleep I heard her muttering all the time. And she went to the other world happy, with the crucifix on her breast and her hands folded over it. That saint! She doesn't need Masses and rosaries. The money for the priest would be thrown away."

"This world is full of troubles!" exclaimed the neighbor. "Also the donkey of Angela, who lives nearby, is dying from the colic."

"My troubles are bigger!" concluded Meno, wiping his mouth with the back of his hand. "No, don't make me eat any more, every mouthful drops into my stomach like a piece of lead. You eat, poor innocent girl, you who don't understand these things. Now you won't have anybody to wash you and comb your hair. Now you won't have your mamma any more to keep you under her wing like a mother hen, and you're ruined too, the same as I am. I found you that one, but you'll never have another stepmother like that, my child!"

The child, moved almost to tears, stuck her lip out again and put her fists in her eyes.

"No, you can't do without one," repeated Sidora. "We've got to find you another wife for the sake of this poor little orphan, who's left in the middle of the street."

"And me, how'm I left? And my colt? And my house? And who'll take care of the chickens? Let me cry, Sidora! It would've been better if I'd died myself, instead of that good soul."

"Quiet, you don't know what you're saying, and you don't know what it's like not to have a head of the house."

"That's true!" observed Meno, comforted.

"Look at poor Angela, rather! First her husband died, then her oldest son, and now her donkey's dying too!"

"The donkey should be bled from the vein under the girth if he's got the colic," said Meno.

"You go over, you know about these things," added the neighbor. "You'll be doing a good deed for the soul of your wife."

Meno got up to go to Angela's, and the little orphan, who didn't have anyone else in the world now, ran after him like a little chicken. Sidora, a good housewife, reminded him:

"And your house? Have you thought about it, now that nobody's there any more?"

"I locked it; and besides, cousin Alfia lives just across the street and she'll keep an eye on it."

Neighbor Angela's donkey was lying in the middle of the courtyard, his nose cold, his ears hanging down and his four legs in the air, kicking from time to time when the colic drew his sides together like a pair of bellows. The widow, as pale as a dead woman, was sitting there on the stones in front of him, watching, her hands in her gray hair and her eyes dry and desperate.

Meno began walking around the animal, touching his ears and looking into his lifeless eyes, and as he saw that the blood was still dripping black, drop by drop, from the vein under the girth, and clotting on the ends of the coarse hairs, he asked:

"So they've bled him then?"

The widow fixed her dull eyes on his face without speaking, and nodded yes.

"Then there's nothing more to do," concluded Meno; and he watched the donkey stretched out on the stones, rigid, his hair all ruffled like a dead cat's.

"It's the will of God, sister!" he said to comfort her. "We're ruined, both of us."

He had sat down on the stones next to the widow, his little daughter between his knees, and they both watched the poor animal who was beating the air with his legs from time to time, just like a dying man.

Sidora, when she had finished taking the bread out

of the oven, in order to chat a little also came to the courtyard with cousin Alfia, who was wearing her new dress and had put her silk kerchief on her head; and pulling Meno aside, Sidora said:

"*Curatolo* Nino won't give you his other daughter, since they die like flies with you and he loses the dowry. Besides, Santa's too young, and there'd be the danger of her filling your house with children."

"If they were boys, one could take it! But there's also the chance of having daughters. I'm so unlucky!"

"There'd be cousin Alfia. She's not young any more and has some property of her own: a house and a piece of vineyard."

Meno fixed his eyes on cousin Alfia, who was pretending to be watching the donkey, her hands on her stomach, and he concluded:

"If that's the way it is, we can talk about it some time. But I'm so unlucky!"

Sidora cut him off:

"Think of those who're more unlucky than you, think of those!"

"There aren't any, believe me! I'll never find another wife like that! I'll never be able to forget her, even if I marry again ten times! And this poor little orphan won't forget her either."

"Calm down, you'll forget her all right. And the child will forget her too. Didn't she forget her real mother? Look at neighbor Angela instead, now that her donkey's dying! And she doesn't own anything else! She's the one who'll never forget!"

Cousin Alfia saw that it was time to come closer, and

with a long face began to praise the dead woman again. She had arranged her in the coffin with her own hands, and had put a kerchief of fine cloth over her face. There was no question about it, she had a lot of white linen. Then Meno, almost moved to tears, turned to neighbor Angela, who sat still, as if she were made of stone:

"Why don't you have the donkey skinned now? At least get the money for his hide."

1881

PROPERTY

If the traveler who was going along the Lake of Lentini spread out there like a piece of dead sea, and along the scorched stubble of the Plain of Catania, and the ever green orange trees of Francofonte, and the gray cork oaks of Resecone, and the deserted pastures of Passaneto and Passanitello,[1] would ask, to while away the time on the long dusty road, under the sky hazy with heat, in the hour when the litter bells sound sadly in the immense countryside, and the mules let their heads and tails droop, and the litter driver sings his melancholy song so as not to let himself be overcome by the sleep of malaria: "Whose land is this?"—he would hear the answer: "Mazzarò's." And passing by a farmstead as big as a town, with storehouses that looked like churches, and flocks of chickens squatting in the shade of the well, and the women who put their hands over their eyes to see who was passing: "And this?"—"Mazzarò's."

And on and on, while malaria lay heavy on your eyes, and the sudden barking of a dog startled you, as you passed through a vineyard that had no end and sprawled

---

1. This story is set in the same region as "Malaria." The Lake of Lentini and the towns and villages mentioned here are either on or near the Plain of Catania.

Property

over hill and plain, motionless, as if the dust lay heavy upon it, and the watchman, lying face down over his gun near the valley, lifted his drowsy head and opened one eye to see who it was—"Mazzarò's." Then came an olive grove as thick as a forest, where never a blade of grass grew, and the crop lasted until March. Those were Mazzarò's olive trees.

And toward evening, when the sun set as red as fire, and the countryside became veiled with sadness, one met the long lines of Mazzaro's plows returning very slowly from the fallow land, and the oxen wading step by step across the ford, with their muzzles in the dark water; and in the distant pastures of Canziria,[2] on the barren slope, one saw the immense whitish blotches of Mazzarò's herds; and one could hear the whistle of the herdsman echoing in the gullies, and the herd's bell resounding from time to time, and the solitary song lost in the valley.—All Mazzarò's.

It seemed as if even the setting sun, and the buzzing cicadas, and the birds flying short flights to go and nestle behind the clods, and the hoot of the horned owl in the woods were Mazzarò's. It seemed as if Mazzarò were stretched out as big as the earth and one walked on his belly.

Instead, he was a puny little man, said the litter driver, and if you saw him you wouldn't have thought he was worth a penny; and the only fat thing he had was his belly, and no one knew how he managed to fill it, because he ate only a few cents' worth of bread,

2. See p. 16, note 6.

and yet he was rich as a pig; but that man, he had a mind that was a jewel.

In fact, with that mind like a jewel, he had piled up all that property, where once he used to come to hoe, to prune, to reap, from morning till night, in the sun, in the rain, in the wind; without shoes on his feet and without even a ragged overcoat; and they remembered having kicked him in the pants, all those who now called him "Your Excellency" and spoke to him cap in hand. Nor had he become conceited because of this, now that all the Excellencies in town owed him money; and he used to say that Excellency means poor devil and bad payer; but he still wore a cap—the only difference was that he wore one of black silk, and this was his only luxury; lately he had even gone so far as to put on a felt hat,[3] because it cost less than the silk cap.

His property reached out as far as the eye could see, and his eyes saw far—everywhere, right and left, in front and behind, on the mountain and on the plain. More than five thousand mouths ate on his land, without counting the birds of the air and the animals of the earth, and without counting his own mouth, which ate less than any other and was satisfied with a few cents' worth of bread and a piece of cheese, gulped down in all haste, as he was standing in a corner of the storehouse as big as a church, in the grain dust where you couldn't see a thing while the peasants unloaded the

---

3. Felt hats were worn in Sicily by the well-to-do and were considered the sign of a higher social class. Caps, instead, were used by the peasants.

sacks, or against a straw rick when the wind swept across the frozen countryside at sowing time, or with his head in a basket on the hot days of the harvest. He didn't drink wine, he didn't smoke, he didn't take snuff, even though his fields along the river produced lots of tobacco with broad leaves as tall as a boy, the kind that sold at ninety-five *lire*. He didn't have the vice of gambling or of women. As for women, the only one he ever had to support was his mother, who had even cost him twelve *tarì*, when he had to have her carried to the cemetery.

The fact was that he had thought and thought again and again about what property means, when he went to work without shoes on the land that was now his own, and he knew what it was like to make three *tarì* a day in the month of July, and to stay with your back bent for fourteen hours, with the overseer on horseback behind you, giving you a whipping if you tried to straighten up for a moment. That is why he hadn't let one minute of his life pass without using it to get property together; and now his plows were as numerous as the long files of crows that come in November; and endless files of mules carried the seed; you couldn't count the women who squatted in the mud from October to March to gather his olives, as you can't count the magpies that come to steal them; and at vintage time entire villages hurried to his vineyards, and all the singing that could be heard in the countryside was for Mazzarò's vintage. Then at harvest time, Mazzarò's reapers looked like an army of soldiers, and to feed all those people with hardtack in the morning and bread and bitter orange for lunch, and to give them the afternoon snack and noodles in the evening, it took handfuls of money, and the noodles were dished up in kneading troughs as big as wash tubs. Therefore, now when he rode on horseback behind the row of his reapers, whip in hand, he didn't lose sight of a single one of them, and kept repeating: "Let's bend over, boys!" All year long he had his hands in his pockets, spending, and for the land tax alone the King took so much that every time Mazzarò got a fever.

But each year, all those storehouses as big as churches were so filled up with grain that the roofs had to be lifted off to hold it all; and every time that Mazzarò sold his wine, it took more than a day to count the money, all in silver coins of twelve *tarì,* because he didn't want filthy paper for his things, and he only went to buy filthy paper when he had to pay the King, or the others; and at the fairs, Mazzarò's herds covered the whole ground and crowded the roads, and it took half a day to let them file by, and the Saint with the band [4] would at times have to give way and go on another street.

He had gotten together all that property himself, with his hands and with his mind, by not sleeping at night, by catching fever from anxiety or from malaria, by toiling from morning till night, and going around in the sun and in the rain, by wearing out his boots and his

---

4. A reference to the frequent and characteristic religious processions in Sicilian villages. A musical band is always an integral part of these processions.

mules—he alone never wore out, thinking of his property, which was all that he had in the world, for he had no children, nor grandchildren, nor other relatives; he didn't have anything but his property. When a man is made this way, it means that he is made just for property.

And property, too, was made for him, who seemed to have a magnet for it, because property wants to stay with those who know how to hang on to it, and who don't waste it like that baron who had once been Mazzaro's master, and who had taken him, poor and in rags, out of charity into his fields, and who had been the owner of all those meadows and of all those woods, and of all those vineyards and all those herds; and when he came on horseback to his lands, with the watchmen behind him, you would have thought he was the King, and they got his lodging and his dinner ready—the fool —so that everybody knew the hour and the minute when he was supposed to come and no one would let himself be caught red-handed. "He's simply asking to be robbed!" said Mazzarò, and when the baron kicked him in the pants, he burst with laughter and rubbed his back with his hands, muttering: "Fools should stay home"; "Property doesn't belong to those who have it, but to those who know how to get it." He, instead, after he had gotten his property, certainly didn't send word to say he was coming to supervise the harvest or the vintage, and when and how, but turned up unexpectedly, on foot or on a mule, without watchmen, with a piece of bread in his pocket; and he slept near his sheaves, his eyes open, and his shotgun between his legs.

So, little by little, Mazzarò became the owner of all the baron's property; and the latter lost first the olive grove, and then the vineyards, and then the pastures, and then the farmsteads, and finally even his palace, because not a day went by but he signed legal papers, with Mazzarò putting his *X* underneath. The baron was left with nothing but the stone shield that had been over the main door, and it was the only thing he hadn't wanted to sell, and he said to Mazzarò: "Only this, of all my property, is not for you." And it was true; Mazzarò didn't know what to do with it, nor would he have given two cents for it. The baron still used *tu* [5] with him, but he didn't kick him in the pants any more.

"How wonderful to have the good luck that Mazzarò has!" people said; and they didn't know what it had taken to grab that good luck: how many worries, how much toil, how many lies, how much danger of going to jail, and how that mind that was a jewel had worked day and night, better than a mill wheel, to get property; and if the owner of a bordering field kept refusing to give it up to him, or wanted to make Mazzarò pay through the nose, he had to devise a trick to force him to sell, and trap him into it in spite of peasant mistrust. He went to him, for example, to brag about the fertility of a holding where not even lupins would grow, and managed to make him believe that it was a promised land, until the poor devil let himself be convinced to

---

5. The familiar form of address was used by landowners when speaking to servants or peasants.

lease it in order to speculate on it, and then he lost the lease, the house and the field, which Mazzarò grabbed for a song.

And how many troubles Mazzarò had to stand! The sharecroppers who came to complain about the poor crops, the debtors who sent their women in a procession to tear their hair and beat their breasts, begging him not to put them out in the street by taking their mule and their donkey, because they didn't have anything to eat.

"See what I eat?" he answered. "Bread and onions! And yet my storehouses are packed and I own all this property."

And if, from all that property, they asked him for a handful of broad-beans, he said:

"What? Do you think I stole them? Don't you know what it costs to sow them, and to hoe them, and to harvest them?"

And if they asked him for a penny, he answered that he didn't have one.

And he really didn't. He never kept more than twelve *tarì* in his pocket—so much money was needed to make all that property pay, and money went in and out of his house like a river. But then he didn't care about money; he said that it wasn't property, and as soon as he got a certain sum together, he bought a piece of land right away, because he wanted to have as much land as the King has, and be better than the King, since the King can neither sell it nor say that it is his own.

Only one thing distressed him: that he was beginning to get old and would have to leave the land there, where

it was. It is an injustice of God, that having worn yourself out all your life to acquire property, when you
finally have it, and you want more, you have to leave it!
And he would sit for hours on a basket, his chin in his
hands, looking at the vineyards that spread out green
before his eyes, and at the wheat fields full of ears that
moved like a sea, and at the olive groves that veiled the
mountain like fog; and if a half-naked boy, bent under
a weight like a tired donkey, passed in front of him,
he threw his stick between his legs, out of envy, and
muttered:

"Look who's got all his days before him! This one,
who doesn't own anything!"

So, when they told him that the time had come to
leave his property and think of his soul, he staggered
out into the courtyard like a madman and went around
killing his ducks and his turkeys with his stick, and
screamed:

"My property, come with me!"

1882

STORY OF THE SAINT JOSEPH DONKEY [1]

They had bought him at the Fair of Buccheri [2] when he was still a colt, and as soon as he saw a she-donkey he would go and nudge her with his nose, looking for her teats; for this he was pounded by her head and was given sound blows on his rump, and in vain they could shout again and again: "Gee! Away! Away!" When Neli saw him so lively and stubborn that at the beating he licked his muzzle and gave his ears a little shake, he said:

"That's just what I want."

And keeping his hand holding the thirty-five *lire* in his pocket, he went right up to the owner.

"It's a beautiful colt," said the owner, "and he's worth more than thirty-five *lire*. Don't pay any attention to that black and white coat like a magpie's. Let me show you his mother; we keep her over there in the grove because the colt always has his nose at her teats. You'll see

---

1. Saint Joseph donkeys are a type of donkey considered the cheapest and least useful. Their coat is black and white and their name probably derives, by popular association, from rustic paintings of the donkey which appears in scenes representing the flight to Egypt.

2. See p. 24, n. 3.

what a beautiful black animal she is! She works for me better than a mule, and she's given me more colts than she has hairs on her back. In all honesty, I don't know where the colt got that magpie coat. But his build's good, believe me! You don't judge men by their faces. Look what a chest he's got! And those legs like pillars! Look how he holds his ears! When you have a donkey who keeps his ears that straight, you can put him to a cart or to a plow, just as you like, and make him carry four *tumoli*[3] of buckwheat better than a mule, I swear by the holy day that's today! Feel this tail; you and your whole family could hang on it!"

Neli knew all this better than he but wasn't foolish enough to say so, and held his ground with his hand in his pocket, shrugging his shoulders and curling his nose, while the owner made the colt go around in front of him.

"Uhm!" muttered Neli. "With that coat of his he looks like the Saint Joseph donkey! Animals that color are no good, and when you ride them through town, people laugh in your face. What should I give you as a present to get that Saint Joseph donkey?"

The owner then became furious and turned his back on him, shouting that people who didn't know anything about animals, or who didn't have money to buy them, shouldn't come to the fair and make Christians waste their time on a holy day like this.

Neli let him swear, and walked away with his brother, who pulled him by the sleeve of his jacket and said that

3. See p. 33, n. 4.

if he was going to throw money away for that ugly animal, he would kick him.

But secretly, they didn't lose sight of the Saint Joseph donkey and of the owner who was pretending to shell green broad beans, the halter rein between his legs, while Neli went wandering around among the rumps of the mules and horses, stopping to look and bargaining for now one and then another of the best animals, without opening the fist holding the thirty-five *lire* inside his pocket, as if he had enough to buy half the fair. But his brother, nodding toward the Saint Joseph donkey, whispered in his ear:

"That's just what we want."

The owner's wife hurried over once in a while to see what had been done, and finding her husband with the halter in his hand, she said:

"Isn't the Blessed Virgin going to send us anyone to buy the colt today?"

And each time her husband answered:

"Nobody yet! One came to bargain, and he liked him. But he's stingy and he's gone away with his money. See, that one with the white cap, over there behind the herd of sheep. But so far he hasn't bought anything, and that means he'll be back."

The woman would have liked to sit down on some stones near her donkey, to see if he would be sold. But her husband said:

"Go away! If they see you waiting, they'll never come to close the deal."

Story of the Saint Joseph Donkey

In the meantime the colt kept nudging with his muzzle between the legs of the she-donkeys passing by, mainly because he was hungry, and as soon as he would open his mouth to bray, the owner would silence him with a good beating since no one had wanted him.

"He's still there!" Neli whispered in his brother's ear, pretending to pass by again only to look for the man who was selling roasted chick-peas. "If we wait till the *Angelus* we can get him for five *lire* less than the price we offered."

The May sun was hot, so that now and then, in the middle of the noise and the bustle of the fair, a great silence fell over the whole fairground, as if there were nobody there any more; and then the owner's wife came back to say to her husband:

"Don't hold out for five *lire* more or less; we don't have money to buy groceries this evening; and then you know that if he's left on our hands the colt eats up five *lire* in a month."

"If you don't go away," her husband answered, "I'll give you a good swift kick!"

So passed the hours of the fair; but none of the people who passed in front of the Saint Joseph donkey stopped to look at him, even though the owner had chosen the most modest place, near the cheap animals, so as not to make him look bad near the fine bay mules and the shiny horses, with that magpie coat of his! It took somebody like Neli to go and bargain for the Saint Joseph donkey that made the whole fair laugh when they saw him. The colt, having waited so long in the sun, let his head and ears droop, and his owner had sat down sadly on the stones, his hands hanging between his knees and the halter in his hands, looking here and there at the long shadows which, in the setting sun, the legs of all those animals that had not found a buyer were beginning to make on the fairground. Then Neli and his brother, and a friend whom they had picked up for the occasion, happened to pass by there, looking up in the air, and the donkey's owner turned his head too, not to let them see that he was there waiting for them; and Neli's friend, his eyes wide open, said casually, as if he himself had gotten the idea:

"Oh, look at the Saint Joseph donkey! Why don't you buy this one, Neli?"

"I bargained for him this morning, but he's too expensive. Besides, everybody would laugh at me with that black and white donkey. You see that nobody's wanted him, so far!"

"That's true, but the color doesn't make any difference for what you need him."

And he asked the owner:

"How much should we give you as a present to get the Saint Joseph donkey?"

The owner's wife, when she saw that the dealing was on again, began to come near once more, very softly, her hands folded under her mantilla.

"Don't talk to me about it!" Neli began to shout, running away on the fairground. "Don't talk to me about it, I don't want to hear about it!"

"If he doesn't want it, leave him alone," answered the owner. "If he doesn't take him, someone else will. 'Unfortunate is the man who doesn't have anything to sell after the fair!'"

"But I want to be heard, damn it!" screamed the friend. "Can't I have my asinine say too?"

And he ran and grabbed Neli by the jacket; then he came back and whispered in the ear of the donkey's owner, who insisted that he wanted to go home again with the little donkey, and he threw his arms around the owner's neck murmuring:

"Listen here! Five *lire* more or less—if you don't sell him today, you'll never find another fool like my friend, who'd buy that animal of yours which isn't worth a cigar."

And he embraced the owner's wife too, and whispered in her ear, to get her on his side. But she shrugged her shoulders, and answered with a surly face:

"It's my husband's business. I haven't got anything to do with it. But if he gives him to you for less than forty *lire* he's a fool, in all honesty! He's cost us more than that!"

"This morning I was crazy to offer thirty-five *lire!*" insisted Neli. "He hasn't found another buyer for that kind of money, has he? The only things left in the whole fair are a few mangy rams and the Saint Joseph donkey. Thirty *lire* now, if he wants them!"

"Take them!" suggested the owner's wife to her husband in a low voice, with tears in her eyes. "We don't have money to buy groceries this evening, and Turiddu has the fever again; we've got to have some quinine."

"Damn it!" screamed her husband. "If you don't go away, I'll give you a taste of this halter!"

"Thirty-two and a half, come on!" shouted the friend at last, shaking them both hard by the collar. "Neither you nor I! [4] This time you've got to do as I say, by all the Saints in Heaven! And you don't even have to give me a glass of wine! Don't you see that the sun's gone down? What are you waiting for, you two?"

And he snatched the halter from the owner's hand, while Neli, swearing, pulled out of his pocket the fist with the thirty-five *lire,* and gave them to him without looking at them, as if his liver were being torn out. The friend drew aside with the owner's wife to count the money on a stone, while the donkey's owner was running over the fairground like a colt, swearing and hitting himself with his fists.

But then he let his wife, who was again very slowly counting the money in the handkerchief, catch up with him, and he asked:

"Is it all there?"

"Yes, it's all here; Saint Gaetano be praised! Now I'll go to the druggist."

"I fooled them! I'd have sold him even for twenty *lire;* donkeys that color are no good."

And Neli, pulling the donkey behind him down the slope, said:

---

4. Here the friend, that is to say the mediator, by "you" means the seller, and by "I" the buyer. In the whole deal he has been trying, somewhat boisterously, to reach a happy medium for both sides.

"I swear to God, I've stolen this colt! The color doesn't make any difference. See those legs like pillars? He's worth forty *lire* with your eyes shut."

"If I hadn't been there," answered the friend, "you wouldn't have gotten anywhere. I've still got two and a half *lire* of yours here. How'd you like to go and drink to the donkey's health with them?"

Now the colt had to stay healthy in order to make the thirty-two and a half *lire* he had cost, and the straw he was eating. Meanwhile, he kept tripping along behind Neli, trying to bite his jacket for fun, as if he knew it was the jacket of his new owner, and as if he didn't care that he was forever leaving the stable where he had been warm beside his mother, where he had rubbed his muzzle on the edge of the manger, or had butted and capered with the ram, and had teased the pig in its little corner. And the first owner's wife, who was again counting the money in the handkerchief before the counter of the druggist, wasn't thinking either that she had seen the colt born, all black and white, his skin as shiny as silk, and he couldn't stand on his legs, and lay curled up in the sun in the courtyard; and all the grass that had made him get so big had passed through her hands. The only one who remembered the colt was his mother, who stretched out her neck braying toward the door of the stable; but when her teats weren't swollen with milk any more, she too forgot about the colt.

"This animal here," said Neli, "you'll see that he'll carry four *tumoli* of buckwheat better than a mule. And at harvest time I'll make him help with the threshing."

Story of the Saint Joseph Donkey

At the threshing, the colt, tied by the neck in a row with the other animals, old mules and lame horses, trotted over the sheaves from morning to night, and he became so tired that he didn't even feel like biting into the pile of straw in the shade where they put him to rest when the breeze came up, while the peasants winnowed the grain, shouting: *Viva Maria!* [5]

Then he let his muzzle and his ears droop, like a full-grown donkey, his eyes lifeless, as if he were tired of looking at that vast white countryside which was clouded here and there with dust from the threshing floors and seemed made only to let you die of thirst and to make you trot around on the sheaves. In the evening, he went back to the village with his saddlebags full, and the owner's boy kept pricking him in the withers, as they went along the path's hedges which seemed alive with the chirping of the titmice and the fragrance of catmint and rosemary, and the donkey would have liked to take a bite, if they hadn't made him trot all the time so that the blood went down to his legs and they had to take him to the farrier; but his owner didn't care at all, because the harvest had been good, and the colt had made his thirty-two and a half *lire.*

"Now he's done his job, and even if I sell him for twenty *lire,* I still have my profit," the owner said.

The only one who loved the colt was the boy who made him trot along the path when they came back from the treshing floor; and he cried while the farrier

---

5. "Long live Mary!" This was the call used by the peasants to urge the animals on during the threshing and it could be heard all over the countryside.

burned the colt's legs with red-hot irons and the poor animal writhed around, his tail in the air and his ears straight up, as when he was running on the fairground, and when the farrier's helper came to change the hot irons that were as red as fire, he tried to break loose from the twisted rope which squeezed his lip, his eyes wild from the pain as if he were human, and his skin smoked and sizzled like fish in a frying pan. But Neli shouted to his boy:

"Jackass! Why are you crying? He's done his job now, and since the harvest's gone well we'll sell him and buy a mule, which'll be better."

Children don't understand certain things, and after the colt was sold to *massaro* Cirino from Licodia, Neli's son used to go to see him in the stable and to pet his muzzle and his neck, and the donkey would turn to sniff at the boy as if his heart were still clinging to him, but donkeys are made to be tied up wherever their owner wants and their fortune changes as their stable changes. *Massaro* Cirino from Licodia had bought the Saint Joseph donkey for little money, because he still had the fetter scar on the pastern, and when Neli's wife saw the donkey pass by with the new owner, she said:

"That was our good fortune; that black and white coat brings cheer to the threshing floor; and now the crops are going from bad to worse, and we've had to sell the mule too."

Massaro Cirino had yoked the donkey to the plow, with the old mare that fitted him like a jewel in a ring; and the donkey cut away at his fine furrow for miles

157

and miles all day long, from the time the skylarks began to trill in the sky white with dawn until the time the robins with their short flights and melancholy whistles hurried to nestle behind the bare stalks that quivered in the cold, while the fog rose like a sea. And, since the donkey was smaller than the mare, they had put a little cushion of straw on his packsaddle under the yoke, and he found it still more difficult to tear up the frost-hardened ground, as he jerked ahead with his shoulders.

"He'll save the mare who's gotten old," said *massaro* Cirino. "This Saint Joseph donkey! He's got a heart as big as the Plain of Catania! And you wouldn't think so!"

And he also said to his wife, who was following him wrapped in her mantilla and was sparingly scattering the seed:

"If an accident should ever happen to him, God forbid! with the crop that's in store for us, we're ruined."

The woman looked at the crop that was in store for them in the stony and desolate little field, where the soil was white and cracked because it hadn't rained for so long, and the water had all come in the form of fog, the kind that eats up the seed; and at hoeing time the wheat was so sparse and yellow that it looked like the devil's beard, as if it had been burned with matches.

"And this, even though I'd left the land fallow!" whined *massaro* Cirino, tearing off his jacket. "That donkey broke his neck working at it like a mule! He's the donkey of bad crops!"

His wife, in front of that scorched wheat field, had a

lump in her throat and while big tears rolled down her cheeks, she answered:

"The donkey doesn't make any difference. To Neli he brought good crops. But we're the ones who're unlucky."

So the Saint Joseph donkey changed owner once again when *massaro* Cirino returned from the wheat field with the sickle on his shoulder, for the wheat didn't have to be reaped that year, although they had put there images of saints stuck on reed stakes, and they had spent two *tarì* to have it blessed by the priest. "The devil's what we need here!" *massaro* Cirino kept swearing in front of those ears of grain which were standing up straight like plumes, and which not even the donkey wanted; and he spat into the air toward that blue sky that didn't have a single drop of water. Just at that time, Luciano, the cart driver, meeting *massaro* Cirino who was pulling behind him the donkey with the saddlebags empty, asked:

"What do you want me to give you as a present to get the Saint Joseph donkey?"

"Give me what you want. To hell with him and the saint who made him!" answered *massaro* Cirino. "Now we don't have any more bread to eat, or barley to feed the animals."

"I'll give you fifteen *lire* just because you're ruined, but the donkey isn't worth that much; he won't drag on for more than six months. See what a state he's in?"

"You could have asked for more!" *massaro* Cirino's wife began to mutter after the deal was closed. "Luciano's mule died, and he hasn't got the money to buy another one. Now if he hadn't bought that Saint Joseph donkey, he wouldn't know what to do with his cart and equipment; and you'll see, that donkey will make him rich!"

The donkey also learned to pull the cart, which all weighed down on his shoulders because the shafts were too high for him, so that he wouldn't even have lasted six months, hobbling up the slopes, and it took Luciano's blows to put a little energy into him; and when he went down it was worse, because the whole load fell on top of him and pushed him in such a way that he had to hold back with his spine bent in an arch and those poor legs gnawed by fire, so that the people who saw him began to laugh, and when he fell it took all the angels of paradise to get him on his feet again. But Luciano knew that he pulled three quintals of stuff better than a mule, and for each quintal carried they paid him five *tarì*.

"Every day the Saint Joseph donkey lives, I make fifteen *tarì*," he said, "and he costs me less than a mule to feed."

Sometimes the people who walked slowly uphill behind the cart, seeing that poor animal push his hoofs into the ground without any strength, and curve his spine, panting hard, his eyes desperate, suggested:

"Put a stone under the wheels and let that poor animal catch his breath."

But Luciano answered:

"If I let him do as he likes, I won't make fifteen *tarì*

a day. With his skin I've got to fix up my own. When he can't do his job any more I'll sell him to the lime man; the animal's good and he'll be all right for him; and it's not true at all that Saint Joseph donkeys are no good. I got him for a song from *massaro* Cirino who's become poor now."

In this way the Saint Joseph donkey happened to come into the hands of the lime man, who had about twenty donkeys, all skin and bones and with one foot in the grave; they carried his small sacks of lime, and lived off those mouthfuls of weeds they managed to crop along the way. The lime man didn't want him because he was all covered with scars worse than the other animals, with his legs seared by fire, and his shoulders worn out by the collar, and his withers gnawed by the plow saddle, and his knees broken by the falls; and then the lime man felt that the black and white coat wouldn't go at all well with the other animals, who were black:

"That doesn't make any difference," answered Luciano. "As a matter of fact, it'll help you recognize your donkeys from far away." And to close the deal, he took another two *tarì* off the seven *lire* he had asked.

But the Saint Joseph donkey was so changed that not even the first owner's wife, who had seen him born, would have recognized him any more, as he walked under the sacks of lime with his muzzle to the ground and his ears like an umbrella, twisting his rump at the blows of the boy who drove the herd. But also the first owner's wife herself had changed by then, with the bad crops there had been, and the hunger she had suffered, and the fever they had all caught on the plain, she, her husband and her Turiddu, without money to buy quinine, because there wasn't a Saint Joseph donkey to sell every day, not even for thirty-five *lire*.

In the winter, when there was less work, and the wood to burn the lime was scarcer and farther away, and the frozen paths didn't have a leaf on their hedges, or there wasn't a mouthful of stubble along the frozen ditch, life was harder for those poor animals, and the owner knew that winter ate up half of them, so he used to buy a good supply in the spring. At night the herd remained in the open beside the kiln, and the animals shielded themselves by huddling close together. But the stars that were shining like swords went right through them, despite their thick hides, and all those harness sores shuddered and quivered in the cold as if they could speak.

And yet there are so many Christians who are no better off, and who don't even have a ragged cloak like that in which the boy who took care of the herd slept all rolled up before the kiln. Nearby lived a poor widow, in a hut more broken down than the lime kiln itself, where the stars went through the roof like swords, as if she were in the open, and the wind made those few ragged bedcovers flutter. In the past, she had been a washerwoman, but that was a poor trade, for people wash their rags themselves, when they wash them, and now that her boy had grown up she made a living by going to sell firewood in the village. No one had known her husband, and no one knew where she got the wood she sold; but her boy knew, because he went to pick it up here and there, at the risk of getting shot by the field watchman.

"If you had a donkey," the lime man said to her in order to sell the Saint Joseph donkey who couldn't do his job any more, "you could carry bigger bundles to the village, now that your boy's grown up."

The poor woman had a few *lire* in a knot in her handkerchief, and she let the lime man wring them out of her, for, as the saying goes, "old things die in the house of the fool."

This way at least, the poor Saint Joseph donkey was better off during his last days, since the widow kept him like a treasure, thanks to the money he had cost her, and at night she went to find straw and hay for him, and kept him in the hut beside her bed, where he gave off heat like a little fire; and in this world one hand washes the other. The woman, pushing before her the donkey loaded with a mountain of wood, so that you couldn't see his ears, was building castles in the air; and the boy broke through the hedges and ventured to the borders of the woods to scrape the load together, and both mother and son believed that they would get rich with that trade, but finally the baron's field watchman caught the boy in the act of stealing boughs, and worked him over from head to foot with a stick. To cure the boy, the doctor ate up the money tied in the handkerchief, the supply of firewood, and all there was to sell, and it wasn't much; so one night when her boy was raving with fever, his burning face toward the wall, and there wasn't a mouthful of bread in the house, the mother went out in a frenzy, talking to herself as if she too had a fever, and broke off all the branches of an almond tree nearby, and you wouldn't have thought that she could reach them, and at dawn she loaded them on the donkey to go and sell them. But the donkey, going up the slope under that weight, knelt down just like the real Saint Joseph donkey in front of the Christ Child, and he didn't want to get up any more.

"Holy Souls of Purgatory!" muttered the woman. "you carry my load of wood!"

And the passers-by pulled the donkey by the tail and pinched his ears to make him get up.

"Don't you see he's dying?" a cart driver finally said; and so the others left him in peace, for the donkey had the eyes of a dead fish, his nose was cold, and a shiver ran through his skin.

Meanwhile, the woman was thinking of her boy who was raving, his face red with fever, and she mumbled:

"Now what'll we do? Now what'll we do?"

"If you want to sell him with all the wood I'll give you five *tarì*," said the cart driver, whose cart was empty.

And as the woman looked at him, her eyes staring wildly, he added:

"I'm buying only the wood, because here's all the donkey's worth. . . ."

And he kicked the carcass, which sounded like a broken drum.

1881

BLACK BREAD

As soon as Nanni closed his eyes, and the priest with his stole on was still there, a war broke out among the children as to who had to pay for the funeral, and they drove the reverend away, the aspersorium under his arm.

Because Nanni's illness had been long, one of those which eat the flesh that is on your bones and the things you have in your house. Each time the doctor spread a sheet of paper on his knee to write a prescription, Nanni looked at his hands beseechingly and mumbled: "At least, sir, make it short, for God's sake."

The doctor was doing his job. Everyone in this world does his job. Doing his, *massaro* Nanni had caught the fever at Lamia, a land blessed by God, which produced wheat as tall as a man. In vain the neighbors could say again and again:

"Nanni, you'll leave your bones down there."

"I'm not a baron, who can do as he pleases," he would answer.

The children were like the fingers of the same hand while the father was alive, but now each had to think of himself. Santo had a wife and children on his hands; Lucia was without a dowry, as if left in the street; and Carmenio, if he wanted to eat, had to seek his bread somewhere else and find himself a master. Then there was the mother, old and sickly, and nobody knew which one of the three of them who had nothing was to support her. It's a good thing to be able to cry over one's dead without other worries!

The oxen, the sheep, and the supply of grain had gone with the owner. All that remained was the dark house with the empty bed, and the orphans' faces, also dark. Santo moved in his things there, with the Redhead, and said that he would keep the mother with him.

So he wouldn't have to pay rent any more—said the others.

Carmenio packed his belongings and went to work as a shepherd for *curatolo* Vito, who had a piece of pasture land at Camemi; and Lucia threatened to go and find a job as a maid, in order not to live with her sister-in-law.

"No!" said Santo, "Nobody's going to say that my sister has to serve others."

"He wants me to serve the Redhead!" muttered Lucia.

The big problem was this sister-in-law who had driven herself into the family like a nail.

"What can I do now that I've got her?" sighed Santo, shrugging his shoulders. "I should have paid attention to the good soul of my father when there was still time."

The good soul had preached: "Leave Nena alone; she has no dowry, no house, no land."

But at Castelluccio, Nena was always at his heels, when he was hoeing, when he was reaping; she would gather wheat for him, and clear the stones from under his feet with her hands; and when he rested beside the farmhouse door, his shoulders against the wall, in the hour when the sun died away over the fields and all was silent:

"Santo, with the help of God you won't have worked for nothing this year!"

"Santo, if the crop is good, you should rent that large field, the one on the plain; sheep have been grazing there, and it's been left idle for two years."

"Santo, if I have time this winter, I'll knit you a pair of long heavy socks that'll keep you warm."

Santo had met Nena while working at Castelluccio; she was the field watchman's red-haired daughter, and no one wanted her. For this reason, the poor girl fawned on every fellow that passed, and went without bread to give Santo a black silk cap each year on Saint Agrippina's Day and to have him find a flask of wine or a piece of cheese when he arrived at Castelluccio.

"Take this, Santo, for my sake. It's the kind the master drinks." Or: "I've been thinking that last week you had to eat dry bread."

He couldn't say no, and accepted everything. At the most, he answered out of courtesy:

"It's not right, Nena, to go without things yourself to give them to me."

"I'm happier if you have them."

Then, every Saturday evening, when Santo went home, the good soul would repeat to his son:—Leave Nena alone, she hasn't this; leave Nena alone, she hasn't that.

"I know that I don't have anything," said Nena, while

she sat on a little wall facing the setting sun. "I have no land, no houses; and I've had to go without bread to get some linen together. My father is a poor field watchman who depends on his boss for a living, and no one will want to take on the burden of a wife without a dowry."

But the nape of her neck was white, as those of redheads are; and while she kept her head bowed, with all those thoughts in it, the sun glistened on the golden hairs behind her ears and on her cheeks that had the soft down of peaches; and Santo looked at her eyes which were as blue as the flower of flax, and at her breasts that filled her corset and moved in waves like the wheat field in the wind.

"Don't worry, Nena," he would say. "You won't have any trouble finding a husband."

She shook her head to say no; and her red earrings that seemed of coral caressed her cheeks.

"No, no, Santo. I know that I'm not beautiful, and that nobody wants me."

"Look!" he said suddenly, as the thought came to his head. "Look how different people's ideas can be! . . . They say red hair is ugly, but now that you have it, it doesn't bother me at all."

When the good soul of his father saw that Santo had so lost his head over Nena that he wanted to marry her, he asked him one Sunday:

"You've got to have the Redhead? Tell me, you've just got to have her?"

With his shoulders against the wall and his hands behind his back, Santo didn't dare lift his head, but nodded yes, yes—without the Redhead he wouldn't know how to get along, and that was the will of God.

"It's up to you, if you feel you can support a wife. You already know I can't give you anything. Your mother here and I, we have only one thing to tell you: think it over before you get married; there isn't much bread and children come in a hurry."

His mother, squatting on a stool, pulled him by the jacket and, with a long face, whispered:

"Try to fall in love with *massaro* Mariano's widow; she's rich and won't ask for much because she's crippled."

"Sure, sure!" muttered Santo, "*massaro* Mariano's widow would take a tramp like me!"

Also Nanni agreed that *massaro* Mariano's widow was looking for a husband as rich as herself, even though she was a cripple. And then there would have been the trouble of seeing lame grandchildren born.

"It's up to you," he repeated to his boy. "Remember that there isn't much bread and children come in a hurry."

Then on Saint Bridget's Day, toward evening, Santo happened to meet the Redhead who was picking asparagus at the side of the path. She blushed when she saw him, as if she didn't know he had to pass by there on his way back to town, and she let fall the hem of her skirt, which she had tucked under her belt to be able to crawl on her hands and knees among the cactuses. The young man also grew red in the face, as he looked at her without saying anything. At last he began to chatter about having finished his week's work, and about going back home.

"Anything you want done in town, Nena? Just tell me."

"If I had to go and sell the asparagus, we could go together said the Redhead. And as he, befuddled, nodded yes, yes, she added, her chin on her heaving breast:

"But you wouldn't want me; women are a nuisance."

"I'd carry you in my arms, Nena, I would."

Then Nena began to chew a corner of the red kerchief she wore on her head. And Santo didn't know what to say either; and he looked at her, looked at her, and shifted his knapsack from one shoulder to the other, as if he didn't know what to do. The catmint and the rosemary were filling the air with gaiety, and up there above the cactuses, the slope of the mountain was all red from the setting sun.

"You'd better go now," Nena told him, "you'd better go, it's late."

And then she began to listen to the noise the titmice were making. But Santo didn't move.

"You'd better go, they might see us here alone."

Santo, about to leave at last, went back to his first idea, after giving his shoulders another twist to arrange his knapsack, and said that he would carry her in his arms, he would, if they could go together. And he looked into Nena's eyes, which were fleeing his and hunting asparagus among the stones, and into her face that was afire as if the setting sun were beating upon it.

"No, Santo you'd better go alone; I'm a poor girl without a dowry."

"God will help us. . . ."

She continued saying no, that she wasn't for him, her face now dark and scowling. Then Santo, discouraged, arranged the knapsack on his shoulders and started to leave, his head bowed. The Redhead at least wanted to give him the asparagus she had picked for him. They would make a fine dish if he would accept them and eat them for her sake. And she stretched out toward him the corners of her apron, which was full. Santo put his arm around her waist and kissed her cheek, his heart melting.

At that very moment the girl's father came and she ran away frightened. The field watchman had his gun on his shoulder, and he didn't know what on earth stopped him from blowing Santo's brains out for that piece of treachery.

"No! I don't do such things!" answered Santo, his hand on his heart. "I want to marry your daughter, I really do. Not because I'm afraid of your gun, but I'm the son of an honest man; and God will help us since we don't do any wrong."

So the following Sunday there was the wedding, with the bride in her holiday dress and her field watchman father in new boots, in which he waddled like a tame duck. Wine and toasted broad beans put even Nanni in a gay humor, although he was already suffering from malaria; and Santo's mother got from the chest a spindle of yarn that she had been saving for the dowry of Lucia, who was already eighteen, and who, before going to Mass each Sunday, groomed herself for half an hour, using the water in the basin as a mirror.

Santo, the tips of his ten fingers stuck in the pockets of his jacket, was beaming with delight looking at his bride's red hair, at the yarn, and at all the gaiety that there was for him that Sunday. The field watchman, his nose red, was jumping in his boots and wanted to kiss everybody, one by one.

"Not me!" said Lucia, grown sullen because of the yarn they were taking away from her. "I don't go for this sort of thing."

She remained in a corner with her face long, as if she already knew what was coming after her father closed his eyes.

Now, in fact, she had to bake the bread and sweep the rooms for her sister-in-law, who went to the fields with her husband as soon as God brought daylight, even though she was pregnant again, since for filling the house with little ones she was worse than a cat. Altogether different things were now needed than the little presents at Easter and Saint Agrippina's Day, and the nice words they exchanged when they saw each other at Castelluccio. That crook of a field watchman had done himself a favor by marrying off his daughter without a dowry, and now it was up to Santo to support her. Since Nena had been with him, Santo saw that he didn't have enough bread for both of them and they would have to snatch it by the sweat of their brow from the land at Licciardo.

While they were going to Licciardo, shouldering their knapsacks and drying the sweat with their sleeves, they always had the wheat fields in their minds and before their eyes and they didn't see anything else among the stones of the path. To them, that wheat was like the thought of one who is sick and is always heavy on your heart: yellow first, engulfed by the mud of continuous rains; then as it began to breathe again, the weeds came, and Nena, pulling them out one by one, had made a pitiful mess of her hands, bending over with such a big belly, lifting her skirt above her knees in order not to cause any damage. And she didn't feel the strain of pregnancy, nor the pains in her back; it was as if with every green stalk she freed from the weeds, she brought a child into the world. And when at last, all out of breath, she would squat down on the embankment, pushing her hair behind her ears with both hands, she thought she saw the tall wheat ears of June, curving in waves in the soft wind, one above the other. And she would figure up the harvest together with her husband, while he removed his badly drenched socks and cleaned his hoe on the grass of the embankment: the seed had been so much; it would have yielded so much if the return was twelvefold, or ten, or even seven; the stalks were not very strong, but there were many of them. It would be enough if March wouldn't be too dry, and if the rain came only when it was needed. Good Saint Agrippina would have to see to that!

The sky was clear, and from the west all in fire, the golden sun lingered over the green meadows, and the skylarks, singing, drifted down like black dots toward the clods. Spring was beginning to burst forth everywhere, as green as hope: in the cactus hedges, in the bushes along the path, among the rocks, on the roofs of the huts. Walking heavily behind his companion, who was bent under a sack of grass for the animals and had such a big belly, Santo felt his heart full of tenderness for the poor woman, and with his voice broken by the steep grade he chatted with her about what he would do if the good Lord blessed the wheat fields until the end. Now it wasn't a case of discussing red hair any more, whether it was pretty or not, and other nonsense. And when the treacherous May came and stole all the year's work and hopes with its fog, husband and wife were again seated on the embankment, looking at the field that was turning yellow before their eyes like a sick man who is leaving for the other world, and they didn't say a single word, their elbows on their knees and their eyes stony in the pallor of their faces.

"This is God's punishment!" muttered Santo. "The good soul of my father told me!"

And the ill humor of the black and muddy path entered the little house of the poor. Husband and wife turned their backs on each other sulkily, arguing each time the Redhead demanded money for groceries and if the husband came home late, or if there was no firewood for the winter, or if the wife became slow and lazy on account of her pregnancy: long faces, curses, and even blows. Santo grabbed Nena by her red hair, and she dug her nails into his face; the neighbors rushed up, and the Redhead screamed that that infidel wanted to cause an abortion and didn't care if he sent a soul to Limbo. Then, when Nena gave birth to a little girl, they made up; and Santo was so happy that he carried the baby in his arms to show her to his relatives and friends, as if he had become the father of a princess. And as long as his wife remained in bed, he prepared her broth, swept the house, cleaned the rice, and planted himself there in front of her, so that she could have everything she needed. Then he stood in the doorway holding the baby in his arms and looking like a wet nurse, and to those who passed by and asked, he said:

"A girl! Hard luck hounds me even this far; it's a girl. My wife can't do any better."

Whenever the Redhead was beaten by her husband, she took it out on her sister-in-law, who didn't do a thing to help around the house; and Lucia retorted that without having a husband she had to bear all the troubles of someone else's children. The mother-in-law, poor woman, tried to bring peace to those arguments, and kept repeating:

"It's all my fault; I'm no good for anything any more. I'm just a burden on you."

She was good only for hearing all those troubles and for brooding over them: Santo's difficulties, his wife's complaints, the thought of the other son, far away—a thought that was sticking in her heart like a nail—and the ill humor of Lucia, who didn't even have a ragged holiday dress and never saw a fellow pass under her window. On Sundays, if her mother called her into the group of women chattering in the shade, she answered, shrugging her shoulders:

"What should I come there for? To show the silk dress I don't have?"

To that group of women neighbors occasionally came Pino the Tome, the frogcatcher, who never opened his mouth and listened with his shoulders against the wall and his hands in his pockets, spitting here and there. No one knew why he came, but when Lucia appeared at her doorway, Pino stole a glance at her, pretending that he was turning to spit. In the evening then, when all the doors were closed, he even risked singing little songs outside her door, supplying his own bass—huum! huum! huum! Sometimes the young fellows who returned home late recognized his voice and croaked like frogs to make fun of him.

Meanwhile, Lucia pretended to be busy in the house, her head low and far from the light so that her face wouldn't be seen. But if her sister-in-law muttered "Now the music starts!" she turned like a viper and retorted:

"So even music bothers you. Sure, in a jail like this there shouldn't be anything for the eyes or for the ears!"

Her mother, who saw everything and also listened, looking at her daughter said that she, on the other hand, felt happy inside hearing that music. Lucia pretended not to know anything about it. But every day at the time the frog catcher passed, she always appeared at the doorway, spindle in hand. As soon as the Tome came back from the river, he wandered up and down the village, always ending in that neighborhood, with his string of

frogs in his hand, shouting: "Singing fish! Singing fish!"
—as if the poor people of those alleys could buy singing
fish.

"They must be good for the sick!" said Lucia, who
couldn't wait to start bargaining with the Tome. But her
mother didn't want them to spend any money for her.

The Tome, seeing that Lucia, her chin on her breast,
was stealing glances at him, slackened his pace before
her door, and on Sundays he gathered up enough courage to draw a little nearer, even going so far as to sit on
a step of the adjoining terrace, with his hands hanging
between his thighs; and to the group of women neighbors he described the manner in which frogs were
caught, how devilishly cunning one had to be. He, Pino
the Tome, was more cunning than a red-haired jackass,
and waited until the women went away before saying to
Lucia:

"We've got to have rain for the wheat!" Or: "There
won't be many olives this year."

"What do you care? You make your living off frogs,"
Lucia said to him.

"Listen, sister; we're like the fingers of the same hand;
like tiles, one sends water to the next. If there isn't any
grain, or oil, money doesn't come to town, and nobody
buys my frogs. Understand?"

That "sister" sank as sweet as honey into the girl's
heart, and she kept thinking about it the entire evening,
while she was spinning silently near the lamp; and she
turned and turned it over in her mind, just like the
spindle whirling before her.

Her mother seemed to read everything in that spindle, and when those little songs had not been heard for a couple of weeks and the frog seller had not been seen passing, she said to her daughter-in-law:

"How sad the winter is! You don't hear a soul in the neighborhood any more."

Now the door had to be kept closed because of the cold, and all you could see through its little opening was the window across the street, black from the rain, or some neighbor going back home in his drenched overcoat. But Pino the Tome didn't come around any more, and Lucia said that if a poor sick person needed some frog broth, there wouldn't be any way to get it.

"He must be trying to earn his bread some other way," answered her sister-in-law. "He had a poor trade, good only for people who can't do anything else."

Having heard such chatter one Saturday evening, Santo, out of love for his sister, gave her a sermon:

"I don't like this business about the Tome. What a fine match he'd be for my sister! One who makes his living off frogs, and has his legs in the mud all day! You've got to find yourself a farm boy; even if he doesn't have anything, at least he'll be made from the same mold you are."

Lucia was silent, her head low and her brows knit, and at times she bit her lips in order not to come out with: "And where am I going to find this farm boy?" As if she could find him by herself! The only young man she had found didn't come around any more, perhaps because the Redhead had been spiteful to him, envious and gossipy woman that she was. And then

Santo was always repeating the words of his wife who kept saying that the frog catcher was a lazy lout; and this had certainly reached the ears of Pino.

So war broke out every minute between the two sisters-in-law.

"I'm not the boss here!" muttered Lucia. "In this house the boss is the one who knew how to lure my brother and grab him for a husband."

"If I'd known what was in store, I wouldn't have lured your brother, you can be sure; because if before I needed one loaf of bread, now I need five."

"And you, what do you care if the frog catcher has a trade or not? If I'd get him for a husband, it'd be up to him to support me."

The mother, poor woman, tried to calm them down with kind words; but she was a person who didn't speak much and could only run from one to the other, with her hands in her hair, stammering:

"For heaven's sake! For heaven's sake!"

But they didn't pay any attention to her, and planted their nails into each other's face, after the Redhead let the bad word "Bitch" escape her.

"You're the bitch, you who stole my brother from me!"

Then Santo came and beat them both to restore peace, and the Redhead, sobbing, muttered:

"I said it for her own good, because if you get married on nothing troubles come fast."

And to quiet his sister, who screamed and tore her hair, Santo repeated:

"What can I do, now that she's my wife? But she loves

you and speaks for your own good. You see what the two of us got out of marriage, don't you?"

Lucia complained to her mother:

"You think I want to get out of life what they did? I'd rather go and find a job as a maid. If a Christian [1] shows himself around here, they chase him away." And she was thinking of the frog catcher, who didn't come around any more.

Later it became known that he had gone to stay with *massaro* Mariano's widow; as a matter of fact, they wanted to get married; for although it was true he had no trade, he was quite a piece of a man, whom nature hadn't begrudged anything, as handsome as San Vito in flesh and blood, no less; and the cripple was rich enough to pick anyone she wanted for a husband.

"Look here, Pino," she said to him, "this is all white linen, these are all gold earrings and necklaces; in this jar are twelve *cafisi* [2] of olive oil, and that wicker-mat is full of broad-beans. If you're satisfied with this, you can live with your hands on your belly, and you won't have to stay up to your knees in the slough catching frogs any more."

"I'd be satisfied," said the Tome. But he was thinking of Lucia's black eyes looking for him from under the cloth window pane, and of the cripple's hips that shook like a frog's as she walked here and there about the house to show him all her things. Once, however, when he hadn't been able to scrape up a cent for three whole days

---

1. See p. 43, n. 11.

2. The *cafiso* was a Sicilian oil measure equivalent to approximately five-eighths of a gallon.

and so had been forced to stay at the widow's eating, drinking, and watching the rain from the doorway, he agreed to say yes, for love of bread.

"It was for love of bread, I swear it!" he said with his hand on his heart, when he looked for Lucia again before her door. "If it hadn't been for the bad year I wouldn't have married the cripple, Lucia!"

"Go and tell that to the cripple!" answered Lucia, green with bile. "I've got only one thing to say to you: don't show your face here any more."

And the cripple also told him not to show his face at Lucia's any more, for if he did she would kick him out, hungry and in rags as she had taken him in. "Don't you know that except to God, you owe the bread you eat only to me?"

Her husband had everything: he was well dressed, well fed, had shoes on his feet, and had nothing more to do than loaf around the square all day, at the vegetable stand, the butcher's, the fish dealer's, with his hands behind his back, his belly full, watching the bargaining.

"That's his trade: a bum!" said the Redhead. And Lucia retorted that he didn't do anything because he had a rich wife to support him.

"If he'd married me he'd have worked to support his wife."

Santo, his head in his hands, was thinking that his mother had advised him to marry the cripple himself, and it was his own fault that he had let the bread slip from his mouth.

"When we're young," he preached to his sister, "we all

have in our heads the same foolish whims that you have
now, and we only look for what we like, without thinking of the future. Ask the Redhead now if we'd do it all
over again! . . ."

The Redhead, squatting on the threshold, nodded her
approval, while her children screamed around her, pulling at her clothes and her hair.

"At least the good Lord shouldn't make us bear the
cross of having children!" she whined.

Of her children she dragged those she could with her
to the fields every morning, like a mare her colts, carrying the baby girl in the knapsack and leading the older
one by the hand. But she had to leave the other three at
home to drive her sister-in-law out of her mind. The
one in the knapsack and the one limping behind
screamed together along the path in the cold of the white
dawn, and their mother had to stop now and then, and
she sighed as she scratched her head: "Oh good Lord!"
And with her breath she warmed the tiny blue hands of
the little girl or pulled the baby out of the sack to nurse
her, while she continued walking. Her husband went
ahead, bent under his load, and hardly turned around to
give her time to catch up with him, all out of breath as
she was, pulling the little girl behind her by the hand,
and her breast nude; and if he did turn it wasn't in
order to look, as at Castelluccio, at the Redhead's hair
or at her breasts that filled her corset and moved in
waves. Now the Redhead jerked those breasts out in
sun and frost, as if they were good for nothing but to
give milk, just like a mare.—A true beast of burden—
and as for this, her husband couldn't complain: at hoe-

ing, reaping, sowing, she was better than a man, when she pulled up her skirts, her legs black to the knees in the wheat field. She was twenty-seven now and had plenty to do without worrying about her shoes and blue stockings.

"We're old," said her husband, "and we have to think of our children."

At least they helped each other, like two oxen under the same yoke. This was marriage now.

"Unfortunately, I know it too!" muttered Lucia, "I've got all the troubles of children without having a husband. When the old woman closes her eyes, if they still want to give me a piece of bread, they'll give it to me. But if they don't, they'll throw me into the street."

Her mother, poor woman, didn't know what to answer and just listened, sitting near the bed, her head wrapped in a kerchief and her face yellow with illness. During the day, she appeared in the sun at the doorway and sat there motionless and silent until the hour when the sunset became pale on the dark roofs across the street and the women called in their chickens.

Only when the doctor came to see her, and her daughter put the candle near her face, she asked with a timid smile:

"For heaven's sake, sir . . . is it going to be long?"

Santo, who had a heart of gold, answered:

"I don't mind spending money for medicine, as long as that poor old woman remains here and I know I'll find her in her corner when I come home. Besides, when she was able to, she did her share of work. And when we're old our own children will do the same for us."

Black Bread

And it also happened that at Camemi Carmenio had caught the fever. If his master had been a rich man he would have bought him medicine, but *curatolo* Vito was a poor devil, who lived off a little flock, and he kept the boy just out of charity, for he could have tended those few sheep himself if it hadn't been for his fear of malaria. Besides, he had also wanted to do the good deed of providing bread for Nanni's orphan in order to curry favor with God, who should help him, he should, if there was justice in Heaven. What could he do, after all, if he had only that piece of pasture land at Camemi, where malaria was as thick as snow, and Carmenio had caught the tertian fever?

One day when the boy felt his bones crushed by the fever and gave in to sleep against a large rock that threw its black shadow on the dusty path, while the horseflies buzzed in the suffocating heat of May, the sheep broke into the neighbor's wheat field, a poor plot the size of a handkerchief, which the scorching sun had already half eaten up. Nevertheless, Uncle Cheli, hidden under a lean-to of branches, treasured it like the apple of his eye, that field which had cost him so much sweat and was the hope of the year. As he saw the sheep run around, he shouted:

"Ah! Don't those Christians eat bread?"

And Carmenio woke up under the blows and kicks of Uncle Cheli, who started to run after the scattered sheep like a madman, weeping and howling. For Carmenio those blows were all he needed, with his bones already crushed by the tertian fever! But, by any chance, could he repay his neighbor just with screams and laments, for the damage he'd done?

"A year's crop lost, and my children without bread this winter! That's the damage you've done, bastard. If I skinned you alive, it wouldn't be enough!"

Uncle Cheli hunted up witnesses to go to court against the sheep of *curatolo* Vito. For *curatolo* Vito, when he was served the summons, it was as if both he and his wife had a stroke.

"Ah! that bastard of a Carmenio has ruined us entirely! You try to help somebody out, and that's the way you get paid back! I couldn't have stayed in the malaria myself to watch the sheep, could I? Now Uncle Cheli will drive us into complete poverty by making us pay for everything!"

The poor man ran to Camemi at noon, blind with despair because of all the misfortunes raining down on him, and at every kick and every punch he gave Carmenio he stammered, gasping:

"You've made us paupers! You've ruined us, you scoundrel!"

"Don't you see what a state I'm in?" Carmenio tried to answer, as he warded off the blows. "What fault is it of mine, if I couldn't stand up because of the fever? It trapped me there under the big rock!"

Nevertheless, he had to pack his belongings on the spot, say good-by to the two *onze* that *curatolo* Vito owed him, and leave the flock. And *curatolo* Vito had to be satisfied with catching the fever again himself, so many were his misfortunes!

Black Bread

At home Carmenio didn't say anything, returning poor and hungry, his bundle on a stick over his shoulder. Only his mother, seeing him so pale and gaunt, felt sad and didn't know what to think. She found out about it later from Don Venerando, who lived nearby and also had some land at Camemi, just next to Uncle Cheli's.

"Don't tell the reason why Uncle Vito sent you away!" the mother suggested to her boy. "Otherwise, no one will hire you."

And Santo added:

"Don't say anything about having the tertian fever; otherwise, if they know that you're sick, no one will want you."

However, Don Venerando hired him for his flock at Santa Margherita, where the *curatolo* was robbing him right in the open, doing more damage than sheep scurrying in the wheat fields.

"I'll give you medicine so you won't have any excuse for going to sleep and letting the sheep run around wherever they want."

Don Venerando had begun to like the whole family, on account of Lucia, whom he saw from his little terrace when he went out for a breath of fresh air after dinner.

"If you want to give me the girl too, I'll pay her six *tarì* a month."

He also said that Carmenio could take his mother to Santa Margherita, for the old woman's health was failing more and more every day, and up there with the flock she would at least have plenty of eggs and milk, and even some mutton broth when a sheep died. The Redhead deprived herself of her best things to make up a small bundle of linen.

Sowing time was now coming; Santo and the Redhead couldn't go back and forth from Licciardo every day, and with winter came the scarcity of everything. This time Lucia was serious about going to work as a maid in Don Venerando's house.

They put the old woman on the donkey. Santo was on one side and Carmenio on the other, and the luggage on the packsaddle; and their mother, letting them do with her what they liked, looked at Lucia with heavy eyes from her pale face, and said:

"Who knows if we'll see each other again? Who knows? They've told me I'll be back in April. Have the fear of God in your heart when you're in your master's house. At least, there you'll have everything you need."

Lucia sobbed in her apron, and so did the Redhead, poor woman. At that moment they had made up, and were embracing, crying together.

"The Redhead has a good heart," her husband said. "The trouble is we're too poor to love each other all the time. When chickens don't have anything to peck at in their coop, they peck at each other."

Now Lucia was well settled in Don Venerando's house, and said that she wanted to leave it only after she died, as one usually says to show gratitude to one's master. She had as much bread and soup as she wanted, a glass of wine a day, and her dish of meat on Sundays and holidays. Meanwhile, her month's pay remained intact in her pocket, and in the evening she even had free time to spin linen for her dowry. She already had the match in the same house, right under her eyes: Brasi, the kitchen-boy, who did the cooking and also helped with the work in the fields when it was necessary. The master had become rich in the same way, serving the baron, and now he was called *Don* and had lots of farms and cattle. Since Lucia came from a well-to-do family that had fallen into poverty, and it was known that she was virtuous, she had been assigned the easier jobs: the dishwashing, the trips to the cellar, and the feeding of the chickens; and she was given a nook beneath the stairs to sleep in, just like a little bedroom, with a bed, a chest of drawers, and everything she needed; so that Lucia wanted to leave only after she died. In the meantime she was making eyes at Brasi, and told him in confidence that in two or three years she would have a nice little pile of money and could "go out into the world," if the Lord called her.

Brasi was deaf in that ear. But he liked Lucia, with her coal-black eyes and all that wealth of curves she had. She liked him too, small, curly-haired, with the fine and cunning face of a fox dog. While they were washing dishes or putting firewood under the kettle, he thought up all kinds of mischief to make her laugh, as if he were tickling her. He sprinkled water on the nape of her neck and stuck endive leaves in her tresses. Lucia screamed in undertones so that the master wouldn't hear. She hid in the corner by the oven, her face as red as embers, and threw dish rags and branches of firewood in his face, while she was thrilled by the water dripping down her back.

"Now it's your turn!"

"Not me!" answered Lucia. "I don't like this sort of thing."

Brasi pretended to be mortified. He picked up the endive leaf she had thrown into his face and stuck it inside his shirt against his breast, muttering:

"This is mine. I won't touch you. It's mine and it belongs here. If you want to put something of mine in the same place, take this." And he made believe that he was tearing out a handful of his hair to offer to her, and stuck out his tongue full length.

She hit him with solid peasant punches that made him bend over and gave him bad dreams at night, he said. She grabbed him by the hair like a little dog and felt certain pleasure in sticking her fingers in that soft curly wool.

"Take it out on me! Go ahead! I'm not touchy like you. I'd let your hands pound me to sausage meat."

Once Don Venerando caught them in those little games and made a scene. He didn't want any dirty business going on in his house; if he caught them again he would kick them both out. But whenever he found the girl alone in the kitchen, he pinched her cheek and tried to caress her.

"No! No!" repeated Lucia. "I don't like this sort of thing. If you don't stop, I'll pack up and go."

"You like it from him all right, you like it from him! But not from me, your master. What's the meaning of this? Don't you know that I can give you rings and gold earrings, and even a dowry, if I want to?"

And he really could, agreed Brasi, for the master had all the money he wanted, and his wife wore a silk mantle like a rich lady, now that she was thin and old, worse than a mummy; for this reason, her husband went down to the kitchen to tell jokes to the girls. He went there also to watch out for his own interests, how much wood they burned and how much meat they cooked. He was rich, yes, but knew what it was like to get that way, and argued all day with his wife, who had put on airs now that she played the rich lady and complained about the smoke of the firewood and the stench of the onions.

"I want to earn my dowry with my own hands," retorted Lucia. "My mother's daughter wants to stay an honest girl, in case a Christian should want to marry her."

"Stay honest then!" answered the master. "You'll see what a fine dowry it'll be and how many will come looking for your honesty!"

If the macaroni was overcooked or if Lucia served a couple of fried eggs that smelled a little burned, Don Venerando gave her a tongue-lashing in front of his wife—another man entirely, his stomach sticking out and his voice loud. Did they think they were making swill for the pigs? With two servants who were eating the flesh off his bones! The next time he would throw the food in her face!—The lady of the house, blessed woman, didn't want that brawling, on account of the neighbors, and screaming in falsetto, she sent the maid back:

"Go to the kitchen; get out of here, you sloppy good-for-nothing!"

Lucia would go and cry in the corner by the oven, but Brasi consoled her, with that cunning face of his:

"What do you care? Let them shout! If we'd listen to the masters, poor us! The eggs smelled burned? Too bad! I couldn't chop wood in the yard and turn the eggs at the same time. They want me to be the cook and do the outside work too, and then they want to be served like kings! Don't they remember when he ate bread and onions under an olive tree and she gathered wheat for him in the field?"

Then the maid and the cook talked about their "bad luck," that they were born of "respectable people," and that some time ago their folks had been richer than the master. Brasi's father was a cartwright, no less! and it was the son's own fault if he hadn't wanted to take up the trade, and had gotten it into his head to tramp from fair to fair behind the cart of the haberdasher, from whom he had learned how to cook and how to feed animals.

Lucia started the litany of her troubles all over again: her father, the cattle, the Redhead, the bad crops; the two of them alike, she and Brasi, in that kitchen; they seemed made for each other.

"The same old story of your brother with the Redhead?" answered Brasi. "No, thanks!" However, he didn't want to insult her this way right to her face. He didn't care at all if she was a peasant. He didn't reject her out of pride. They were both poor and it would have been better to throw themselves into the well with a stone around their necks.

Lucia gulped those bitter words down without saying anything, and if she wanted to cry, she hid herself in the nook under the stairs, or in the corner by the oven when Brasi wasn't around. By now she loved that Christian, after having been together with him before the fire all day for such a long time. She took the rebukes and the scoldings of the master upon herself, and left the best dish of food and the fuller glass of wine for Brasi, and went out into the yard to chop wood for him and had learned to turn the eggs and dish out the macaroni when they were cooked just right. Seeing her make the sign of the cross before eating, the bowl on her knees, Brasi said:

"What's the matter? Haven't you ever seen food before?"

He was always complaining about everything: that it was like a jail there, and that he had only three hours in the evening to take a walk or go to the tavern; and Lucia, blushing and her head low, sometimes would go so far as to say:

"Why do you go to the tavern? Leave the tavern alone, it's not for you."

"It's obvious that you're a peasant!" he would answer. "You people think the devil's at the tavern. I come from a family of craftsmen, my dear. I'm not a clumsy peasant!"

"I say it for your own good. You spend your money, and then there's always a chance of getting into a fight with somebody."

Brasi was touched deep inside by these words and by those eyes which avoided looking at him. And he wanted to prolong the pleasant feeling:

"What do you care?"

"I don't care. I say it for your own good."

"And you, don't you get sick of staying here in the house all day?"

"No, I thank God I can stay here and I wish my whole family could live this way; I have everything I need."

She was drawing wine from the barrel, squatting with the pitcher between her legs, and Brasi had gone down into the cellar with her to hold the light. Since the cellar was big and dark like a church, and there wasn't even the buzz of a fly in that place underground, and Brasi and Lucia were alone, just the two of them, he put his arm around her neck and kissed her coral-red lips.

The poor girl had been waiting for it in dismay as she was bent down, with her eyes on the pitcher; neither one was speaking, but she could hear his heavy breathing and the gurgling of the wine. And yet, she gave a stifled cry, and jumped backwards, shaking all over, so that she spilled some af the red foam on the floor.

"What's the matter?" exclaimed Brasi. "You act as

if I'd slapped you in the face! Then it isn't true that you love me?"

She didn't dare look him in the face, though she was dying to. Embarrassed, she watched the spilled wine and stammered:

"Oh, poor me, poor me, what have I done? The master's wine . . ."

"Never mind; the master's got lots of it. Pay attention to me instead. Don't you love me? Tell me, yes or no!"

Without answering, she let him take her hand this time, and when Brasi asked her to return the kiss, she gave it to him, and was red with something that wasn't only shame.

"What? Haven't you ever been kissed before?" asked Brasi, laughing. "Oh, fine! "You're shaking as if I'd said that I'd kill you."

"Yes, I love you too," she answered, "and I couldn't wait to tell you. If I'm still shaking, don't pay any attention. It's because of the wine."

"Is that so? You too? Since when? Why didn't you tell me?"

"Since that talk about being made for each other."

"Ah!" said Brasi, scratching his head. "Let's go upstairs, the master might come."

After that kiss, Lucia was happy as could be; she felt as if Brasi had stamped her lips with the promise to marry her. But he didn't even talk about it, and if the girl harped on that string, he would answer:

"What's your hurry? Besides, there's no use putting

the yoke on our necks when we can be together as if we were married."

"No, it's not the same. Now you're on your own and I'm on my own, but when we get married we'll be only one."

"A fine couple we'll make! Besides, we're not of the same breed. If you had a little dowry, at least!"

"Ah! What a black heart you have! No, you've never loved me!"

"Yes, I have too. And here I am, all yours, but without talking about that other business."

"No! I'm not that kind! Leave me alone, and don't look at me again!"

Now she knew what men were like. All liars and traitors. She didn't want to hear anything about them any more. She'd rather throw herself into the well, head down; she wanted to become a Daughter of Mary; she wanted to take her good name and fling it out of the window! Of what use was it to her without a dowry? She wanted to go to wrack and ruin by giving in to that rotten old man, the master, and get her dowry together with her shame. What difference did it make by now? By now! . . .

Don Venerando was always around her, sometimes kind and sometimes mean, under the pretext of watching out for his own interests: to see how much wood they were putting on the fire, how much oil they were using for frying; and he would send Brasi away to buy some snuff and try to pinch Lucia's cheek, chasing her around the kitchen on tiptoes, so that his wife wouldn't hear, and chiding the girl for not having any respect for him, making him run like that.

"No! No!"

You'd think she was a wildcat.

She'd rather pack up and go!

"And what are you going to eat? And where are you going to find a husband, without a dowry? Look at these earrings! And I'd make you a present of twenty *onze* for your dowry. For twenty *onze,* Brasi'd let both his eyes be gouged out!"

Ah, that Brasi! What a black heart he had! He left her in the master's filthy hands, which shook while they touched her! He left her with the thought of her mother who couldn't live long, of the house stripped of everything and filled with troubles, of Pino the Tome who had jilted her to go and eat the widow's bread! He left her with the temptation of the earrings and the twenty *onze.*

And one day she came into the kitchen with her face all upset, the long gold earrings beating against her cheeks. Brasi opened his eyes wide and said:

"How beautiful you are this way, Lucia!"

"Ah! you like me this way? That's fine! That's fine!"

Now that Brasi saw the earrings and all the rest, he left no stone unturned and was always ready and anxious to be helpful, as if she had become another mistress of the house. He left her the fuller plate and the better place by the fire. With her, he gave vent to his feelings openheartedly: they were both poor and it was good for

your soul to confide your troubles to a person you love.
If he could only get twenty *onze,* he would open up a
little tavern and get married. He in the kitchen and she at
the counter. That way one wouldn't have to take orders
from anybody. If the master wanted to help them out,
he could do it without any trouble, because to him
twenty *onze* were like a pinch of snuff. And Brasi
wouldn't be squeamish, not he! In this world, one
hand washes the other! And it wasn't his fault if he had
to earn his bread any way he could. Poverty is no sin.

But Lucia turned red or pale, or her eyes became
swollen with tears, and she hid her face in her apron.
After a while she didn't even show herself outside the
house, not at Mass, not at confession, not at Easter, not
at Christmas.

In the kitchen she withdrew into the darkest corner,
her head low, bundled up in the new, loose-fitting dress
the master had given her.

Brasi consoled her with kind words. He put his arm
around her neck, and he felt the fine material of her
dress and praised it. Those gold earrings seemed to have
been made just for her. One who is well dressed and has
money in her pocket has no reason to be ashamed and
to keep her eyes lowered, especially when they are as
beautiful as Lucia's. The poor girl, still bewildered,
mustered enough courage to raise those eyes to his, and
stammered:

"Really, *mastro* Brasi? Do you still love me?"

"Yes, yes, I do!" answered Brasi, with his hand on
his heart. "But what fault is it of mine if I'm not rich

enough to marry you? If you had twenty *onze* for a dowry, I'd marry you with my eyes shut."

Now Don Venerando had begun to be good also to Brasi, and gave him his worn out clothes and boots. Whenever he went down to the cellar, he gave him a big glass of wine, saying:

"There, drink to my health."

And his big belly danced with laughter, as he saw the faces Brasi made and as he heard him mumble, pale as a corpse, to Lucia:

"The master is a real gentleman, Lucia! Let the neighbors talk; they're all envious, miserable people, who'd like to be in your place."

Her brother, Santo, heard about it in the square a few months later. And all out of breath, he ran home to his wife. Poor they had always been, but honorable. The Redhead was appalled too, and ran to her sister-in-law so completely upset that she could hardly say a word. But when she came back home, she was altogether different, calm and with rosy cheeks.

"If you could only see! A big chest full of linen, and rings, earrings, and necklaces of real gold! Then there are twenty *onze* for her dowry. Truly a providence of God!"

"I don't care!" her brother kept repeating from time to time, who couldn't quite take it. "If at least she'd waited until our mother closed her eyes! . . ."

And this happened the year that it snowed, when

many roofs crumbled and in the region a great number of cattle died, God save us!

At Lamia and on the mountain of Santa Margherita, as they saw that colorless evening drift down, so loaded with massive ominous clouds that the oxen turned their heads suspiciously and mooed, the people appeared before their huts to look far off down toward the sea, their hands over their eyes, without saying anything. The bell of the Old Monastery at the top of the town was ringing to avert the evil night, and on Castle Hill there was a thick swarm of women, black against the pale horizon, who had come to see the Dragon's Tail in the sky, a pitch-colored streak that smelled of sulphur, they said, and it promised to be a bad night. The women were conjuring the dragon away with their fingers, and they showed it the scapulars of the Virgin on their nude breasts and spat at its face, making the sign of the cross on their navels, and they prayed to God, to the souls in Purgatory, and to Saint Lucy, whose eve it was, to protect their fields and their animals, and those whose men were away from town prayed for them too.

Carmenio had gone to Santa Margherita with the flock at the beginning of winter. That evening his mother didn't feel well and lay restless in her bed, her eyes wide open, and she didn't want to stay quiet as she used to, and she wanted this, and she wanted that, and she wanted to get up and she wanted to be turned on the other side. For a while, Carmenio had run here and there, paying attention to her and trying to help her. Then, bewildered, he had planted himself before the bed, with his hand in his hair.

The hut was on the other side of the creek, at the end of the valley, between two big rocks that climbed over its roof. Opposite, the slope, standing high up barren and black with stones among which the whitish path became lost, began to disappear in the darkness that came up from the valley. At sundown, the neighbors tending the flock in the cactuses had come to see if anything was needed for the sick woman, who didn't move in her bed any more, her face in the air, and her nose dark.

"That's a bad sign!" said *curatolo* Decu. "If I didn't have my sheep up there, with this bad weather brewing, I wouldn't leave you alone tonight. Just in case anything happens, call me."

Carmenio answered yes, his head leaning against the doorpost; but seeing him walk away step by step and become lost in the night, he felt a great desire to run after him, to cry out, to tear his hair—he didn't know what.

"Just in case," shouted *curatolo* Decu from the distance, "run up to the flock in the cactuses; there are people up there."

The flock could still be seen on the high rocky slope, against the sky, in the remaining twilight that lingered at the top of the mountains and pierced the cactus bushes. Far, far away, at Lamia and toward the plains, you heard the howling of dogs—ah-oo! . . . ah-oo! . . . ah-oo! . . .—that reached even there, and chilled your bones. And the sheep, pushing one another, began to run wild in the corral, seized by mad terror as if they smelled the wolf nearby, and with the brusque tinkling of their bells, the darkness all around seemed to be lit up with many fiery eyes. Then the sheep halted and stood still, huddling together with their muzzles to the ground, and the watchdog, seated on his tail, ended his barking with a long lamenting howl.

"If I'd only known!" thought Carmenio, "I should have told *curatolo* Decu not to leave me alone."

Outside, in the darkness, now and then you could hear the bells of the flock quiver. The dim light from the little opening framed the square of the door, black as the mouth of an oven; nothing else. And the slope opposite and the deep valley and the Lamia plain—all sank into that bottomless darkness, and you seemed to see only the noise of the creek down there, rising swollen and threatening toward the hut.

If he had only known—this too! Before dark he would have run to town to call his brother; and certainly by this time Santo would have been here with him, and Lucia and his sister-in-law too.

Then his mother began to talk, but you couldn't understand what she was saying, and she groped around in the bed with her bony hands.

"Mamma! Mamma! What do you want?" asked Carmenio. "Tell me, I'm here with you!"

But his mother didn't answer. Instead, she shook her head as if trying to say no! no! nothing! The boy put the candle near her nose and burst out crying from fear.

Black Bread

"Oh, Mamma, Mamma!" whined Carmenio. "I'm alone and can't do anything for you."

He opened the door and called those who were with the flock in the cactuses. But no one heard him.

A dense glow was everywhere: on the slope, in the valley, down there on the plain—like a silence made of cotton. Suddenly the stifled sound of a bell came from the distance—'nton! 'nton! 'nton!—and it seemed to thicken in the snow.

"Oh, Blessed Virgin!" sobbed Carmenio. "What can that bell mean? You with the flock in the cactuses, help! Good Christians, help! Help, good Christians!" he began to shout.

Finally, from up there, at the top of the mountain with the cactuses, a voice was heard, distant like the bell of Francofonte.

"Ooooh . . . what i-ii-iis it? What i-ii-iis it?"

"Help, good Christians! Help! Here at *curatolo* Decuu-u's! . . ."

"Ooooh . . . chase the shee-ee-eep! . . . chase them around!"

"No! no! It's not the sheep. . . no-o-o!" At that moment an owl came and started to screech on top of the hut.

"That's it!" whispered Carmenio, making the sign of the cross. "The owl has smelled a dead person! Now mamma's going to die!"

All alone in the hut with his mother, who didn't speak any more, he felt like crying.

"Mamma, what's wrong? Mamma, answer me! Mamma, are you cold?"

She wasn't breathing, her face dark. He lit the fire between two stones in the fireplace and began to watch how the branches were burning, flaming first and then wheezing and blowing as if saying words of their own.

When he had been with the flocks at Resecone, in the evening he used to hear the man from Francofonte tell certain stories of witches who ride on broomsticks and weave magic spells over the flames of the fireplace. Carmenio still remembered the farm hands gathered together to listen wide-eyed in front of the little lantern hanging on the pillar of the big, dark storeroom, and that night no one had the courage to go to his corner to sleep.

Fortunately, under his shirt he had the scapular of the Virgin, and around his wrist the ribbon of Saint Agrippina, which had become black with time. In his pocket he had his reed whistle that reminded him of the summer evenings—ee-oo! ee-oo!—when you let the sheep go into the stubble that is yellow as gold everywhere, and at noon the grasshoppers crackle, and at sunset the skylarks drift down chirping to nestle behind the clods, and the fragrance of catmint and rosemary wakes in the air. —Ee-oo! ee-oo! Child Jesus!—at Christmastime, when he had gone to town, they had played this way for the novena, before the little altar lit up and decorated with branches of orange trees, and just outside the door of every house children were playing pitch-and-toss with stones, the good December sun on their backs. Then they had started out for the Midnight Mass, in a group with the neighbors, bumping one another and laughing along the dark streets.

Ah! Why did he have such a thorn in his heart now? His mother, who didn't say anything any more! It was still long before midnight. Each hole between the stones of the plasterless walls seemed to be filled with eyes, frozen and black, peering inside toward the fireplace.

On his straw mattress in a corner, a jacket had been thrown and lay spread out long, and its sleeves seemed to be swelling up; and in the picture of the Archangel Michael that was pasted at the head of the bed, the devil, in the middle of the red zigzags of Hell, gnashed his white teeth, his hands in his hair.

The next day, as pale as corpses, came Santo, the Redhead with her children behind her, and Lucia, who in that time of distress didn't think of hiding her condition. Around the bed of the dead woman they tore their hair and hit themselves on the head with their fists, without thinking of anything else. Then when Santo noticed his sister who had such a big belly that it was a disgrace, he began to say in the middle of all that wailing:

"If at least she had let the poor old woman close her eyes before! . . ."

And for her part Lucia said:

"If I'd only known, only known! Now that I've got

twenty *onze* I wouldn't have let her be without a doctor and medicine."

"She's in Heaven praying to God for us sinners," concluded the Redhead. "She knows that you've got your dowry and she's happy, poor woman. Now *mastro* Brasi will marry you for sure."

1882

FREEDOM

They hung the tricolor kerchief from the campanile, sounded the alarm with the bells, and began to shout in the square: "Hail to freedom!"[1]

Like the sea in the thick of a storm. The crowd foamed and swayed before the rich men's club, in front of the City Hall, on the steps of the church—a sea of white caps. Axes and sickles glistened in the sun. Then they burst into an alley.

"You first, Baron! who had people whipped and lashed by your field watchmen."

At the head of the group there was a witch, her old hair standing on end, armed with nothing but her nails.

"You, priest of the devil, who sucked our souls out of us!"

"You, wealthy pig, who can't even run away, so fat you are with the blood of the poor."

"You, cop, who brought to justice only the poor because they didn't own anything."

---

1. This story is based on an actual incident which took place in the town of Bronte, on the western slopes of the Etna, in 1860, when Giuseppe Garibaldi and his "red shirts" conquered Sicily. The "tricolor" is, of course, the red, white, and green flag of the kingdom of Piedmont, and from 1861 to 1946 the flag of the Kingdom of Italy; after 1946 it remained the flag of the Republic of Italy. The "General" referred to later in the story is Nino Bixio, Garibaldi's lieutenant.

"You, woods-keeper, who sold your own flesh and your neighbor's flesh for two *tarì* a day!"

And blood smoked, and made them drunk. The sickles, the hands, the rags, the very stones, everything red with blood.

"Get the rich men!"—"Get the *Hats!*" [2]—"Kill them all!"—"Kill them all!"—"Let's get the *Hats!*"

Don Antonio was slinking away toward home on the shortcuts. But at the first blow he fell, his face bleeding against the sidewalk.

"Why? Why are you killing me?"

"You too! Go to hell!"

A lame urchin picked up his greasy hat and spat into it.

"Down with the *Hats!*"—"Hail to freedom!"

"Take that! That's for you!"—It was for his reverence the priest, who preached hell for everyone who stole a piece of bread. He was just coming from celebrating Mass, the consecrated Host in his big belly:

"Don't kill me; I am in mortal sin!"

Lucia was his mortal sin; Lucia, who had been sold to him by her father when she was fourteen, during the famine winter, and who now filled the Cloister Wheel [3] and the streets with starving urchins. If that dog meat were worth anything, they could have gorged themselves

---

2. See p. 141, n. 3.

3. A cylinderlike device rotating on its axis in a wall, with an opening designed to transmit any item from the parlor to the inner cloister. Unwed mothers often put their babies in the device and then turned it so as to bring the opening to the other side of the wall, whereby the babies were given over to the care of the nuns.

with it, while they were hacking it to shreds with their axes on the thresholds of the houses and on the stones of the streets. Just like a starving wolf when he happens into a flock of sheep; he does not think of filling his belly, he just slaughters right and left in a fury.—The Lady's son, who had run there to see what was happening; the pharmacist, while he was locking up the store as fast as he could; Don Paolo, who was coming back from the vineyard on his donkey, his saddlebags half empty. He was even wearing an old little cap his daughter had embroidered some time ago, before the disease hit the vineyard. His wife saw him fall in front of the door, while she and their five children were waiting for the meager soup he was carrying in the saddlebags. "Paolo! Paolo!" The first man hit him in the shoulder with an ax. Another got him with a sickle and disemboweled him while his bleeding arm was reaching for the door knocker.

But the worst happened when the notary's son—an eleven-year-old boy, as blond as gold—fell, no one knows how, as he was swept away by the crowd. His father had gotten up two or three times before dragging himself into the garbage heap to die, and had called to him: "Neddu! Neddu!" Neddu was running away in terror, his eyes and his mouth wide open, unable to cry out. They knocked him down. He too got up on one knee, just like his father. The torrent rushed over him; one man stepped with hobnailed boots on his cheek and smashed it; yet the boy still asked for mercy with his hands. He didn't want to die, no, not the same way he had seen his father killed; it tore your heart out!—Out of pity, the woodcutter, grabbing his ax with both hands, gave him a tremendous blow, as if he had to fell a fifty-year-old oak tree—and he shook like a leaf. Another man shouted:

"Eh! After all, he would have been a notary too!"

Who cared? Now that their hands were red with that blood, the rest of it had to be spilled. All of them! All the *Hats!* It wasn't any more the starving, the beatings, the abuses, that made anger boil over. It was the innocent blood. The women were still more ferocious, as they shook their lean arms and screamed with rage in falsetto, their flesh tender under the shredded clothes:

"You, who came to pray to the good God in a silk dress!"

"You, who loathed kneeling next to the poor!"

"Take that! Take that!"

In the houses, on the stairways, inside the bed chambers, while they tore silk and fine linens. How many earrings on the bleeding faces! and how many gold rings on the hands that were warding off the ax blows!

The Baroness had had the main door barricaded: beams, country carts, full wine kegs against it; and the field watchmen shooting from the windows, determined as they were to sell their skins dear. The crowd ducked their heads at the gunfire, because they had no firearms with which to respond. For there was the death penalty for those with firearms in their possession.

"Hail to freedom!" And they broke the main door down. Then into the courtyard, up the steps, over the wounded. They didn't bother the field watchmen for the moment. "The field watchmen later!" First they wanted the baroness's flesh, her flesh made of quails and good wine. She ran from room to room, dishevelled, her baby at her breast—and the rooms were many. You could hear the crowd howling in that maze, while getting closer and closer like an overflowing river. Her older son, sixteen years of age, his flesh still as white as hers, tried to hold the door closed with shaking hands, while crying out: "Mother! Mother!" With the first push they crashed the door down on him. He clung at the legs trampling him. He no longer cried out. His mother had sought safety on the balcony, clutching her baby tightly, shutting his mouth with her hand so that he would not cry—a mad woman. Her other son, wild-eyed, wanted to defend her with his own body; he tried to grasp all those axes by the blades, as if he had a hundred hands. They tore them apart in a flash. One man seized her by the hair, another by her hips, another by her dress; they lifted her over the balcony rail. The charcoal man wrenched the baby away from her arms. The other brother couldn't see anything but black and red. They trampled on him, they ground his bones with blows of hobnailed heels; he had set his teeth into a hand that was gripping his throat and wouldn't let go. The axes couldn't strike into the heap and glistened in the air.

And in that savage carnival of the month of July, above the drunken howlings of the crowd that was still going on empty stomachs, the bell of God kept sounding the alarm all day long, without noon *Angelus,* without evening *Angelus,* as if in a land of Turks. They were beginning to disperse, tired of the slaughter, quiet and puzzled, everyone avoiding his companion. Before nightfall all the doors were shut, from fear, and in every house a lamp was keeping watch. Along the alleys you could hear only the dogs, rummaging in the corners, and a sharp gnawing of bones, in the moonlight which washed over everything and pointed at the wide open doors and windows of the empty houses.

It was daybreak; a Sunday without people in the square and without ringing for the Mass. The sacristan had hidden out of sight; no priest could be found. The people who first began to gather in front of the church looked at each other suspiciously, each one thinking of what the other must have on his conscience. Then, as they grew into a larger group, they began to mumble. —They couldn't go without Mass, on a Sunday, like so many dogs.—The rich men's club was barred up, and they wouldn't know where to go to get their masters' orders for the week. From the campanile the tricolor kerchief, flabby in the yellow heat of July, was still dangling.

And as the shadow slowly grew shorter in front of the church, the crowd clustered in a corner. Between two small houses on the square, at the end of a steeply sloping little road, you could see the yellowish fields of the plain and the dark woods on the sides of the Etna.

Freedom

Now they had to split those woods and those fields. Each one was figuring on his fingers what his share would be and scowled at the man next to him.

—Freedom meant that all should have their share!— Nino the Jackass and Ramurazzo would have wanted to carry on with the *Hats'* abuses!—If there was no more surveyor to measure the land, and no notary to put it on paper, everyone would have gotten it by hook or by crook!—And if you eat up your share at the tavern, we have to split up the land all over again?—One a thief and the other a thief.—Now that there was freedom, whoever wanted to eat enough for two would be taken care of just like the rich men!—The woodcutter brandished his hand in the air as if he were still holding the ax.

The day after they heard that the General—the one who made people tremble—was on the way to town to do justice. They could see the red shirts of his soldiers slowly climbing up the ravine. It would have been enough to roll down rocks from the top to crush them all. But no one made a move. The women screamed and tore their hair. Now the men, their faces dark with long beards, sat on the hill with their hands between their thighs, watching the arrival of those tired boys bent under their rusty rifles, and of the tiny General on his big black horse, alone in front of them all.

The General had straw carried into the church and put his boys to sleep, just like a father. In the morning, before dawn, if they did not get up at the sound of the bugle, he rode into the church on horseback swearing like a Turk. He was that kind of man. And he quickly ordered five or six of them shot—Pippo, the dwarf, Pizzanello—the first ones to be caught. The woodcutter, while they were making him kneel against the cemetery wall, cried like a child, because of some words his mother had spoken to him, and because of the howl she had given out when they had torn him away from her arms. From far away, in the most distant alleys, behind the doors, you could hear those gunshots, one after the other, just like fireworks on a holiday.

Then came the honest-to-goodness judges—gentlemen with glasses on, perched on the mules, exhausted from the trip, still complaining about the fatique even while they were questioning the accused in the monastery dining room, as they were seated sideways on benches saying "Ah!" each time they changed sides. Such a long pretrial that it would never come to an end. The guilty ones were taken to the city, on foot, chained two by two, between two lines of soldiers with cocked rifles. Their women followed them, running along the endless country roads, in the furrows, in the midst of the cactuses, in the midst of the vineyards, in the midst of the golden wheat fields; out of breath, limping, they kept calling their names each time the road made a bend and the prisoners' faces could be seen.

In the city they were locked up in the great big jail, as high and huge as a monastery, all riddled with grated windows; and if the women wanted to see their men, they could do so only on Mondays, in the presence of the wardens, behind the iron gate. And the poor men grew yellower and yellower in the endless shade, never seeing the sun. Every Monday they were more silent, they complained less, and they hardly answered. On the other days the women, if they hung around the square by the jail, were threatened by the sentinels with rifles. And then never knowing what to do, where to find work in the city, or how to earn their bread. The bed in the stables cost two *soldi;* the white bread went down in a gulp and did not fill their stomachs; if they crouched down to spend the night on the threshold of a church, they were picked up by the police. Slowly, one by one they went back home, the wives first, and then the mothers. A beautiful broad lost herself in the city and was never heard from again.

All the others in town had gone back to the same things they had done before. The rich men could not work their lands with their own hands, and the poor could not live without the rich men. They made peace. The pharmacist's son stole Neli Pirru's wife and thought it was a good thing to do to avenge himself on his father's killer. If every once in a while the woman had qualms, and was afraid that when he got out of jail her husband would cut up her face, he said: "Don't worry, he'll never get out." No one thought of them any more; except a few mothers, and a few old men, if their eyes ran toward the plain where the city was, or on Sundays, when they saw the others calmly talking business with the rich men, before the club, their caps in their hands; and they became convinced that only the poor get the worst of it.

It took three years before coming to trial, no less! three years in jail without ever seeing the sun. So that, each time they were taken handcuffed to the court, the accused look like so many dead men out of the grave. All those who could had come from the town: witnesses, relatives, curious people who were going there as if to a festival, to see the townsfolk, after such a long time, crammed into the capon coop—you really became capons in there! And Neli Pirru had to find himself face to face with the pharmacist's son, who had become a relative of his in such a tricky way!

They made them stand up one by one. "What's your name?" And each one heard about himself: first name, last name, and what he had done. The lawyers, in wide loose sleeves, busied themselves with their jabberings, gesturing in excitement, foaming at the mouth, quickly wiping themselves with a white handkerchief, and then sniffing up a pinch of snuff. The judges dozed behind the lenses of their glasses, which froze your heart. In front were seated twelve rich men, who were tired, bored, and yawned and scratched their beard or prattled among themselves. They were certainly saying that they were quite lucky not to have been rich men in that town up there when freedom arrived. And the poor devils tried to read their faces. Then they all went away to consult one another, and the defendants waited white-faced, their eyes fixed on the closed door. As they came back in, their foreman—the one who spoke with his hand on his belly—was almost as white-faced as the accused, and said: "On my honor and on my conscience! . . ."

The charcoal man, while they were handcuffing him again, stammered: "Where are you taking me? To jail? Why? I didn't even get a foot of land. And they had said there was freedom! . . ."

1882

PART THREE

BUDDIES

"Malerba?"

"Here!"

"There's a button missing there, where is it?"

"I don't know, Corporal."

"Confined to the barracks!"

It was always that way: his overcoat was like a sack, his gloves bothered him, he didn't know what to do with his hands any more, his head was harder than a stone during instruction and on the drill field. And was he a clodhopper! In all the beautiful cities where he was stationed, he never went to see the streets, or the palaces, or the fairs—not even the side shows or the merry-go-rounds. He spent the time of his pass wandering along the streets in the outskirts of the city,[1] his arms hanging down, or he watched the women who were squatted on the ground ripping up the grass in Castle Square; or he planted himself in front of the little chestnut cart, without ever spending a cent. His buddies laughed at him behind his back. Gallorini drew his picture on the wall with a piece of charcoal and put his name under it. He let them do it. But when, for a joke, they stole the cigar butts he kept hidden in the barrel of his gun, he flew

[1] An unidentified city in northern Italy, probably Milan.

into a rage, and once he went to the guardhouse on account of a punch that half blinded the Lucchese[2]—you could still see the black mark—and as stubborn as a mule he kept repeating:

"It's not true."

"Well then, who was it that punched the Lucchese?"

"I don't know."

Then he would sit on his bed of hard boards, in his cell in the guardhouse, his chin in his hands.

"When I get back to my home town . . ." That's all he said.

"Count the days then, go on. You've got a girl friend back home?" asked Gallorini. Malerba stared at him suspiciously and wagged his head. Neither yes nor no. Then he would look far away. With the stub of a pencil, every day he made a mark on a small calendar which he carried in his pocket.

But Gallorini had a girl friend. A great big woman with a mustache, who had been seen sitting with him at the café one Sunday, each one with a glass of beer, and she had been the one who wanted to pay. The Lucchese found out about it hanging around there with Gegia, who never cost him anything. With his smooth and pleasant line of chatter, he could find Gegias anywhere; and in order that they wouldn't get insulted by all being put in the same bunch even by name, he said it was the custom of his home town, when you love a girl, to call her Teresa, Assunta, or Bersabea.

[2] A "lucchese" is a person from Lucca (an ancient city in Tuscany), or from the surrounding region.

At that time, the word was beginning to spread that there was going to be a war with the Germans.[3] Soldiers coming and going, crowds on the streets, and people who came to see the exercises on the drill field. When the regiment filed by through the bands and the hand clapping, the Lucchese marched boldly and proudly as if the whole show were for him, and Gallorini never stopped greeting friends and acquaintances with his arm constantly in the air, and he wanted to come back either dead or an officer, he said.

"Aren't you glad you're going to war?" he asked Malerba when they stacked their guns at the station.

Malerba shrugged his shoulders, and continued watching the people who were shouting and yelling: "Hurrah!"

The Lucchese saw Gegia too; she was watching, curious, from a distance in the middle of the crowd, and she had at her side a crude-looking boy wearing a rough jacket and smoking a pipe.

"That's what you call being prepared!" muttered the Lucchese, who couldn't break ranks, and he asked Gallorini if his girl had joined the grenadiers in order not to leave him.

It was like a fiesta everywhere they went. Flags, towns all lit up, and peasants running to the railroad embankment to see the train go by packed with kepis and guns. But sometimes in the evening, in the hour when the

---

[3] During the last century, Italy had to fight to free herself from the domination of Austria, and Italians usually meant Austrians when they said Germans.

trumpets sounded taps, they felt overcome by nostalgia for Gegia, for their friends, for all the faraway things. As soon as the mail arrived at the camp, they ran up all together to stick their hands out. Only Malerba stayed aside in a daze, like someone who didn't expect anything. He always made this mark on the calendar, day after day. And from a distance, he listened to the band, and thought of God knows what.

Finally one night, there was a lot of activity in the camp. Officers who were coming and going, wagons that were filing by toward the river. Reveille sounded two hours after midnight; nevertheless, they were already giving out the rations and pulling down the tents. Soon after, the regiment began to march.

The day was going to be hot. Malerba, who knew about these things, felt it by the gusts of wind that lifted up the dust. And then it rained big, scattered drops. From time to time, as soon as the shower stopped, and the rustle of the corn died down, the crickets began to chirp loudly in the fields on both sides of the road. The Lucchese, who was marching behind Malerba, amused himself at his buddy's expense:

"Up with your hoofs, buddy! What's wrong, why don't you talk? Thinking of your will maybe?"

With a twist of his shoulders, Malerba arranged his knapsack and muttered:

"Shut up!"

"Leave him alone," said Gallorini, "he's thinking of his girl who'll get somebody else if the Germans kill him."

"You shut up, too!" answered Malerba.

Suddenly in the night, the trotting of a horse and the tinkle of a saber passed between the two ranks of the regiment, which were marching on either side of the road.

"Have a good trip!" said the Lucchese, who was the company clown. "And say hello to the Germans if you meet them."

To the right, a group of houses made a patch of white in a huge dark spot. And the watchdog barked furiously, running along the hedge.

"That's a German dog," observed Gallorini, who wanted to joke like the Lucchese. "Can't you tell from the barking?"

It was still deep night. On the left, sticking out above a black cloud that must have been a hill, there was a shining star.

"What time do you think it is?" asked Gallorini. Malerba lifted his nose in the air, and answered immediately:

"It must be at least an hour before sunrise."

"What fun!" muttered the Lucchese. "They make us get up in the middle of the night for no reason at all!"

"Halt!" a curt voice ordered.

The regiment was still stamping, like a flock of sheep gathering close together.

"What are we waiting for?" muttered the Lucchese after a while.

Another group of cavalrymen went by. Now in the dawn that was beginning to break, you could see the banners of the lancers waving in the air, and a general, up front, his hat with gold braid all the way to the top and his hands stuck in the pockets of his field jacket. The road began to grow white, stretching straight ahead in the middle of the fields which were still dark. The hills seemed to rise one by one in the dim twilight; and you could see a fire burning below—made by some woodcutters, perhaps, or by peasants who had run away in front of that flood of soldiers. At the murmur of voices, the birds woke up and began to twitter on the branches of the mulberry trees, which outlined themselves against the dawn.

Shortly afterward, as daylight began to increase, you heard a deep rumble toward the left, where the horizon spread out in a glow of gold and pink; it was like thunder, and coming from that cloudless sky, it startled you. It could be the murmur of the river or the sound of marching artillery. All of a sudden they said:

"Cannon fire!"

And everyone turned to look toward the golden horizon.

"I'm tired!" muttered Gallorini.

"By now they should call a halt!" agreed the Lucchese.

The chatter was dying out as the soldiers marched on in the hot day, between stripes of dark earth, green wheat fields, vineyards prospering on the hills, rows of mulberry trees, stretching straight ahead as far as the eye could see. Here and there were abandoned houses and stables. As they drew near a well to get a sip of water, they saw some tools on the ground beside the door of a farmhouse and a cat that stuck his nose out between the ramshackle door leaves, miaowing.

"Look!" remarked Malerba. "Their wheat's ripe, poor people!"

"You want to bet that you won't eat any of that bread?" said the Lucchese.

"Shut up, hoodoo!" answered Malerba. "I've got the scapular of the Virgin on me." And he crossed his fingers.

At that moment you could hear thundering on the left too, toward the plain. At first, rare shots that echoed from the mountain, and then a crackling like rockets, as if there were a fiesta in the village. Above the green that crowned the summit, you could see the bell tower, calm against the blue sky.

"No, it's not the river," said Gallorini.

"And it's not wagons going by either."

"Listen! Listen!" exclaimed Gallorini. "The fiesta's started down there."

"Halt!" was ordered again. The Lucchese listened, arching his brows, and didn't say anything else. Malerba was near a road post and had sat down on it, with his gun between his legs.

The cannon bombardment must have been down on the plain. You could see the smoke of every shot, like a dense little cloud rising just above the rows of mulberry trees and breaking apart slowly. The quiet meadows sloped down toward the plain, while the quail sang among the clods.

The colonel, on horseback, looking toward the plain from time to time with a telescope, was talking with a group of officers at a standstill at the side of the road. As soon as his horse began to trot away, all the trumpets of the regiment blared out together:

"Forward march!"

To the right and to the left you could see bare fields. Then some more patches of corn. Then vineyards, ditches full of water, and finally some dwarf trees. The first houses of a village[4] began to appear; the road was packed full of wagons and carts. A maddening confusion and clamor of voices.

At a gallop a courier came up, white with dust. His horse, a squat black animal all hair, had red and smoking nostrils. Then an officer of the general staff passed, shouting, as if possessed, to clear the road, hitting out left and right with his saber at the poor civilian mules. Through the elms on the edge of the road, you could see the black *bersaglieri* run by with their plumes in the wind.

Now they were walking on a little road that turned to the right. The soldiers broke into the wheat—and so Malerba's heart wept. On the slope of a little mountain they saw a group of officers on horseback with an escort

---

[4] Probably a village near Custoza, a small town in the hilly region on the eastern bank of the Mincio River, about fifteen miles southwest of Verona. A bloody battle took place there on the 24th of June, 1866. The Italian army, led by General La Marmora, had moved into Austrian territory, was attacked unexpectedly and suffered heavy losses. It was an episode of the third war for Italian Independence. Eventually Italy won the war, and as a result annexed Venetia. The battle occurring in the present story is almost certainly the battle of Custoza.

of lancers behind them, and the pointed hats of the *carabinieri*.[5] Three or four steps ahead, on horseback and with his fist on his hip, there was a big shot, whom the generals answered with their hands on their visors, and the officers passing by saluted with their sabers.

"Who's that?" asked Malerba.

"Vittorio,"[6] answered the Lucchese. "Haven't you ever seen him on money, you fool?"

The soldiers turned to look as long as they could see him. Then Malerba observed to himself:

"That's the King!"

A little farther on, there was a small dry creek. The bank on the far side, covered with bushes, climbed up toward the mountain which was scattered with topped elms. The bombardment wasn't heard any more. In that peacefulness of the clear morning, a blackbird began to whistle.

Suddenly it all exploded like a tornado. The summit, the bell tower, everything was wrapped in smoke. Tree branches creaked and dust rose from the earth here and there at every cannon ball. A grenade swept away a group of soldiers. At the top of the hill, from time to time you heard immense shouts, like hurrahs.

---

[5] A special military corps founded in Piedmont by Victor Emmanuel I in 1814. The *Carabinieri* have fought in all the Italian wars and at the same time they have been—and still are—the national police of Italy.

[6] Victor Emmanuel II (1820–1878), the king of the unification of Italy. In 1849 he became king of Piedmont and Sardinia, and in 1861, after Garibaldi had conquered all the southern part of the peninsula, king of Italy.

Buddies

"Blessed Virgin!" stammered the Lucchese. The sergeants ordered the soldiers to put their knapsacks on the ground. Malerba obeyed reluctantly because he had two new shirts and all his other things in his.

"Hurry up! Hurry up!" the sergeants were saying. Artillery guns arrived at a gallop from the stony little road, with an uproar, as if there were an earthquake: the officers ahead, the soldiers bent over the rigid manes of the smoking animals and whipping with all their might, the cannoneers grabbing the axles and spokes of the wheels and pushing them up the steep grade.

In the middle of the violent noise of the bombardment, you could see a wounded horse with hanging traces rolling down the slope, neighing, topping vines, shooting out desperate kicks. Farther below, there were groups of soldiers, bloody, their clothes torn, without kepis, waving their arms. Finally, whole platoons backing up step by step, stopping to open scattered fire among the trees. Trumpets and drums sounded the charge. The regiment plunged up the steep grade at a run, like a torrent of men.

The Lucchese felt it coming:

"Why all this rush for what's in store for us up there?"

Gallorini shouted:

"Savoia!" [7]

---

[7] "Savoy." The House of Savoy ruled first the kingdom of Piedmont and Sardinia, and then, from 1861 to 1946, the kingdom of Italy. —In battle, while charging the enemy, Italian soldiers cried *Savoia*—a word that epitomized the concepts of liberty, independence, and unity.

And to Malerba, who had a heavy step:

"Up with your hoofs, buddy!"

"Shut up!" said Malerba.

As soon as they got to the summit, to a rocky little meadow, they found themselves facing the Germans who were advancing in close ranks. A long flash of light ran over those swarming masses; the gunfire crackled from one end to the other. A young officer, fresh from the academy, fell at that moment, saber in hand. The Lucchese groped in the air a little with his hands, as if stumbling, and he fell too. Then you could no longer see what was going on. The men fought hand to hand, with blood in their eyes.

"Savoia! Savoia!"

At last the Germans had enough, and began to retreat step by step. Bands of gray-coats[8] ran after them. Malerba, in the rush, felt something like a stone that hit him and made him limp. But soon he noticed that blood was dripping down his pants. Then, furious as an ox, he plunged forward with his head low and struck right and left with his bayonet. He saw a big blond devil who was coming at him with his saber overhead and Gallorini who was aiming the mouth of his gun at his back.

The trumpet sounded muster. In bands and in groups, all that remained of the regiment now ran toward the village which was smiling under the sun, in the green. However, at the first houses, you could see the slaughter that had taken place there. Cannons, horses, wounded

---

[8] At the time, gray was the color of the uniform of the Italian Army.

bersaglieri, everything upside down. Doors broken in, window shutters hanging like rags in the sun. At the end of a courtyard there were a bunch of wounded men on the ground and a cart, still loaded with firewood, with its shafts in the air.

"And the Lucchese?" asked Gallorini out of breath.

Malerba had seen him fall; nevertheless, he turned around instinctively, toward the mountain that was swarming with men and horses. The weapons were glistening in the sun. In the center of an esplanade you could see some officers on foot looking far away with a telescope. The companies were coming down the slope one by one and flashes of light ran along the ranks.

It might have been ten o'clock—ten o'clock in the month of June, under the sun. As if burning, an officer had thrown himself on the water in which they were washing the breechblocks of the cannons. Gallorini was lying on his stomach against the wall of the cemetery, his face in the grass; at least there in the thick grass, a little coolness came from the nearby ditches. Malerba, seated on the ground, was trying his best to tie his leg with a handkerchief. He was thinking of the Lucchese, poor fellow, who had remained along the way spread out flat on his back.

"They're coming again! They're coming again!" somebody shouted. The trumpet sounded the call to arms. Ah! This time Gallorini was really fed up! Not even a minute to rest! He got up like a wild animal, his clothes all torn, and grabbed his gun. The company rushed into position at the first houses of the village, behind the walls, behind the windows. Two cannons stretched their black throats out in the middle of the road. You could see the Germans coming in close ranks, endlessly, one battalion after the other.

There Gallorini was hit. A bullet broke his arm. Malerba wanted to help him:

"What's the matter?"

"Nothing, leave me alone."

The lieutenant, too, was firing away like a private, and you had to run and give him a hand, and Malerba said at every shot:

"Let me do it, it's my job!"

The Germans disappeared again. Then retreat was ordered. The regiment couldn't stand any more of it. Lucky Gallorini and the Lucchese who were resting. Gallorini was sitting on the ground against the wall, and didn't want to move. It was about four o'clock; they had been in that heat more than eight hours with their mouths burned by the dust. Malerba, however, had begun to enjoy it all and asked:

"Now what do we do?"

But nobody listened to him. They were going down toward the little creek, still accompanied by the music that the cannon shots were making on the mountain. Later, from far away, they saw the village swarm with canvas uniforms. You couldn't figure anything out, neither where they were going nor what was happening. At the turn of an embankment, they ran into the hedge behind which the Lucchese had fallen. Gallorini wasn't with them any more either. They were coming back in disorder behind the limping officers—faces that didn't know one another, grenadiers and front-line infantry, their clothes torn, dragging their feet, the heavy guns on their shoulders.

Evening drifted down calmly in a great silence, everywhere.

You kept meeting wagons, cannons, and soldiers, going along in the dark, without trumpets and without drums. When they were beyond the river, they found out that they had lost the battle.

"What?" said Malerba. "What?" And he couldn't figure it out.

Then, at the end of his enlistment, he went back to his home town and found Martha already married, tired of waiting for him. He didn't have any time to waste either and married a widow with property. Some time later Gallorini, who worked on the nearby railroad, came by, and he had a wife and children too.

"Look! Malerba! What're you doing here? I'm doing contract jobs. I learned my business abroad, in Hungary, when they took me prisoner, remember? My wife brought me a little money . . . It's a hell of a world, eh? Did you think I got rich? And we've done our duty for sure. But we aren't the ones to wallow in luxury. We've got to have a good clean up and start all over again." [9]

---

[9] The approximate time of this section of the story is the early 1870's, when Socialist ideas were already widespread in northern Italy.

On Sundays at the tavern, he preached the same thing to his workmen too. The poor men listened and nodded, sipping the bitter, cheap wine, resting their backs in the sun, like brutes, like Malerba, who didn't know anything more than how to sow, to reap, and to breed children. He nodded his head just to be polite, when his buddy spoke, but he didn't open his mouth. Gallorini, instead, had seen the world and knew all about everything, what was right and what was wrong; above all, he knew the wrong they were doing him, driving him crazy by forcing him to wander around and work in any old place, with a brood of children and a wife on his hands, while so many wallowed in luxury.

"You don't know anything about the way the world goes! If they have a demonstration and shout long live this and death to that, you don't know what to say. You don't understand at all what we need!"

And Malerba always nodded yes. —He needed rain for the wheat fields now. This coming winter he needed a new roof for the stable.

1883

CONSOLATION

"You'll be happy, but first you'll have troubles," the fortuneteller had told Arlia.

Who would have imagined it when she married Manica, who had his fine barbershop on Fabbri Street, and she was a hairdresser too—both of them young and healthy? Only Father Calogero, her uncle, hadn't wanted to bless that marriage—had washed his hands of it like Pilate, as he said. He knew they were all consumptive in his own family, from father to son, and he had been able to put a little fat on himself by choosing the quiet life of a parish rector.

"The world is full of troubles," Father Calogero preached. "It's best to keep away from it."

The troubles had come, in fact, little by little. Arlia was always pregnant, year after year, so that her clients deserted her shop, because it was sad to see her come all out of breath and cursed with that big belly. Besides, she didn't have time to keep up to date with fashions. Her husband had dreamed of a big barbershop on the Avenue, with perfumes in the window, but in vain he could go on and on shaving beards at three *soldi*[1] each. The

---

[1] The *soldo* was a copper coin worth one-twentieth of a *lira*. It ceased to exist on account of the inflation that resulted from World War II.

children became consumptive one after the other, and before going to the cemetery gobbled up the small profit of the year.

Angiolino, who didn't want to die so young, complained during his fever:

"Mamma, why did you bring me into the world?" Just like his brothers who had died before him. The mother, thin and wan, standing before the little bed, didn't know what to answer. They had done the impossible; the children had eaten all kinds of things, cooked and raw: broths, medicines, pills as small as the head of a pin. Arlia had spent three *lire* for a Mass, and had gone to hear it on her knees in Saint Lawrence's, beating her breast for her sins. The Virgin in the picture seemed to be winking yes to her. But Manica, more sensible, would laugh with his crooked mouth, scratching his beard. Finally, the poor mother grabbed her veil like a crazy woman and ran to the fortuneteller. A countess, who had wanted to have her hair cut off out of desperation over her lover, had found consolation there.

"You'll be happy, but first you'll have troubles," answered the fortuneteller.

In vain her uncle, the priest, could say over and over again:

"It's all a fraud of Satan!"

You have to feel what it is like to have your heart black with bitterness as you wait for the verdict, while that old woman reads your whole destiny in the white of an egg. Afterward, it seemed to her that at home she would find her boy up, saying to her happily: "Mamma, I'm all better."

Consolation

Instead, the boy was slowly wasting away, all skin and bones in his little bed, his eyes getting bigger and bigger. When Father Calogero, who knew about dead people, came to see his nephew, he called the mother aside and said:

"I'll take care of the funeral myself. Don't worry!"

But the unfortunate woman, beside the bed, went on hoping. Sometimes, when also Manica, with an eight-day beard and his back bent, came upstairs to see how his boy was doing, she pitied him because he didn't believe. How the poor man must have suffered! She, at least, had the words of the fortuneteller in her heart, like a burning lamp, till the moment when her uncle, the priest, sat at the foot of the bed with his stole on. Then when they carried her hope away inside her son's coffin, she felt a great darkness in her breast, and mumbled before the empty little bed:

"And what did the fortuneteller promise me?"

Because of all the heartache, her husband had taken to drinking. Finally, a great calm came slowly into her heart. Just like before. Now that all the troubles had fallen on her shoulders, happiness would come. That's the way it often is with the poor!

Fortunata, the last one of so many children, got up in the morning, pale and with rings the color of mother-of-pearl under her eyes, like her brothers who had died of consumption. The clients deserted Arlia one by one, the debts piled up, the shop became empty. Manica, her husband, waited for customers all day long, his nose against the clouded window.

Arlia asked her daughter:

"Does your heart tell you that what fate promised us will really come true?"

Fortunata didn't say anything, her eyes circled with black like her brothers', and fixed on a point that only she could see. One day her mother caught her on the stairs with a young man, who slipped away quickly when he saw somebody come, and the girl was left there all red in the face.

"Oh, poor me! . . . What are you doing here?"

Fortunata lowered her head.

"Who was that young man? What did he want?"

"Nothing."

"Tell your mother who's your own flesh and blood. If your father knew! . . ."

The girl's only answer was to raise her forehead and fix her blue eyes on her mother's face.

"Mamma, I don't want to die like the others!"

May was in flower, but the girl wore a different look on her face and had become uneasy under the anxious eyes of her mother. The neighbors warned:

"Arlia, watch your girl."

Even her husband, frowning, one day had taken her aside face to face, in the dark little shop, in order to repeat:

"Watch your daughter, understand? Let's at least not have our flesh and blood disgraced!"

The poor woman, seeing her daughter so wild-eyed, didn't dare question her. She only fixed her eyes on her with looks that went through to the heart. One night, in front of the open window, while the song of spring came up from the street, the girl buried her face in her mother's breast and confessed everything, crying bitter tears.

The poor mother fell into a chair, as if her legs had been cut off. And she kept stammering with her colorless lips:

"Ah! what'll we do now?"

She seemed to see Manica warmed by wine, his heart hardened by misfortune. But worst of all were the eyes of the girl when she answered:

"See that window, Mamma? . . . See how high it is? . . ."

The young man, who was an honest fellow, had sent someone to see the uncle, the priest, to sound him out in order to know which way to turn. Father Calogero had purposely become a priest so that he wouldn't have to listen to the troubles of the world. It was no secret that Manica wasn't rich. The young man understood the refrain and sent word that he was sorry that he wasn't rich himself and wouldn't be able to do without a dowry.

Then Fortunata became really sick and began to cough as her brothers had done. Holding her arm around her mother, she often whispered, with her face red, and repeated:

"See how high that window is? . . ."

And her mother had to run here and there, to comb rich women's hair for the theater, the terror of that window always before her eyes if she couldn't find a dowry for her daughter, or if her husband learned about the blunder.

From time to time the fortuneteller's words came back into her mind, like a ray of light. One evening, passing before a lottery window as she was going back home tired and discouraged, the printed numbers fell under her eyes, and for the first time she got the idea of gambling. Then, with the little yellow slip in her pocket, it seemed to her as if she had her daughter healthy, her husband rich and her home peaceful. She also thought with tenderness of Angiolino and the other children who had long been underground in the Porta Magenta[2] cemetery. It was a Friday, the day of the afflicted, and the spring twilight was serene.

And so it was every week. By going without food, she got together the few cents needed for the lottery ticket, so that she could live with the hope of that great happiness which was to come to her all at once. The blessed souls of her children would take care of it from up above. Manica, one day when the little yellow slips jumped out of the drawer as he was secretly looking for a few *lire* to drown his ill-humor at the tavern, flew into a terrible rage:

"So that's the way the money's been going! . . ."

His wife, trembling all over, didn't know what to answer.

"But listen, what if the Lord should send us the right numbers? . . . We have to leave the door open to luck."

And in her heart she was thinking of the words of the fortuneteller.

"If that's the only hope you've got . . . ," muttered Manica with a bitter smile.

"And what hope have you got?"

---

[2] The name of the western entrance into the center of Milan.

"Give me two *lire!*" he answered bluntly.

"Two *lire!* Holy Virgin! . . . What do you want them for?"

"Give me just one!" insisted Manica, his face distorted.

It was a dark day with snow everywhere and dampness that you felt in your bones. That night Manica came back home with his face shining and gay. Fortunata, instead kept saying:

"I'm the only one who can't find any consolation."

At times, she would have liked to have been under the grass in the cemetery, like her brothers. They, at least, weren't suffering any more, and even their parents, poor people, had become hardened.

"The Lord won't abandon us completely," stammered Arlia. "The fortuneteller told me so. And I've got an idea."

On Christmas Day they set the table with flowers and their best tablecloth, and this time they had invited her uncle, the priest, who was the only hope they had left. Manica rubbed his hands together and said:

"Today we've got to be happy and gay."

But the lamp hanging on the ceiling swayed sadly.

They had beef, roast turkey, and even a *panettone*[3] that had a picture of the Cathedral of Milan. At dessert, the poor uncle, a good glass of *barbera* wine in his hand, seeing them lament on such a day, couldn't resist any more and had to promise the girl a dowry. The lover—

---

[3] A type of sweet bread made with flour, sugar, eggs, and dried fruit, and used especially at Christmas.

Silvio Liotti, a clerk in a store, and well-informed—was heard from again: he was ready to make amends for the wrong he had done.

Manica, holding up a glass in his hand, said to Father Calogero:

"See this, sir? It cures many ills."

It was destiny, though, that where Arlia was, happiness didn't last. The son-in-law, a really fine fellow, ate up his wife's dowry, and after six months Fortunata, hungry and beaten, went back to her parents' home to tell her troubles and to show her bruises. Every year she too had a baby, just like her mother, and each one was bursting with health and ate like a horse. To the grandmother it seemed as if she were having babies again herself, because each one brought more trouble, even without dying of consumption. Having become old now, she had to run as far as Borgo Degli Ortolani and to Porta Garibaldi in order to earn four *lire* a month doing little jobs for the shopkeepers. Her husband, whose hands trembled, made hardly ten *lire* on Saturday, by cutting his customers and using spider webs to stop the blood. The rest of the week, he either sulked behind the dirty window or was at the tavern with his hat slanted over his ear.

And Arlia now spent the lottery money on brandy, secretly, hiding it under her apron; her consolation was to feel it warm her heart, as she sat before the window thinking of nothing, looking out at the wet, dripping roofs.

1883

THE LAST DAY

Just past Sesto,[1] the travelers in the first cars of the train for Como felt a bump, and an old marchioness, who to her misfortune happened to be sitting between a young man and one of those rich girls wearing a big, broad-brimmed hat, opened her eyes wide and curled up her nose.

The young gentleman had a beautiful fur coat, and out of gallantry he wanted to share it with his younger neighbor, although it was late spring. After many yeses and noes, they were just about to reach an agreement when the train bounced. Luckily, the marchioness was known at the Monza station, and so she was given a seat in a special compartment.

The evening papers read:

"An unidentified body was found today on the railroad tracks in the vicinity of Sesto, the authorities report."

That was all the newspapers knew. A crowd of peasants returning from the fiesta at Gorla had suddenly found the body under their feet on the railroad embankment and had gathered around, curious to see what it looked like. Someone in the group said that coming across a dead man on a holiday brings bad luck; but

[1] A town in the outskirts of Milan.

most of them got numbers for the lottery out of it.[2]

To clear the line, the trackman had laid the body among the bushes in the meadow and had put a handful of weeds over his badly smashed face which made an ugly sight for those who passed. Between trains, the chief magistrate, the police, and the neighbors came hurrying up, and since it was Ascension Day, you could see in the green fields, the red plumes of the *carabinieri* and the new clothes of the curious.

The dead man was wearing torn, ragged pants, a worn-out canvas jacket, and shoes held together with twine, and he had a lottery ticket in his pocket. With his eyes wide open in his livid face, he looked up into the blue sky.

The police tried to find out if it was murder—for robbery or for some other motive.

And they made their report according to all the regulations, just as if a hundred thousand *lire* had been in those pockets. Then they wanted to know who he was and where he came from: his name, address, occupation, and the name of his father. There were no clues except his week-old red beard and his dirty, wasted hands; two hands that hadn't done anything and had been hungry for a long time.

From these characteristics, a few had recognized him —among others, a group that had been having a noisy party at Loreto.

---

[2] Italians often derive the numbers they bet on the National Lottery from seeing a corpse or from dreaming of a dead person.

The Last Day

The girls who were dancing, all excited and with their skirts flying in the air, had said:

"That fellow there doesn't feel like dancing!"

He was going his own way, with his arms hanging down, his legs weak, and had a hard time dragging along those two shoes that didn't hold together. For a moment, he stopped to listen to the accordion as if he really wanted to dance, and watched without saying anything. Then he continued along the boulevard, which stretched out white and dusty as far as the eye could see. He was walking on the right, under the trees, his head low. A horsecar missed running over him by a hair, and the driver threw a curse and a lash of the whip after him. He jumped back desperately, in order to get away from the danger.

Later he was seen sitting on the ground, at the edge of a farm, looking suspicious. He seemed to be pondering the corn patch or counting the stones in the irrigation ditch. One of the farm hands hurried over with a club, and crept up to him softly. He wanted to see what that tramp was plotting, since the ears of corn wouldn't be ripe for a long time yet and in the whole field, try as you might, there wasn't a cent's worth to steal. When he got close to him, he saw that he had taken off his shoes and was holding his chin in his palms. The farm hand, with the club behind his back, asked him what he was doing there on other people's property, and looked at his hands suspiciously. The man stammered without being able to answer and dejectedly put his shoes on once more. Then he left again with his back bent, like a criminal.

He was walking along the bank of the irrigation ditch, under the mulberry trees that were getting their first leaves. To the right and to the left, the meadows were all green. The water flowed black in the shade and from time to time glistened in the sun—a beautiful spring sun that made the birds twitter.

The farm hand added that he had remained there on the lookout more than an hour, to see if that tramp would come back; and he never could have imagined that he was making so much fuss just in order to go and end under a locomotive. He had recognized him from those shoes that wouldn't even hold together with twine and that had jumped off his feet, one to this and one to that side of the track.

"Those feet must have done a lot of kicking when the wheels ran over them!" observed the tavern waiter who, at the odor of the dead man, had rushed there like a raven, in his black jacket and with a napkin on his arm. He had seen that stranger pass by the tavern about noon: one of those hungry faces that, when they pass, devour with their eyes the soup that's boiling in your pot. Even the dogs had smelled him and barked behind those shoes that were falling apart in the dust.

As the sun was setting, the shadow of the body stretched out like a scarecrow from those shoeless feet, and the birds flew away silently. The gay sound of voices and the Barbapedana song came from the nearby taverns. At one end of a courtyard, behind a row of thin little plants, you could see the girls jumping and dancing with their hair in disorder. And when the cart carrying the remains of the suicide passed, the lit-up windows immediately darkened with a curious crowd that looked out to see. Inside, the accordion was still playing the waltz from *Madame Angot*.[3]

Later, they found out a few more things about him. The landlady of the cheap inn at Porta Tenaglia had seen that red-bearded man arrive one rainy night a month earlier. He was dead tired and under his arm he had a little bundle that must not have given him much trouble, and before saying yes, she had weighed it with her eyes to see if the two *soldi* for the bed were in it. He had first asked how much it cost to sleep with a roof over his head. Then, every day that God sent to earth, he waited for a letter to come and at dawn he started out to go and look for that answer, his shoes full of holes, his back bent, already tired before he began. Finally, the letter had come. It said that there was no job for him at the workshop. The woman had found it on the mattress, because that day he had sat on the bed until late, with the letter in his hands and his legs hanging down.

No one knew any more about him. He had come from far away. "Milan's a big city," he had been told, "you'll

---

[3] *La Fille de Madame Angot,* an operetta in three acts by Charles Lecocq, was premiered in 1872 and immediately became very popular throughout Europe.

find something there." He didn't believe it any more, but he looked as long as he had a few cents left.

He had had all kinds of jobs: stonecutter, brickmaker, and finally bricklayer's helper. But after he had broken an arm, he wasn't the same man any more, and the contractors sent him from one to the other to get him out from under their feet. Then, when he got tired of hunting for his bread, he laid himself down on the railroad tracks. What was he thinking about as he waited, stretched out on his back, looking at the clear sky and at the tops of the green trees?

The day before, when he was going back to his room with his legs aching all over, he had said: "Tomorrow!"

It was a Saturday night: there were people packed to the doors in all the taverns of Bonaparte Square, crowded in the clear gaslight, before the booths of the clown shows, at the peddlers' benches, and losing themselves in the shadow of the boulevards, with a soft and caressing whisper of voices. A girl in a flesh-colored sweater played a drum under a painted poster. Farther on, a young couple, sitting with their backs to the boulevard, were embracing. A peddler of baked apples tempted your stomach with his wares.

He passed before a half-closed shop; in the rear there was a woman nursing a baby, and a man in shirt sleeves was smoking at the door. Walking along he looked at everything, but he didn't dare stop; he felt that they were chasing him away, away, always away. It seemed as if the Christians already smelled the odor of the dead man, and they avoided him.

The Last Day

Only a poor woman who was going to Sesto bent under a large back-basket, and was grumbling, sat down to rest on the edge of the road beside him; and she began chattering and complaining, as old people do, prattling of her troubles: that she had a daughter in the hospital and her son-in-law made her work like an animal, and that she had to go all the way to Monza with that big basket, and that she had a steady pain in her back as if dogs were biting it. Then she too went her own way, to cook *polenta*[4] for her son-in-law, who was waiting for it. The village clock struck noon, and all the bells rang out joyously for Ascension Day. When they became silent, a great peace fell suddenly all around over the countryside. All at once, you heard the shrill, threatening whistle of the train that was passing like a flash of lightning.

The sun was high and warm. On the other side of the road, toward the tracks, the meadows became lost in the distance under the shady rows of mulberry trees and were crisscrossed by the irrigation ditch that glistened among the poplars.

"Come on, let's go! It's time to end it all!" But he didn't move, his head between his hands. A hungry, stray mongrel went by, the only dog that didn't bark at him, and half hesitating and half afraid it stopped to look at him; then it began to wag its tail. Finally, since it wasn't given anything, it went away too; and for a while, in the silence you could hear the poor animal

---

[4] A type of mush made with finely milled corn flour.

tramping around, with its stomach thin and its tail drooping.

The accordions went on playing, and the noise in the taverns lasted until late at night. Then, when the voices grew hoarse and the girls were tired of dancing, they began talking of the day's suicide again. A girl told the story of a friend of hers, who was as beautiful as an angel and had killed herself for love, and who had been found with the picture of her lover on her lips—a traitor who had jilted her in order to marry a shopkeeper. She knew every detail; they had been sewing together at the same table for two years. The other girls listened half stretched out on the couch, fanning themselves, still red and all excited. A young man said that if he had reason to be jealous, he would fix both of them, first her and then him, with that shoemaker's knife that he carried even when he wasn't in the shop, because you never know! And with his hands in his pockets he posed before the girls, who listened to him intently—handsome young man that he was, his curly hair breaking loose from under a tiny, tiny hat.

The waiter brought some more bottles; and with their elbows leaning heavily on the tablecloth, they all talked of tender things, their eyes shiny while squeezing each other's hands.

"In this damned world there's nothing but friendship and a little love. *Viva!* One bottle drives away a week of the blues."

The Last Day

Some of them stepped in to break up a fight between two burly young men who wanted to knock each other's brains out because of the eyes of a little brunette, who was shamelessly going from one to the other.

"It's the wine! It's the wine!" somebody cried. *"Viva!"*

The peacemakers almost came to blows with the tavern keeper over a few bottles too many that they saw on the bill. Then they all went out into the fresh air and into the night that was already far gone.

The tavern keeper spent some time barring all the doors and windows, and figuring out the day's income in his big, greasy old book. Then he went to join his wife, who was dozing in front of the counter with the baby in her lap. You could hear rare and sudden bursts of gaiety as the voices were becoming lost along the street, far in the distance. And a great silence fell all around under the starry sky, and a cricket began to chirp on the railroad embankment.

1883

TEMPTATION

Here is how it happened. —I swear to God it's true!

There were three of them: Ambrogio, Carlo, and Pigna, the saddle maker, the one who had dragged them out to go and have a good time: "Let's take the horse-car to Vaprio." And without even taking a woman of any kind along, because they wanted to enjoy the holiday in peace.

They played bocce ball,[1] took a long walk as far as the river, bought drinks for one another and finally dined under the trellis at the Merlo Bianco. There was a big crowd there, and an accordion player, and a guitar player, and girls screaming on a swing, and lovers seeking the shade—a real fiesta.

Pigna had begun to fool around with one of the girls at the big table next to him, a flirt with her hand in her hair and her elbows on the tablecloth. And Ambrogio, who was a quiet boy, pulled him by the jacket, saying in his ear:

"Let's go, or there might be a fight."

Later, in jail, he thought he would go crazy when he turned over in his mind how the terrible mishap had come about.

---

[1] A type of bowling played with small wooden balls on an alley made of hard soil.

Temptation

Toward evening, they went a long way on foot to catch the horsecar. Carlo, who had been in the service, claimed he knew the short cuts and made them take a little road that zigzagged across the meadows. This was their ruin.

It might have been seven o'clock on a beautiful fall evening—the fields still green and not a living soul around. They were walking along singing, happy about their picnic, all three of them young and without worries.

If they had been without money, or work, or if they had had other troubles, perhaps it would have been better. And to think that Pigna kept saying they had spent their money well that Sunday!

As young men do, they were talking about women in general, and each one about his own sweetheart. And even Ambrogio, who seemed a timid greenhorn, told in detail what happened with Filippina when they were together every night behind the wall of the factory.

"Wait and see," he muttered at last, because his shoes were hurting him. "Wait and see, Carlo will make us take the wrong road!"

Carlo instead insisted: No! The horsecar was going to be there for sure, behind that row of topped elms; you couldn't see it yet because of the evening haze.

L'è sott'il pont, l'è sott'il pont a fà la legnaaa . . . [2]

---

[2] "She's under the bridge, she's under the bridge, gathering firewood . . ." This is the refrain of a Milanese folk song that tells about a girl who, pretending to go and gather firewood, goes to make love under a bridge.

Ambrogio, limping behind them, accompanied in a deep bass voice.

After a while, they caught up with a peasant girl who was going the same way and had a basket under her arm.

"What luck!" exclaimed Pigna. "Now we'll ask directions."

Wow! She was really something, one of those girls who fill you with temptation when you meet them alone.

"Baby, is this the right way to go where we're going?" asked Pigna laughing.

She was an honest girl, and so she lowered her head and quickened her pace without paying any attention to him.

"What legs, eh!" muttered Carlo. "If you're going this fast to see your boy friend, he's sure a lucky guy!"

The girl, seeing that they were sticking too close to her, stopped suddenly, the basket in her hand, and began to scream:

"Let me go on, and mind your own business."

"Eh!" answered Pigna. "What the hell! We don't want to eat you!"

She started on her way again, her head low, like the stubborn peasant that she was.

Carlo, in order to break the ice, asked:

"Where're you going, you beautiful girl? . . . What's your name?"

"My name is what it is, and I'm going where I'm going."

Temptation

Ambrogio wanted to join in too:

"Don't be afraid, we don't mean to hurt you. We're good fellows who want to get to the horsecar and go on about our business."

And since he had the face of a good man, and because it was getting dark and she risked missing the ride, the young woman let herself be persuaded. Ambrogio wanted to know if that was the right way to get to the horsecar.

"They told me it is," she answered. "But I don't know my way around here." And she told them that she was going to the city to look for a job. Pigna, who was gay and lighthearted by nature, pretended to understand that she was looking for a job as a wet nurse,[3] and if she didn't know where to go, he would find her a nice and warm place himself, that very night. And since he was free and loose with his hands, she gave him such a blow with her elbow that she almost crushed his ribs.

"Christ!" he muttered. "Christ, what a punch!" And the others laughed out loud.

"I'm not afraid of you or anybody else!" she answered.

"Not of me?"

"And not even of me?"

"And what about all three of us together?"

"And if we'd take you by force?"

Then they looked around the countryside, where not a living soul could be seen.

"What about your boy friend?" said Pigna, to change

---

[3] Wet nurses had the reputation of being easy prey for men.

the subject. "What about your boy friend? How come he let you leave?"

"I don't have a boy friend," she answered.

"Really? Beautiful as you are?"

"No, I'm not beautiful."

"Come on, come on, don't tell me that!" And Pigna started to play the gallant, his thumbs in his vest. —By God! Was she beautiful! With those eyes, and those lips, and with this, and that and the other!

"Let me go," she was saying as she laughed in her sleeve, her eyes low.

One kiss, at least, what's one kiss after all? She could at least let him give her one kiss to seal their friendship. After all, it was beginning to get dark, and no one would see them. She tried to protect herself with her raised elbow.

"God! What a view!" Through her bent arm, Pigna devoured her with his eyes. Then she planted herself in front of him, threatening to slam the basket in his face.

"Go ahead! Hit all you want. Coming from you, it'll be a pleasure!"

"Let me go, or I'll call for help."

"Nobody can hear. Come on, let me give you this one kiss," he stammered, his face burning.

The other two were dying with laughter. Finally, since they pressed up close to her, the girl, half laughing, half serious, began to hit hard, at this one and that one, any way the blows happened to fall. Then she began to run, her skirt flying in the air.

"Ah! you want me to force it on you! You want me to force it on you!" shouted Pigna, panting as he ran after her.

And all out of breath, he caught up with her and threw one of his big hands over her mouth. So they clutched each other and knocked each other here and there. Fuming, the girl bit, scratched, kicked.

Carlo found himself caught in the middle as he was trying to separate them. Ambrogio had grabbed her legs so that she wouldn't cripple anyone. Finally Pigna, who was pale and panting, forced her under him and put his knee on her breast. And then the three of them, one after the other, drunk with woman at the contact with that warm flesh, as if they were overpowered all at once by a savage madness . . . God help us!

She got up like a wild animal, without saying a word, and rearranged the shreds of her dress and picked up her basket.

The men looked at one another with a strange smile. As she started to go, Carlo planted himself in front of her, his face dark:

"You're not going to say anything!"

"No! I'm not going to say anything!" promised the girl in a dull voice.

At these words, Pigna grabbed her by the skirt. She began to scream:

"Help!"

"Shut up!"

"Help! Murder!"

"Shut up, I say!"

Carlo grabbed her by the throat:

"Do you want to ruin all of us, damn you!"

Under that grasp she couldn't scream any more, but she still threatened them with her wide open eyes in which one could see the *carabinieri* and the gallows. She was becoming livid—her tongue sticking all the way out, black, enormous, a tongue that could no longer fit in her mouth. And at that sight all three of them became frightened and lost their heads. Carlo pressed her throat harder and harder as the woman relaxed her arms, and grew limp and inert, her head thrown back on the stones, the whites of her eyes showing. Finally they slowly drew aside one by one, terrified.

She remained motionless, stretched out on her back on the edge of the path, her face up and her eyes wide open and white. Pigna, surly and without saying a word, grasped Ambrogio, who hadn't moved, by the shoulder; and Carlo stammered:

"It was all three of us, eh! All three of us! . . . Or, by the blood of the Virgin! . . ."

It had gotten dark. How much time had gone by? Across the whitish path you could still see that black thing on the ground, motionless. Fortunately no one passed. Behind a patch of corn there was a long row of mulberry trees. A dog had begun to bark in the distance. And the three friends thought they were dreaming when they heard the whistle of the horsecar, which they had been going to catch half an hour before—a century seemed to have passed.

Pigna said that they had to dig a deep hole to hide what had happened, and they forced Ambrogio to drag the dead woman into the meadow, since it had been all three of them who had made the blunder. That body was like lead. Besides, it wouldn't fit in the grave. Carlo cut off the head with a little knife that Pigna happened to be carrying. When they had pressed the dirt down, stamping on it, they felt calmer and started out along the little road. Ambrogio, suspicious, kept an eye on Pigna who had the knife in his pocket. They were dying of thirst, but they took a long way around in order to avoid a country tavern that was becoming visible in the dim light of dawn; a rooster crowing in the cool morning air made them start. They were walking cautiously and without saying a word, but they didn't want to part, as if they were tied together.

The *carabinieri* arrested them one by one a few days later: Ambrogio in a brothel, where he was staying from morning to night; Carlo near Bergamo, where they had begun to watch him because of his aimless wandering; and Pigna at the factory, in the middle of the crowd of workers and the rumble of the machine, and as he saw the *carabinieri* he grew pale and immediately became tongue-tied. In court, in the defendant's box, they gave one another dirty looks, and called one another Judas.

But later, in jail, they thought they would go crazy when they turned over in their minds how the disaster had come about, and how, one thing leading to the other, you can start with a joke and end up with blood on your hands.

1884

NANNI VOLPE

Nanni Volpe had spent the best years of his life thinking of nothing but getting property together. He had the sharp mind of a peasant, and big broad shoulders—big and broad from carrying the hoe and the knapsack in the sun and in the rain, for thirty years. When the other young men of his age were chasing skirts or going to the tavern, he was "feathering the nest," as he put it: today he got a piece of land, tomorrow a house—all of it bread that he took out of his mouth, all of it his very blood, which turned into land and bricks. When the nest was finally ready, Nanni Volpe was fifty, his back broken and his face full of furrows like a field; but he had good holdings on the plain, a vineyard on the hill, a house with an attic,[1] and everything else you could think of. On Sundays, when he went down to the square, with his blue suit on, everyone made way for him, even the women, both widows and girls, for they knew that now that the house was ready a wife was needed.

He didn't say no; on the contrary, he was thinking about it. But he did things slowly, like a man who wasn't used to biting off more than he could chew. He didn't

---

[1] In Sicily, at the time of this story, only rich people could afford a house with an attic.

want a widow because widows throw their first husbands in your face every minute; he didn't want a
spring chicken either, "so as not to join the club right
away," [2] as he put it. He had set his eyes on the daughter
of Senzia, the Dwarf, a quiet girl of the neighborhood,
who was always glued to her loom and didn't even
show herself at the window on Sundays, and until she
was twenty-eight there hadn't even been a dog barking
after her. As for a dowry, he didn't care: he didn't mind
having worked for two! With the Dwarf, it was all
right; the girl said neither yes nor no, but it must have
been all right with her too. Only a few malicious gossips
kept saying behind her back:

"Still waters swallow up mills." Or: "This time the
fox[3] is going to be eaten up by the wolf."

At Easter finally came the time for the "explanation."
The wheat was this tall, the olive trees were loaded,
Nanni Volpe had just paid the last installment on the
mill. "Everything as it should be." He put on his blue
suit, and went to have a talk with Senzia. The girl was
behind the kitchen door, listening. When her mother
called her, she appeared, freshly groomed and blushing,
her chin nailed to her breast and her knitting in her
hands.

"Raffaela, *massaro* Nanni's here and says he wants to
marry you," said her mother.

---

[2] A southern Italian expression meaning cuckold. The
"club" is an imaginary society to which betrayed husbands
automatically belong.

[3] This is a play on words based on the Italian for "fox,"
volpe, Nanni's last name.

The girl kept her head bowed and went on knitting, while her breasts were heaving. *Massaro* Nanni added:

"Now we're waiting for you to tell us what you think."

The mother then came to the help of her daughter:

"As far as I'm concerned, it's all right."

And Raffaela raised her eyes, as tender as a lamb's, and answered:

"If it's all right with you, mother . . ."

They were married without much fanfare, because Nanni Volpe didn't have foolish ideas in his head and knew that "it takes twenty *grani* to make a *tarì*." But he didn't forget the closest relatives and the neighbors; he served sweets made by the nuns and white wine. Among the guests there were also Nanni Volpe's future heirs, all poor devils who stuffed themselves with everything and would even have liked to devour the bride with their eyes. She, with a gold necklace around her neck, was standing stiff as a poker in her wool and silk dress, and was already looking after her own interest, keeping an eye on everything and having her holiday smile and a good word for everyone, friends and enemies. Nanni Volpe rubbed his hands, happy as could be, and said to himself:

"If a wife like this doesn't turn out to be a good one, there are no saints nor paradise!"

And Carmine, a distant cousin, who called him uncle for love of his property and now had to act friendly toward the new aunt who had come to take that property away, kept saying to her, each time he grabbed a handful of wedding candies:

Nanni Volpe

"If I had known what a beautiful aunt I was going to get! . . . I wish I had my uncle's age and ailments tonight!"

After everybody had gone and the door was closed, Nanni showed his bride the rooms, the granary, even the stable, and all the good things he had. Then he put the lamp on the chest of drawers by the bed, and said:

"Now you're the boss."

Raffaela, who knew where things were, for her mother had talked so much about the place, locked her jewelry in the drawer and the wool and silk dress in the closet; then, standing in her petticoat, she tied the keys together in a bunch and stuck them under her pillow. Her husband nodded his approval, and concluded:

"Fine! That's the way I like you to be!"

Everything was going well. Nanni Volpe, as tough as the soil, took care of the fields, and when he came home on Saturday evenings his wife made sure that he found a fresh shirt on the bed, the macaroni made, and the bread for the following week already leavening. She kept count of the things her husband sent home: so many *tumoli* of wheat, so many quintals of sumac—all notched on the sticks that hung in bundles below the crucifix. As a God-fearing housewife, on Sundays and other holidays she went to Mass with her husband, twice a month she went to confession, and the rest of the time she was completely devoted to her home, so much so that she gave her husband a sermon whenever Carmine, his poor nephew, came buzzing around him:

"Don't give anything to that good-for-nothing, or

you'll never be able to shake him off your back. If you'd let your relatives have their way, they'd eat you alive."

And Nanni rubbed his hands and answered:

"Fine! That's the way I like you to be!"

Carmine finally had smelled which direction the wind was blowing and had begun to stick to his aunt's skirts in order to snatch from her some measures of broad beans or some bundles of firewood, during the winter when the weather was severe enough to freeze hell over.

"If you let your own flesh and blood die of starvation you must have a heart of stone. With all the good things you have in your house . . . If you say 'yes' Uncle Nanni won't say 'no.' "

"What can I do? You know he's the boss."

"If you had children I'd understand! But what'll you do with all that property when you're dead, both of you?"

"If we have no children it's because that's the will of God!"

The rascal then scratched his head, looking at his aunt with cat's eyes. One day, to touch her heart, he went so far as to say:

"You're so beautiful and young, it's really a pity that that's the will of God."

"What do you care?"

Carmine thought about it a minute, and then answered rubbing his hands:

"I wish I were in Uncle Nanni's shirt; then I'd show you what I care!"

"Quiet, you damn fool! Or I'll tell your uncle what you come and say to me."

"Will you give me that bottle of wine, then?"

"Yes, to get you out from under my feet. But don't tell Nanni anything."

Carmine, having finally found the note that had to be sounded, would repeat to his aunt, whenever he needed something:

"You're as beautiful as the sun. You're as plump as a quail. The Lord doesn't do things right when he gives bread to those who don't have teeth any more."

Aunt Raffaela became red with anger; she scolded him for being such a rascal, and to make him get out of her sight she gave him something. Once she even slapped him.

"Go ahead, go ahead!" said Carmine. "To me, anything that comes from your hands is sweet."

"Don't come here again! Don't make me sin because of you! Then each time I have to go and tell the father confessor."

"What's wrong with it? I'm your nephew, your own flesh and blood."

"No, no, I don't want you to come. If they see you here all the time, people will talk. Besides, I don't want you to!"

"I only come to see you. I won't ask you for anything any more, that's all. You've cast a spell over me; you can't blame me for that!"

One day, during the harvest, when Carmine was helping to unload the barley in the granary, and Raffaela, all red in the face and wearing her bodice, was holding the lamp, the scoundrel, just like the animal that he was, grabbed her by the hair and didn't want to let go of her, no matter how she hammered his shins with her wooden shoes and planted her fingernails in his face.

"I swear by the holy day that's today! . . ." puffed Carmine breathing heavily. "This time I won't let you go, no, I won't!"

Raffaela, her face distorted, her clothes disorderly, and her breasts panting under the bodice that seemed to be tearing apart, was groping about on the floor to find the lamp that had fallen, and stammered with her lips still moist:

"You made me spill the oil. Something bad is going to happen."[4]

Nanni Volpe, tilling the fallow land after the first rains, had caught malaria. His land was finally eating him up—and so were the doctor and the druggist. Raffaela, poor woman, deserved a monument under those circumstances: she was busy all day, she and her nephew, boiling herb teas and preparing medicine for the sick man. And he, entirely helpless in his bed, kept thinking of all the money that was flying away, and of his interests that were in the hands of this one and that one—of the men who ate and drank his things and sat in the yard without doing anything, now that the boss' eye wasn't there; of the *curatolo* who certainly robbed him of a cheese every other day; of the warehouse door

---

[4] In Sicily, to spill oil was considered a bad omen.

that needed a new lock because the field watchman must have known how to work the old one . . . —During the night he didn't dream of anything but thieves and robberies, and woke with sudden starts, covered with the sweat of death. Once he thought he heard a noise in the next room, and jumped out of bed in his nightshirt with the shotgun in his hand. There actually were two feet coming out from under the big bench and Raffaela, in her underclothes, was hurrying to cover them with everything she could find.

"Thief! Help! Thief!" Nanni Volpe began to shout, as he searched under the bench with the barrel of his shotgun.

"Don't kill me; I'm your own flesh and blood!" stammered Carmine, as pale as his shirt, as he was getting up on his feet; and Raffaela, making the sign of the cross, muttered:

"Didn't I say so? Spilling oil brings something bad!"

Then, after slamming the door on Carmine, who was more dead than alive and still half undressed, Raffaela busied herself taking care of her husband, to help him get over the fright, giving him teas and mixed wine, warming his feet with the hot-water bottle, tucking the blanket under his back:—in all honesty, she didn't know how that rascal had stuck himself there. Before dark, it's true, she had told him to help her with the laundry; but she thought that by now he had been gone for some time.

Nanni, softened by the bed and by the disease, let her talk and have her way with him. But, his nose under the sheet, with the sharp mind of a peasant, he was thinking of his business and of a way of getting his feet out of that slough without losing his shoes.

"Listen," he said to his wife as soon as it was daylight, "I've decided to make my will."

"What kind of ridiculous ideas are you getting into your head now?"

"No, no, my daughter. I have one foot in the grave. I've worn myself out getting property, and now I want 'to settle accounts before leaving the farm.'"

"Could I know, at least, how you intend to do it?"

"Don't worry about that. You know the saying? 'Soul and property shall go to whom they belong.'"

"God will remember all the good you've done and are doing for me!" answered Raffaela, moved. "You married me, poor and in rags like an orphan; and you can be sure I've always respected you like a father."

"Yes, yes, I know," nodded her husband, and the tassel of his cap seemed to join in and say yes too. He also asked for a father confessor and wanted to receive communion, in order to be at peace with God and man when the Lord called him. He even sent for his nephew, and said to him:

"Why did you run away, you jackass? Were you afraid of me, your own flesh and blood?"

Carmine, like a fool, swayed on his legs, his hat in his hands, and didn't know what to answer.

"Put your hat back on," concluded Uncle Nanni. "This is your own house, and you can come whenever you want to; as a matter of fact, it's better for you to be here, so you can look after your own interest."

And while Carmine opened his eyes as wide as an ox's:

"Yes, yes, go and ask the notary about the will, thankless wretch! 'The soul goes to God, and property to whom it belongs.' "

Then Raffaela jumped up in a fury:

"Your soul will go to the devil because you're a thief! Yes, a thief! What did I marry you for, then?"

"That's another business," answered Nanni while he was getting undressed to go back to bed; "another business that can't be changed like a will, in case . . ."

"Hey!" shouted Carmine, facing his aunt who wanted to plunge forward with her claws ready. "Hey! Don't touch my uncle! Or I'll wring your neck like a chicken's!"

Like a wild animal, Raffaela left the house, swearing that she was going to sue her husband to get her due, and that she wanted to let him die alone and desperate, like a dog.

"Never mind!" said Carmine, the nephew. "If you want me to, I'll stay here to take care of you; I'm your own flesh and blood."

"Fine!" answered Nanni. "And you'll watch over your own interest too."

But Raffaela was welcomed by her mother like a dog who comes to eat from someone else's bowl.

"Don't you have your own home now? Aren't you married? What do you want here?"

She wanted at least alimony from her husband. But Nanni knew the law better than a lawyer.

"Did I throw her out of the house, by any chance?" he answered the judge. "If she wants to come back the door's open."

Carmine kept on telling him that taking his wife back was a big mistake; with all the hatred she must be nursing inside, one of these days she was going to poison him in order to get him out of her sight.

"No, no," answered his uncle with a candid smile. "The will is in your favor, and she won't gain anything by poisoning me. On the contrary!" He scratched his head wondering if he should say the rest, but finally he kept it to himself, laughing very quietly.

Finally, Raffaela came back home as meek as a lamb. Her mother, Senzia, and the other relatives accompanied her.

"Oh, it's nothing, nothing. These are things that happen between husband and wife; but now peace is made and you'll see that your wife will regain all your affection, Nanni."

"I didn't take it away from her," answered Nanni Volpe. "She deserves it: I won't take anything away from her."

Raffaela, to deserve it, became so good and loving that it didn't seem true: always around her husband, taking care of him, anticipating every wish and trying to prevent every ailment. The old man said:

"You're doing the right thing. Because if something happens to me before I have the time to change my will, it will be so much the worse for you."

He let her watch over and cherish him and keep him in cotton, and he felt like a king.

"One of these days," he said again, "if the Lord gives me enough time, I want to change my will. I've worked all my life; my skin has become like shoe leather, but now I'm getting my reward. What's important is to be wise enough to get this reward."

The only things that bothered him now, in that bliss, were the continuous quarrels between Carmine and Raffaela. Screams and terrific blows all day long, and he couldn't even get up to quiet the two of them.

Sometimes Raffaela came in all disheveled, foaming with rage, blood dripping from her nose, and showed him the scratches and the bruises:

"Look what that bastard's done to me!"

"Hey, hey, Carmine, what did you do to your aunt, you rascal?"

"Why don't you kick that loafer out?"

"No, no; we must have a man in the house, now that I'm nailed to the bed."

"Wait and see! Wait and see! One of these days, not to leave you time to change your will, he'll make you die the death of a rat. He'll poison you, I swear to God!"

"Then what are you doing here, if you aren't looking after my life and your own interest?"

Always that business of the will; Carmine was happy about what his uncle had told him, and Raffaela was not. Nanni Volpe, who found himself between the two of them, never got around to changing it—he would say every time he felt worse; so that Raffaela, seeing that he was sinking more and more every day and that he and his cotton cap had now become only one yellow thing, was gnawed away by anger, and was feeling sick herself, so that finally she blurted it out, in the presence of Carmine, who was feeding his uncle and holding the spoon with one hand and Nanni's head with the other.

"You're doing the right thing to think so much of your own flesh and blood; you don't know what kind of help your nephew's given you!"

Carmine wanted to throw the bowl and the candlestick in her face; but the old man, moving the tassel of his cap very slowly two or three times, said:

"Yes, yes, I know."

So he went to the other world, leisurely and waited on like a king. When Carmine wanted to kick Raffaela out of the house, which was supposed to be his own now, he had the will read, and then you saw how shrewd had been Nanni Volpe, who had fooled him, his wife, and even Christ in paradise. His property had all been left to the hospital, and aunt and nephew had a good fight— before the notary, this time.

1887

DONNA SANTA'S SIN

This time, to shake up those mules who actually had to be dragged to the sermon by the harness and who then went and behaved worse than before, the Lenten preacher thought up a good stunt, and if that wasn't going to help, sermons or preaching would all be like flinging words to the wind. He had the sacristan and two or three others, whom he had earlier taught their roles, hide in the old tomb under the floor of the church, and he said:

"Leave it to me."

The sermon on hell happened to be scheduled for the end of the mission, and the church was packed with people; some had come for one reason, some for another, some by order of the judge (for at that time fear of God was taught by the police), and some for love of the skirt. The men on one side, to the left, and the women on the other. On the pulpit the preacher painted hell in a lifelike manner, as if he had been there. And at every detail, he thundered with a deep terrifying voice:

"Woe! Woe!"

Like so many cannon shots. The women, herded together inside the enclosure to the right of the nave, bowed their heads in dismay at every shot, and even Don Gennaro Pepi, who was Don Gennaro Pepi! beat his breast in public and muttered out loud:

"Have mercy on me, Lord!"

But you couldn't trust them, because every day, before skinning his fellow men face to face, in private, Don Gennaro Pepi put himself back in the grace of God by going to Mass and to confession, and you knew that all those at the sermon would go and behave the same way they always had.

"Woe to you, rich glutton! You who've fattened yourself with the blood of the poor! —And you, Scribe and Pharisee, spoiler of the widow and the orphan . . ."

This was for Zacco, the notary. And there was something for all the others: for Baron Scampolo, who had a lawsuit with the Reverend Capuchin Fathers, for Don Luca Arpone, who lived in concubinage with his factor's wife, for the factor, who got even with his Master by stealing from him, for the liberals, who plotted against the Bourbons in the Mondella Pharmacy; in short, for everybody, rich and poor, maidens and married women. And each one in the village, knowing the faults of his neighbor, said in his own heart: "It's a good thing it's falling on *him!*" at every sin the preacher dealt with, and people turned to look in that direction.

"And when you are in the eternal fire, then what will you do? . . . Woe!"

"What's the matter?" muttered Donna Orsola Giuncada in the ear of her daughter, who was squirming around on her seat, as if she were really on the hot coals, to ogle Ninì Lanzo way in the back. "What's the matter? Are you getting the itch now? Watch out, or I'll slap it out of you!"

Meanwhile, you felt you were suffocating, cooped up in there. With the heat, the darkness, the heavy odor of the crowd, those two flimsy candles winking pitifully at the Christ on the altar, the whining of the altar boy who roughly stuck the collection basket under your nose, the preacher's deep voice booming through the church and giving you goose pimples, you felt your breath taken away. And then it seemed that all the fleas of your conscience, old and new, came back to bite you —especially when you heard the scourging which that good Christian, Cheli Mosca, famous thief, was giving himself down there in the dark; he had come to set a good example and to show that he was changing his ways, there under the very eyes of the judge and the Chief of Police—wham-wham—with the belt from his pants. And if a chicken was missing in the village, they went looking for him right away, damn it! As for the men, they sat still and took it as well as might be expected. But in the enclosure of the women, the word of God worked miracles, no less: sighs, grumbling, endless nose blowing; and those who had a clean conscience thanked the Lord in front of everybody—*coram populo* —and so much the worse for some others who didn't dare raise their noses from the prayer book: Donna Christina, the judge's wife, for example, or Caolina, who, with all her finery and smell of musk that poisoned the air, was being kept aside as if she had the plague.

"What good will your hair perfumed with myrrh and incense, and your impudent charm do you, impenitent Magdalene? . . ."

Donna Orsola held her nose, disgusted by the scandal that Caolina brought to church, since for women of that sort men neglect even the sacrament of matrimony and let your daughters grow moldy at home; and then there are the other troubles that come from all this: the girls, who to help themselves even latch on to a penniless tramp without ways or means, like Ninì Lanzo; the men with families, who still go gallivanting when they're fifty years old . . .

"Woe to you, adulterous and lustful! . . ."

"Uhm! Uhm!"

Now that the preacher had thrown himself on the seventh mortal sin, and called a spade a spade, poor Donna Orsola felt herself sitting on thorns for her daughter, who opened her eyes wide and didn't miss a single word of the sermon. She coughed, she blew her nose, and finally she began to preach to her in her own fashion: in church girls must be poised and collected, listening only to what's right for them, without making such silly faces, as if the servant of God were speaking Greek.

Instead, the preacher was speaking like Saint Augustine, and you could have heard a pin drop; even Caolina had lowered her veil on her eyes and seemed to be contrite.

The listeners were so taken by the subject of the sermon that old women of fifty began to blush again like young maids, and those who had warmed up the most looked disdainfully at Donna Santa Brocca, the Doctor's wife, who had come to the sermon with an eight-month stomach that was pitiful, and who felt as if she were dying under those looks, poor woman.

She was really a saintly woman, though, God-fearing, always with priests and going to confession, completely devoted to her home and her husband, so much so that she had filled up that home with children. And her husband—a liberal, one of those who plotted in the Mondella Pharmacy—every time his wife went to bed with labor pains, raved against God and against sacraments, especially that of matrimony, so that the poor woman wept for nine months whenever she was in that condition again.

This time, however, Donna Santa fixed him worse than ever before. It's true that the devil and the preacher had a hand in it—with that hell of a scene the priest had prepared—meaning well, of course. While he strained his throat shouting "Woe to you, lustful! . . . Woe to you, adulteress!" the flames of burning resin and sulphur appeared right in the middle of the church, and you heard the sacristan and his friends scream "Alas! Alas!" What did you see then? Some said it was really the devils, some wept out loud, some threw themselves on their knees. The widow Rametta, whose husband had recently been buried there, fainted from fright, as did two or three others out of sympathy. And poor Donna Santa Brocca, already weak in the mind because of the pregnancy, the fasting, and the prayers, shaken by the rebukes of her husband and the invectives of the preacher, suffering from the heat, from shame, from the stench of sulphur, was suddenly seized by qualms of conscience, or God knows what, and began to get hysterical and wild-eyed, pale as a dead woman, groping in the air with her hands, and moaned:

"Lord! . . . I'm a sinner! . . . Have mercy on me! . . ."

And all at once, bang, she did it.

Imagine the commotion: wild shouts, screams, mothers hurrying out and pushing in front of them their girls who were curious to see: in short, pandemonium. In the confusion, the men invaded the reserved enclosure, in spite of the judge, who was brandishing his bamboo cane and shouting as if he were in the middle of the public square. Punches and pinches were felt in the crush. That was when, as a matter of fact, Betta, the possessed, made up with Don Raffaele Molla, after they had had so many arguments and made so many shameful scenes, and Caolina, jumping over chairs and benches better than a goat, let anyone who liked see her embroidered bloomers. The mess was such that you had to look out for your wallet or watch chain, if you had one, but just in case, the judge gave Cheli Mosca a crack on the shoulder with his cane, to make him behave.

Finally, a few well-meaning men, helped by the judge and other authorities, scolding, yelling, grabbing people by the front of their clothes, and running here and there like dogs around a flock, managed to restore a little

order and to start off the procession that was supposed
to go to the Matrice, as usual, to give thanks to the Lord
—the rabble ahead, disorderly, pushing and slipping on
the precipitous little road, and the rich men behind, two
by two, with the scourge on their shoulders and wearing
crowns of thorns, so that people came from all around
to see the best blue bloods of the town, barons and big
shots, pass by like that with their eyes low; and the
windows were crowded with beautiful women—a temptation for those who passed in the procession with
crowns of thorns on their heads. On the balcony of the
courthouse, Donna Christina, the judge's wife, chatted
with her lady friends, and did the honors of the house
as if she were the mistress there.

"Sure! Donna Santa Brocca! She must really have a
filthy conscience! Would you have imagined it? A big
fake like her! And she passed herself off as a saint! Her
husband had better open his eyes in his own house,
instead of saying nasty things about everything and
everybody!"

Doctor Brocca was a real radical, one of those back-
biters of the Mondella Pharmacy, and he went around
making his calls instead of listening to the sermon and
following the procession; when he heard of the curse
that had fallen on him, and his wife was brought home
more dead than alive, he began yelling and raving
against the Lenten preacher, against the mission, and
against the government that permitted such frauds, saying that they wanted to butcher a pregnant woman with

those farces; till the judge called him to the courthouse *ad audiendum verbum,* and gave him a good raking over the coals:

"It's the government that's the boss, and you, dear friend, won't be the one to tell them what to do. Is that clear?" —And the Lenten preacher belonged to that order of Reverend Redemptorist Fathers,[1] who made themselves heard as far as Naples[2] and went around preaching and noting down the good and bad citizens in the book for their superiors, just as Saint Peter does in paradise. —"You already know you're not on the good page, dear Don Erasmo! Perhaps you're tired of making your calls now, and would like to rest in one of His Majesty's[3] prisons? Mind your own business, instead. Is that clear?"

His own business was that his wife was about to leave him a widower, with five children on his hands, poor Don Erasmo, and in addition, in her delirium she blurted out right in front of him certain things that made him prick up his ears, and how!

"Woe to you, adulteress! Woe to you, lustful! . . . I'm in mortal sin! . . . Lord, forgive me! . . ."

In short, what she had heard at the sermon. But Don

---

[1] A religious order founded in Naples by St. Alfonso Maria De' Liguori in the 18th century.

[2] At the time of this story Naples was the capital of the kingdom of the Two Sicilies.

[3] Ferdinand II of the Bourbons, king of the Two Sicilies. He died in 1859, a year before Garibaldi conquered his kingdom.

Donna Santa's Sin

Erasmo, who hadn't been at the sermon, didn't know what to say; he opened his eyes wide and turned all the colors of the rainbow, muttering anxiously:

"Eh! What're you saying? Eh?"

Not that his wife had ever given him occasion to suspect her, poor woman, with that face of hers! And it would really have been only a dirty trick for someone to do such a thing to Doctor Brocca, someone who didn't have the duty, that is, as he did, for love of peace, to satisfy the wishes of his wife, whose head was filled with the devilry of the priests, and who received all five sacraments with fervor . . . He knew what it was like to have a brood of children on his hands! Sure, priests don't have to pay for all this! And if a woman starts losing her head over something, then . . . He had seen all kinds of things!—

"Eh? What're you saying? Speak clearly, damn it!"

But the sick woman, all red in the face, didn't pay any attention, looking God knows where with her wide-open eyes. And on top of this, Donna Orsola Giuncada who, with the pretext of taking care of her cousin Donna Santa, was always under his feet, would cut him short:

"Is this the way to act? After a miscarriage? I'm surprised at you! You, a doctor!"

"Let her talk, damn it! My own interest is at stake! . . ."

The lady friends who came to visit the sick woman acted astounded! . . .

"Is it possible? A thing like this? She was so healthy! And she had come to the sermon! A model mother!

What could she have had on her conscience?"

"Well! . . . Well! . . ."

Then some of them shook their heads discreetly and some looked at one another, and then they left without asking anything else. A few jokers even shook Don Erasmo's hand in a certain way that seemed to mean: "Too bad! It's happened to *you* . . ."

At least that's what he thought! For when an idea like this gets into his head, an honest man doesn't know what to think any more. And hadn't Vito 'Nzerra come to report the talk which the judge's wife, Donna Christina, that gossip, spread around, dragging him in the mud too, poor man?

The talk had no end: perhaps Donna Santa had gone out not feeling well that day, or perhaps her pregnancy had taken a bad turn, or she had been pushed around in the crowd, or this or that or the other; or she had had an argument with her husband:

"Tell the truth, eh, Don Erasmo! . . ."

"The truth . . . the truth . . . One can't know the truth!"

Don Erasmo, who was ready to explode, finally gave vent to his feelings in front of *Signora* Borella and two or three others whom he could trust:

"They don't want the truth to be told! . . . Priests, police, and all those who're in the puppet show! . . . Who lead fools around by the nose! . . . Just like marionettes! . . . And they want to butcher a pregnant woman with such clowning! . . ."

"But no! No! We were all at the sermon . . . I was

there too . . . Nothing happened to anybody else! . . ."

"Well! . . . Then! . . ."

Then poor Don Erasmo didn't know what to say, his eyes wild and his mouth bitter. He started entreating his wife again, trying to be sweet to her, with half a smile on his lips, while he prepared herb teas and filled her up with medicine:

"Tell the truth to your darling husband . . . What's this sin? What is it I have to forgive you for?"

Like talking to a wall. Sometimes Donna Santa didn't even pull her teeth apart to swallow the medicine; or if she talked she sang the same old song about punishments, grave sins, tongues of fire that she always had before her eyes.

"Ah! Can't I even know what's been going on in my own house, ah?" Don Erasmo fumed then, turning to Donna Orsola who was always there, under his feet.

He, who knew all the stories about everybody else's houses: Donna Christina's scandalous behavior, the scenes of the widow Rametta, who went to cry over the death of her husband in the arms of this one and that one! —He had had some good laughs about all this with the pharmacist and Don Marco Crippa. He thought he could see Don Marco Crippa now, winking his crosseye; now that the misfortune had happened to him, he had become the fodder for the conversation.

"You understand, Donna Orsola, that I've got a right to know what's been going on in my own house!"

"What's been going on! What do you see? Don't you see that she's delirious, poor woman? It's the words of the sermon that have stuck in her mind . . ."

Right! Why precisely those words had stuck in her mind, that's what Don Erasmo wanted to know! In his own house there had never been such filthy goings on! . . . As far as he knew, at least! As far as he knew, good God!

"Good God! Leave me alone, or I'll have to think that you've gotten together on this, you two! And you, talk, explain yourself, damn it!"

"What do you want? Forgive me! . . ."

Ah no! First Don Erasmo wanted to know what it was he had to forgive! . . . And whom to thank for the trick played on him, if there was one! . . . For "the domestic theft!" . . . Yes sir, "the domestic theft!" because if an honest man isn't even safe in a house like his own, a real fortress, and with a wife like his own . . . And to play a trick like that with such a wife must really have come from deep hatred! . . . But who? Muzio, the only one who hung around his place? . . . And more than sixty years old . . . True, Donna Santa was no spring chicken herself any more, and the sin could be old too . . . And then? Then? Those children with whom he had filled his house in observance of the seventh sacrament? Was there some thief among them too? . . . Gennarino, or Sofia . . . or Nicola? . . . All the saints of the calendar were there in his house! Of all ages and all colors . . . Even with red hair like Zacco, the notary, who lived just across the street and was perfectly capable of having played such a trick on him out of pure and simple villainy, *gratis et amore Dei!*

Donna Santa's Sin

The poor man was going crazy with these suspicions, and was being gnawed inside, while he had to help the sick woman, and run around here and there in the disorderly house, forced to do everything himself: make the bread soup for Concettina, wash Ettore's face— perhaps the domestic thieves, poor innocents! . . . No, it couldn't go on this way! Donna Santa would finally have to talk, would have to tell the truth, to ease her conscience—if it was true that she was a saintly woman.

But instead, she didn't confess anything, not even at the point of death, not even to the priest who came to bring her the viaticum. Don Erasmo got him face to face in private afterward, in order to find out the blessed truth, as he followed him down the stairs, his legs faltering under him . . .

—If it's true that there is the world beyond . . . If it's true you have to get there with a clean conscience . . . Especially about certain things that take sleep and appetite away from an honest man forever . . . Ready to forgive though . . . like a good Christian . . .

Nothing! Not even to the father confessor had his wife told anything. —"A true saint, dear Don Erasmo! You can be proud of her . . ." —Either his wife really didn't have anything to say, or even saints know how to lie about some things.

And if Doctor Brocca couldn't remove it then, he could never remove that thorn from his heart, that bitter doubt, that suspicion that made his blood boil when a man came to look for him or even if a man just walked along the street; and it caught him unawares if he stopped for fifteen minutes in the Pharmacy, and it made his house a hell and poisoned the very bread he ate, as he sat at the table in the middle of that brood of children, God knows how many of them by treachery, who devoured bread by the basketful, and that wife who, having come back from death to life, wanted also to go back to being the same way she was before, completely devoted to her home and her husband, and always with priests and father confessors.

"What kind of confessions do you make? What do you go and tell the father confessor, you women? . . . If you never tell the truth! . . ."

The poor woman wept, was desperate, gave a thousand assurances, and swore a thousand oaths. Sometimes, at the shouting, cousin Orsola ran over and gave him a piece of her mind:

"But what do you want from her anyway? Do you want her to invent sins? Are you absolutely determined to be a cuckold?"

And he had to swallow this too, and keep quiet!

And when all of them, together with Don Marco Crippa and the pharmacist, laughed about the other unfortunate husbands, he had to lower his head and change the subject.

1891

THE MARK X

An example of Verga's early work

THE MARK X

That fatal tendency toward the unknown that dwells in the human heart and reveals itself in great as well as in small things, in the thirst for knowledge as well as in the curiosity of the child, is one of the main characteristics of love, I should say its main appeal: a sad appeal imbued with troubles and tears—the sad knowledge of which dries up your heart before its time. Would this love, then, that has inspired so many masterpieces and filled half the prisons and the hospitals, have within itself all the reasons for existing only if used as a transitory means to ends that are much loftier—or much more modest, according to one's point of view—and would it come only last in the scale of sentiments? Would the reason for its transience lie in its very essence? And would that terrible dissolvent inherent in satiety, or in marriage, protect one from the senseless satisfaction of a dangerous curiosity? Would the gravest fault of the child-man consist in the insane avidity of that desire which makes him search with caresses and kisses the hidden mechanism of the toy-woman, who until yesterday made his heart in his chest tremble like a leaf?

During the last Ball at La Scala, in the midst of that whirlwind of frenetic joy, I met a masked woman, whose face I did not see, whose name I did not know, whom, perhaps, I would have never seen again, and who made my heart beat faster when her eyes met mine, and who made me spend a sleepless night, her smile always before my eyes, and the rustle of her satin domino in my ears.

She was leaning on the arm of a handsome young man, and was surrounded by the elegant members of the Club, flattered, courted, carried in triumph; she was tall, elegant, somewhat thin; she had two graceful hollows at her shoulders, delicate arms, a rosy chin, black and shining eyes, an ivory neck which was a little too long and slender, shaded with vague nuances where rebellious curls moved in charming disorder; her smile was fascinating; she was dressed all in white, except for a pink ribbon on her hood, and she trailed the hem of her dress on the carpet, as a queen would have done with her mantle. All this together with that little piece of black satin which was hiding her face where her eyes were sparkling, and was embroidered with all the question marks of curiosity, and behind which the imagination could see all the woman's beauty and could place her on any step of the social scale. In the midst of a group of men where a woman of good reputation would not have ventured even with a mask, she conveyed the innocence, grace, and modesty of a young girl from a convent school.

Her back turned to the hall, she was sitting beside her young man and was speaking to him in the way women in love do, devouring him with her eyes and making him guess the fascinating smile and the blushes running beneath her mask; she caressed him with her fan while resting her hand on his shoulder; with a tender and caressing insistence, she seemed to be making him promise something.

I would have given anything to be in the place of that young man, who seemed to be only moderately flattered by that preference; I would have liked to guess everything I could not hear, everything that stirred in her heart; I would have liked to penetrate the silk of that mask; the riddle of that face, of that person, and of that modest romance that had flowered under the gas lamps of La Scala had a thousand attractions for an observer. My warm interest, or my curiosity, must have penetrated her like an electric current, for she turned to look at me two or three times, with those big black eyes of hers; then she rose, took her companion's arm and went away.

The gaiety of the Ball seemed to have turned into an inexplicable gloom, and something seemed to be missing; I was looking for her with the avid hope of seeing her again, as if this unknown woman had already become someone of importance to me.

Toward the end of the evening, we saw each other again, face to face, by the door, while she was leaving the hall and I was returning. We remained motionless, looking at each other at length, fixedly, like two persons who are acquainted, as if I too, after having looked at her three or four times during the evening, had become someone of importance to her; my heart was beating fast, and I felt that hers must have been doing the same; it seemed that each of us drank something from the other's eyes; I savored her smile already long before her lips parted: she did smile at me, in fact—an effusion of good humor and warmth, which said: "I know you like me, and I also like you!" The tenderest of all words, the sweetest tongue in the world, could not have expressed the eloquence of that smile; the most eminent thinker, the most experienced man of the world, could not have analyzed that feeling born suddenly in a glance between two persons, who met amid a crowd in the same way as two travelers who are about to leave in opposite directions meet in a railway station—the one beside a man whom perhaps she still loved, the other, who had seen her arm on that man's shoulder. Two or three times she turned to look at me with that same smile, and I followed her without knowing what was luring me. The crowd made me lose sight of her; in vain I looked for her in the foyer, in the corridors, in the lounge, in the orchestra, at Canetta's, in those boxes that I could survey, everywhere.

I had the fever of a strange desire; with my eyes I devoured all the white dominoes, all the gracefully moving gowns. Suddenly, I saw her before me, or rather I met her gaze that was searching for me. I was then giving my arm to a woman whom I had not seen for a long time. In the gaze of the unknown woman there was a mute question; she smiled at me again; I could do nothing more than nod to her as she passed by; she turned abruptly, throwing a quick gaze and smile at me, and said: *"Addio!"* I shall never forget that voice and that tone!

I did not see her again that evening. I remained to digest my ill-humor and the idle chatter of my companion. All night, without closing an eye, I dreamt of that face I did not know; I felt as if her gaze had left a luminous groove in my heart. The possibility of tracing that unknown woman lent her apparition the prestige of the extraordinary; in her smile I could imagine a poem of love which gained all its fascination from being cut off forever at its flowering. *Forever!* Is this not the word that shakes the human heart more than any other? I continued that dream for the entire day. I felt as if there were something new in me, as if I had received the sacrament of an immense loss. When my imagination grew tired of wandering in the blue immensity of the unknown, through a natural mental reaction I looked into my heart with surprise, and asked myself if I had fallen in love with that little piece of black satin which was hiding a face I did not know.

That unknown woman's gaze had put my heart in a turmoil, while I was giving my arm to another woman whom I had once loved like a madman and who, at that very moment, was exposing herself to the most serious danger for me. I was cursing the obstinacy of her affection, which did not let me run after the unknown one with all the selfishness of a new love.

For two or three days I looked anxiously for that lover I did not know, and I felt that if I saw her again something of her would be taken away from me. I saw her in Galleria Vittorio and I recognized her by that look and that smile, which said to me: "It is I, do you remember me?" I felt fatally driven toward her and twenty times I was at the point of taking her arm, right in front of those who accompanied her.

In Piazza Della Scala she turned around two or three times to see if I was following her. The vague uncertainties, the tumultuous joys, the feverish desires of the love of a twenty-year-old flooded my heart all at once: the swaying of her dress seemed to have something caressing about it; her white overcoat and the scarf that protected her face from the cold, had luminous radiations. I would never be able to describe the emotion I felt thinking that I could give her my arm or that I could touch the fringe of her scarf. Suddenly she crossed the street, accompanied by her friend and followed by a group of relatives; walking on tiptoes and lifting the hem of her dress, she came near me. She looked into my eyes, as if expecting something of me. I felt an acute pain, and turned away.

I saw her again several times, and her eyes kept asking: "What's the matter?" I did not dare say: "I do not like you any more." She grew tired of soliciting my looks, and when we met she turned her head elsewhere. One evening under the portico of La Scala, a trembling hand clasped mine and put a tiny piece of paper between my fingers. I turned around abruptly: I saw only unfamiliar faces, and a little farther off, my unknown woman who was walking away without looking at me; although she was now rather far, and although for some time now she had diverted her gaze from mine with a show of indifference whenever we met, my thoughts flew to her without a moment of hesitation, and at the same time, in strange contradiction, I accused my conjecture of folly.

Only two words filled the entire piece of paper: *"Follow me."* Whom? Where? Why? These questions gave those simple words colors of fire; the mystery enclosed in them tied itself with irresistible logic to that unknown woman, and restored to her all that vague and indefinable appeal which seeing her near me under the gas lamp had dissolved in a flash; the possibility of being in error made me impatient in a thousand ways. She did not even seem to notice me. I followed her. When the door of her house was closed in my face, I remained standing there without the strength to go away, my feet in the snow, all the windows on both sides of the street staring at me, and the policemen passing close by. From eleven in the evening until two in the morning I did not experience a moment of hesitation or of weariness; I did not doubt for an instant. I heard the door open very slowly, and I saw a white form in the shadow of the entrance. She was trembling like a leaf when I touched her hand; she seemed to be shaking with fever; and with her voice stifled by emotion, she said:

"What's the matter? What have I done to you? Tell me"—as if we had known each other for ten years.

Certain situations, certain words, certain inflections of the voice have evident, irresistible meanings; the young woman I had met at the Ball, amid a group of men who carried Cora Pearl [1] in triumph, and who was throwing her arms around my neck in the darkness of a stairway, was giving the most luminous proof of candor in the expansion of her warm feelings: it was a strange feeling which I could not explain and about which I did not dare ask her the reason. In her trust there was so much innocence that I would have liked to steal her earrings to teach her to be wary of men. I felt her poor trembling hands in mine, and her whispered words seemed to caress my face like a kiss. Certain inexplicable feelings have an essentially material foundation; all the charm of that hour of paradise lay in the darkness of that stairway. It seemed to me as if all the phantoms of the Ideal had taken solid form and were pressing my hands.

"You liked me even though you did not see my face," she said. "That's why I love you." And she did not even ask my name.

She made me promise to return the following night. Alas! senseless promise which reduced desire to the petty proportions of a vulgar rendezvous. We should have invented all the obstacles that were missing for our happiness, or never have seen each other again. The following night I went back to her with a feeling of pain, as if I had lost something. I saw her in her parlor; she was radiant with beauty and my heart swelled with joy, as

---

[1] Cora Pearl was the pseudonym of Emma Elizabeth Crouch (1842–1886), a famous courtesan. In this story the author associates her name with the dazzling woman he had seen at the Ball, in order to stress the contrast between what she had appeared to be and what she really was.

if I found pleasure in the first sensations of tragedy; I admired avidly the graceful features that were blushing for *me*, and I felt a vague unrest insinuate itself into the festive joy of my heart—my Ideal was fading; everything that was in that truly enchanting beauty was taken away from my dreams; it seemed to me as if my mind had become impoverished by being confined within the limits of reality.

"What's the matter?" she said.

"Nothing," I answered, "there is too much light."

She, poor girl, turned down the lamp. She was not aware of the unrest within me and was not afraid of the tragic avidity with which my eyes were devouring her. She spoke smilingly, gaily, like a lovesick little bird singing on a branch; she told me her story, one of those stories to which a guardian angel listens with a smile. She had been in love with the cousin with whom I had seen her at the Ball, and for him she had come from Lecco[2] with her aunt; the cousin, after two or three days of hesitation, had made it clear that he did not love her any more. Then, when the first tears had passed, she had thought of the unknown young man who had looked at her in that special way during the Ball at La Scala.

"I read in your eyes that you liked me," she said, "and I smiled at you because it made me so very happy; at that moment there was a great pain in my heart. If my cousin had continued loving me, I would have never told you this, but I would have always loved you like a

---

[2] A town on the southwestern tip of Lake Como.

brother. Now that my cousin doesn't want to have anything more to do with me, I too want to love whomever I like most!"

She coughed from time to time; her cheeks grew red and her eyes moist.

"Don't say that you'll marry me if you intend to leave me, as the other one did . . . I've been so sick!"

"Addio!" I said to her.

"Will you come again tomorrow? My aunt is going to see my cousins; don't be afraid. Will you come?"

"Addio!"

I never saw her again. I felt that I would have found myself humble and base before the trust and enthusiasm of that love which I no longer shared. And at the same time I felt that I had irrevocably lost a treasure.

In November I received a letter edged in black; it was in the same handwriting as the *"Follow me"*; my hands trembled as I opened it: "If you want to repeat the *Addio* you said to a little masked girl at the last La Scala Ball," she wrote, "go to the cemetery in a week, and look for a cross marked with an X."

Because of a coincidence which seemed the work of fate, that letter had been misplaced at the post office, and arrived after a few days' delay. I flew to that house that I had not seen any more; when I noticed that the window shutters were closed, my heart ached painfully. I ran to the cemetery without daring to believe in the tragic presage of that letter; on the first lane that I entered, as if destiny were guiding my steps, at the first mound of freshly turned earth, on an iron cross, I read

the sign she had wanted on her tomb, the sad hiero-
glyphic of her love; and there, with my knees in the
dust, it seemed to me as if I were looking into an immense darkness, filled with the image of my unknown
woman, her smile, the sound of her voice, the words she
had said to me, the places where I had seen her. I felt
an intense cold.

1874